THE WOODWITCH

About the Author

After training as a lawyer and then working as a teacher for 10 years, Stephen Gregory moved to the mountains of Snowdonia to write his first novel. *The Cormorant* was greeted by the *New York Times* as 'a first-class terror story with a relentless focus that would have made Edgar Allan Poe proud'. *Publishers Weekly* recognised its 'nightmarish horror reminiscent of the tales of Poe, in a tale that could become a classic'. Iain Banks called the book 'intelligent and well-written, with a natural feeling for the avian vandal of the title which brings to mind the poetry of Ted Hughes'.

The Cormorant won the Somerset Maugham Award in 1987 and was made into a critically-acclaimed feature film for the BBC's Screen Two series starring Oscar-nominated actor Ralph Fiennes.

A second novel followed, set again in the brooding atmosphere of a Snowdonian winter. *The Woodwitch* provoked similar reactions: *Publishers Weekly* commented that 'Gregory writes with the hypnotic power of Poe', while the *Washington Post* called the book 'an ambitious attempt to use the conventions of the contemporary horror novel to say something compelling about the irrational side of human nature'. *The Woodwitch* was the subject of a television documentary for the BBC's Statements series.

The Blood of Angels completed a trilogy of novels in which an English incomer confronts the mysteries and vagaries of winter in Wales. It was recognised by Oscar-winning director William Friedkin (*The Exorcist*, *The French Connection*) as the work of an unusually original horror writer, and the author was flown to Hollywood where he spent an exhilarating, often gruelling year writing stories and script for Friedkin at Paramount Pictures.

THE PERILS AND DANGERS OF THIS NIGHT

Stephen Gregory

Published by Virgin Books 2008

2 4 6 8 10 9 7 5 3 1

First published in Great Britain in 2008 by
Virgin Books Ltd
Thames Wharf Studios
Rainville Road
London, W6 9HA

www.rbooks.co.uk

Addresses for companies within
The Random House Group Limited can be found at:
www.randomhouse.co.uk/offices.htm

The Random House Group Limited Reg. No. 954009

A CIP catalogue record for this book is available
from the British Library.

ISBN 9780753513798

The Random House Group Limited supports The Forest
Stewardship Council [FSC], the leading international forest
certification organisation. All our titles that are printed on
Greenpeace approved FCS certified paper carry the FSC logo.
Our paper procurement policy can be found at
www.rbooks.co.uk/environment

Typeset by TW Typesetting, Plymouth, Devon
Printed and bound in Great Britain by
CPI Bookmarque, Croydon, CR0 4TD

For Chris, with all my love

FOREWORD

Strange: for over forty years, no one ever asked me to tell a fuller story of what happened at Foxwood Manor in the week before Christmas 1966.

I was questioned very gently at the time, and over the following weeks, but once I had explained in the simplest terms how things had ended so tragically, they left me alone. The police had been able to see for themselves, from evidence at the scene they discovered that Christmas Day, and by piecing together a story of the events that preceded it. And I was a boy, just thirteen years old: they must have thought I was so disturbed, so traumatised by what had happened, that it was inappropriate to press me further.

Until recently, no one asked me about the killings at Foxwood Manor. More than forty years passed by, and

I often sat and thought, I lay awake at night, and I recalled that long-ago week in such vivid detail that every whisper and creak of the old house, the whiff of the dust, the lingering touch of the cobwebs, the very reek of fear and blood, became real again.

Now I have been asked to write it down. At first I did not put my real self into the story. Somehow I could not. I wrote and wrote, the words came slowly as the story began and faster and faster as it hurried towards a horrid end, but the boy was not me: he was always 'the boy', he was 'Alan', he was 'Alan Scott', he was a third person separate from the boy I had been, the I who had really been there at the time. And so the reader of my bundled manuscript, leafing through page after page in search of the truth, straining for the voice of someone who had not only witnessed the sensational events but been a part of them, asked me with a note of professional exasperation if I had been at Foxwood Manor or not, in the week before Christmas 1966? And if I had been there, and seen everything, why was I not in the story?

I have rewritten my account in the first person. If the style is mannered, it is the voice and vocabulary of a middle-aged man recalling a week of his life as a child.

It all began with a dream. And then there was a boy, a choirboy, running through the woods on a wintry afternoon . . .

Alone. Angry. Afraid.

It was me. I was there. I saw everything.

ONE

I woke very suddenly and sat up in bed. I was trembling and breathing hard. I felt a keen pain on the palms of both my hands and a scalding sensation on my neck.

I got out of bed. The nine other boys in the dormitory were sleeping. I stood in the moonlight from the tall window and looked at my hands, blew on them, rubbed them: they prickled and itched, like a nettle rash. There were rows of narrow stripes like cuts across my palms and fingers. I leaned to the glass to catch my own reflection, and saw a reddening on my neck, like a deep wound all the way round and across the bump of my Adam's apple, which mottled and blurred as I touched it with my fingertips.

I didn't know what the marks were. I think I was afraid. I shivered, barefoot, in my striped pyjamas, looked up and saw that the top of the window was ajar. A flutter of cold air came through it. Dr Kemp must have left it open, after the prayer, before he turned off the dormitory light. I stretched up and pushed the window closed, then I sat on my bed and pulled a blanket around me.

I placed my hands open on my lap and examined the marks. And it was as though I could read from them the dream I'd had . . . I saw a place I'd never seen before and yet so real that I wondered how I could have conjured it: a gloomy study, with shabby furniture and a huge gleaming black piano, curtains half-closed on leaded windows; every inch of every surface of tables and armchair and sofa, the piano and the floor, strewn with papers and books and sheet music; bottles and glasses and pieces of clothing, the dishevelled aftermath of a party. I heard music, lurching and swooping haphazardly, maddeningly familiar and yet barely recognisable. As I sat on my bed and looked from one of my palms to the other, the face of a young man swam into view. He said '*I disgust myself*' in a perfectly matter-of-fact voice, and moved away again. A girl appeared, blew a kiss and ran her tongue around her lips and tried to smile; but the smile was a fake, it quivered and disintegrated; she burst into tears and disappeared. '*I disgust myself*', a voice said again, although I couldn't find the man who'd spoken as the room turned slowly around me . . .

And then the room was different. A small difference, but something so terrible that it filled me with an unexplainable fear.

The top of the piano was wide open. Someone had opened it. I moved towards it and I saw in its glassy shine a reflection of myself: a schoolboy in striped pyjamas, moving closer towards me, closer and closer, as though I and the reflection would meet and fuse into one if we kept on walking. Until, at the last moment, when I held out my hand to the mirrored boy and our fingers nearly touched, I saw that the boy was not me, but a boy I didn't know and had never seen before in all my life.

He handed me a piece of paper, rolled tightly into a ball. It burned my hand so much I dropped it, and it fell in flames into the black hole of the piano. I leaned into the hole, and my stomach and throat were suffused with a horror of what I might see if I looked inside. Worse than that, there was a pain in my throat so keen and sudden that my hands flew to my neck to try and prevent it. A gagging, suffocating dream . . . I recoiled from the piano with a wrenching jolt.

I sat on my bed, trembling again, and I rubbed at my hands. The stripes had gone, as suddenly as the dream had disappeared. The pain in my neck had gone. I breathed deeply, exhaling long and hard to calm myself, and my breath was a plume of silver in the cold air.

I wondered if I'd cried out. I thought I'd heard a cry. Instinctively I looked around me. One of the sleeping boys was muttering and turning over, and then once more the dormitory was silent. I slipped into bed with a feeling of great exhaustion and was quickly asleep again.

It was the first time I'd had this dream. I would have it

again and I would learn to understand it over the following few days.

'I hate you I hate you I hate you . . .'

I was running through the woods, so hard and so fast that the words I was hissing kept time with my footsteps.

I crashed through the bare undergrowth, splintering branches with my arms as I forced my way through. I struggled through dead bracken and dry nettles as tall as myself. As I ran I glanced over my shoulder and saw the chimneys of the school behind me. Still I ran, until my breathing was hoarse. Once I fell, launched headlong when my foot snagged and then slipped on a root, and I landed so hard, flat on my chest with my face in the dead wet leaves, that I lay for a few seconds, winded and breathless. Then, when my breath came back at last, my words were more like sobbing – 'I hate you I hate you I hate you' – and there were tears on my face, smudged with dirt and sweat.

I got up and ran further, slower now that I was far away from the school. When I turned to look, the chimneys and roofs of the old house and its scattered outbuildings were hidden by the deep woods. A bramble, as vicious as barbed wire, reached out for me as I blundered past: it caught at my neck, the thorns cut into my skin, snagging and tearing, and I clutched at it with both hands as though I were being strangled. The wire tightened round my throat, and I cried out in panic until I wrenched it away . . .

And then I stood there panting. My white cassock was smeared with the black soil of the forest. The red surplice I wore under it was torn, and there was blood on the white ruff from a long, raw scratch on my neck. Still I hurried further, and when at last I stopped, hardly able to breathe, I fumbled in the pocket of my surplice and pulled out a letter.

I smeared my face with the back of one hand and stared at the letter through a blur of tears. It was a blue air-mail envelope. I tugged a single sheet of air-mail paper out of it, crumpled the envelope in my fist and then threw it as far as I could into the undergrowth. So angry that every part of the real world was blurred and grey and all I could see was the flimsy piece of blue paper in my hand, I tore it once, twice, three times. Then, as I threw the bits up into the air and they whirled like confetti around me, I wheeled round and round, giddy with rage, and I yelled with all my strength, 'I hate you! I hate you! I hate you!'

A gunshot rang out.

The woodland erupted with the cries of the rooks which wheeled from the high bare branches. I stared into the surrounding trees, and for a second I saw a figure moving there, a dark figure which seemed to melt and disappear into the shadows. Suddenly afraid, brought back to my senses by the shot as though it were a slap on my smeary face, I looked down at my dirty hands. I frowned as I saw my dirty cassock and surplice, and I felt at the crumpled ruff and suddenly knew how strange it was for a choirboy to be standing deep in the woods on a winter's afternoon – and when a second shot rang out and the trees seemed to echo with the violence of the sound, I turned and started to run, back the way I'd come.

It was getting dark. Cold woodland. Late afternoon in December. Dusk and an early twilight. The trees swayed and shook the last of their leaves to the forest floor. A flock of rooks clacked and croaked, blown into the air like cinders from a wintry bonfire. Then, when silence settled and the birds returned to their roost on the highest branches, it was as though I'd never been there, shouting and hissing, as though the explosions of the gun had never happened.

Only, among the wet black leaves where I'd been standing, there was a crumpled blue envelope and a few scattered pieces of thin blue paper . . .

I ran back to the school. As I got closer, as I crossed the football fields and then the lawns in front of the house, the building was warmly lit with the glow from upstairs dormitories, with streaks of soft golden light through the wooden shutters of the library downstairs and the great hall. I caught the movement of boys, up and down the long corridors, and the thought that they were excitedly packing for the end of term filled me with dismay. I moved past the house itself and hurried around it to the stable-yard, where I skidded to a standstill on the cobbles and leaned on one of the stable doors.

It was dark in the yard. I pressed my forehead on the door, trying to control my breathing. The anger felt like a bubble inside my chest. Then I fumbled with the latch and flung myself inside.

I closed the door quietly behind me. Still careless of my cassock and surplice which were already so dirty from the wet woodland, I felt my way through pitch blackness until I found a shelf on the opposite wall.

There was a rustling movement in the darkness. A shuffling, a flutter, a scratching, and the shivering tinkle of a little bell. 'Ssshhh,' I said very softly. I felt along the shelf until my fingers fell on a box of matches, and, fumbling a little because my hands were slippery and cold, I took out a match and scraped it three times until it flared alight. 'Ssshhh,' I said again, because the sound of the match and the suddenness of the light brought another scratching and fluttering and tinkle from the far corner of the stable.

I applied the match to an oil lamp, and the room was bathed in a yellow light which threw great black moving shadows everywhere: to the rafters of the roof, to the empty stalls where horses had stood and stomped years and years ago, over a dusty jumble of old school trunks, broken desks and abandoned cricket bats. I blew softly on the match until it plumed a little feather of smoke, then I carried the lamp across the room.

My bird was in the furthest stall, tethered to the iron framework of a horse's manger.

It ducked and bobbed and stared, as I approached with the lamp. It hopped as far as the leather jesses would allow, and a little bell tinkled as it hopped. I shaded the light with my other hand and crossed the stall very

7

slowly, with hardly a sound of my feet on the cobbled floor.

'Ssshhh,' I whispered, 'my little imp.'

When I set the lamp down on a long wooden bench, the bird stared at the flame as though transfixed. And its eyes were bright and black, like pinpricks of darkness. It shuffled its feathers, shivering and bristling. It hissed like an owl. Like an owl, it angled its head from side to side, the black eyes unblinking.

Not an owl. A jackdaw, with a head too big for its poor, scrawny body, its feathers dull and dishevelled. A cripple, a cringing hunchback, it sprang along its perch on one black scaly leg. It snorted through bristly nostrils, so that a tiny bubble of mucus stood up for a second and then burst.

'My imp,' I whispered again.

The bird peered at me, askance. Its eyes fixed on the lamp and then swivelled to watch me as I bent to the floor and straightened up again.

I'd picked up a feather, one of the jackdaw's own tail feathers. So gently that at first the bird could not have felt the slightest touch, I caressed its breast with the tip of the feather. Then, with a soft insistent rhythm, I stroked from the tip of the beak to the softest spot on the belly, down and down the one leg to the sharpest tip of each claw. I stroked and stroked, and the bird just stared at me. It felt the movement and pressures of its own feather through the movements of my hand, and it heard the gentle hypnotic rhythms of my voice.

It felt the warmth of my breath on its face as I whispered, 'I love you I love you . . .'

TWO

It was Wednesday, 21 December 1966, the last day of the Christmas term. The whole school, boys and teachers and parents, had assembled in the little chapel. The last light of the shortest day of the year fell feebly through the stained-glass windows, so that the reds and greens of the school crest and motto were a splash of colour on the cold stone floor.

'Sing up, Scott,' the headmaster whispered, leaning so close that I could smell the mixture of sherry and mint on his breath, the bitter odour of his body and the pomade on his thinning, slicked-back hair. 'This is an honour for you.'

And then, signalling with a twitch of his ivory baton that everyone should stand up for the beginning of the carol service, Dr Kemp waited for a moment and swept the room with a smile of welcome. Forty-nine boys between the age of seven and twelve, in short trousers and grey jackets, their hair neatly cut for the special occasion; seven assorted teachers and a matron, dutifully attentive; at the back of the chapel, the parents, shivering in stiff dark overcoats, who'd driven to the school for the service and to take their sons home for the Christmas holiday; they all stood up at the flicker of the headmaster's baton and flinched from his smile.

Cold, as cold as a tomb.

In the middle of the aisle, Mrs Kemp sat in her wheel-chair, the fur collar of her coat turned up to her throat, a rug wrapped tightly around her legs. A gleam of scarlet from the stained glass coloured her fine blonde hair and the pale skin of her face. She seemed as fragile and as beautiful as the glass through which the wintry sunlight fell.

At her feet there lay a very old black dog. He groaned so loudly that everyone in the chapel could hear it, and some of the boys giggled. At a glance from Mrs Kemp, the slightest lift of an eyebrow from Dr Kemp, the room was silent again.

'So,' the headmaster whispered, turning back to me. He adjusted the baton into the crook of his fingers and he caressed my knuckles with it. He pinged a tuning fork so softly that only I could hear it. I took a deep breath and started to sing.

Unaccompanied, I sang the opening verse of 'Once in Royal David's City', pure and clear in the icy air of the chapel: Alan Scott, twelve years old, head chorister at

Foxwood Manor School, scrubbed and polished in a clean cassock and surplice, my ruff starched and stiff around my throat. With an anxious white face, a sprinkle of freckles and a bristle of red hair, I stood on the front row of the choir with the other choristers beside and behind me.

And a curious thing happened just then. The tiniest prickling on my palms began. Not enough to make me itch them, but enough to bring to my mind the face of the boy I'd seen in that dream: the boy I'd thought at first was me, who became a boy I didn't know.

He was there with me. He was inside my head, as though a droplet of icy water had splashed onto my scalp and trickled down my neck. It was he who was singing, not me. In the purity of his voice all the lives of every living thing in the chapel stopped still – his was all the breath in the room and there was none left for anything else. Even the dust, which had swirled through the shafts of sunlight with the movement of people standing and shuffling, hung still, motionless sparks of red and green, and the breath that had trickled from the mouths of all the people present stopped for those few moments, while he sang.

Dr Kemp stroked my knuckles with the baton, keeping time. For everything and everyone else, time stood still.

I came to the end of the verse. Dr Kemp waited for the final breath of the last note, and, in the hush which filled the chapel, his eyes held mine. He frowned, as if he'd noticed something different in my voice, and he pressed the baton on my knuckles as if to prolong the moment by pinning me to the choir-stall. Then, turning to the body of the chapel, with a wide sweep of both arms he brought the congregation and the rest of the choir into the second verse.

I sang too, relieved that my big moment was over. I turned over my hands, half-expecting to see the faintest of stripes on my palms. But there was nothing, and the prickling had stopped. The boy had gone.

I touched the purpling scratch on the side of my neck, where the bramble had snagged me, and, still singing, I moved my hand from the scratch and felt for a tiny ear-piece I'd tucked into my ruff. I angled my head so that the headmaster couldn't possibly see it or the wire that ran into my ruff, and I adjusted the ear-piece into my ear. Then I dropped my hand to my pocket and pressed the switch of a little transistor radio.

The music erupted in my ear, so loud that it felt as though my head would explode.

Still I mouthed the words of the Christmas carol, especially angelic whenever Dr Kemp turned and caught my eye. But inside my head it was the Kinks, *'you really got me, you really got me –'* raw and ragged and blasting hard, *'– you got me so I don't know what I'm doin' . . .'*

Through the rest of that Christmas carol, I tapped my foot and swayed to the driving beat, and just as the chapel echoed with the last note of the last verse of 'Once in Royal . . .' I felt in my pocket and switched the radio off.

The congregation sat down, coughing and shuffling. Dr Kemp turned to the choir and gestured at us to sit down too. 'Good,' he mouthed at me. For a horrible split-second, he narrowed his eyes and stared at my neck. I touched it with my hand and felt a trickle of blood runing from the scratch to the perfect whiteness of my collar. At the same time, I took out the ear-piece and snuggled it into my ruff.

Upstairs in the main house, along the corridors of the first floor and the second floor, it was the noisiest afternoon of the term.

In every dormitory the boys were crushing the final items of clothing or boots or shoes into their trunks and struggling to close them. Some were helping one another, one standing or sitting on the lid to force it shut while the other squeezed the clasp shut or tugged at belts and buckles to get it closed. The matron was on the first floor, Miss Hayes, a dumpy middle-aged spinster, usually a stickler for quiet and orderliness in the dorms but this time relaxing and allowing herself a little smile as she reminded this boy or that boy to strip his bed properly and fold the sheets and blankets neatly, to remove the pillow slip and fold it carefully on top of the pillow, to check the cupboards and drawers and the wardrobe to make sure nothing was left behind. Upstairs, at the top of the house, Mr Buxton was on duty, balding, effete, so genuinely nice that the boys took advantage of him in equally nice ways which had, over the seven years he'd been at Foxwood, made him an almost completely ineffectual teacher. He wandered from dorm to dorm and smiled gamely at the boys as they shoved and hustled around him, no doubt wishing with all his heart that they'd soon be gone and he could go too. It was chaotic, but the end was in sight as, one after the other, the trunks were shifted out of the dorms and manhandled along the corridors, then bumped down the stairs to the ground floor.

Some of the dorms were already empty. It was nearly dark, only three o'clock on a midwinter's afternoon.

There was a jam in the second-floor corridor. At the top of the narrow stairs a couple of trunks were stuck, as a number of boys jostled with Mr Buxton to turn the corner. Someone shouted, 'Come on, what's the hold-up?' and another voice, shrill with excitement and emboldened by the thrill of this longed-for moment, called out, 'Hey, let's get out of this dump!'

A sudden silence followed. Mrs Kemp had emerged unnoticed from her door at the further end of the corridor and wheeled herself towards the confusion.

The boys who'd cried out were embarrassed, and one of them, a fat boy with a silly fat face, said lamely, 'Sorry, Mrs Kemp,' as she spun her wheelchair up to the lift door. 'Sorry, Mrs Kemp,' he said again in the hush which had fallen, and, contrite, he came forwards and helped her open the door of the lift and eased her chair inside. She smiled up at him – the shy, foolish, harmless boy who'd blurted so loudly and was sorry to have upset her, just as he was going home for the holiday – and she said, 'Thank you, Jonathan.' The boy glowed with relief. He stepped out of the lift, closed the door, and everyone, Mr Buxton too, watched and waited as the lift went down.

Then the shoving and the bustling resumed, the jam unjammed. The school was emptying fast.

Mrs Kemp went down in the lift. She emerged at the ground floor, tugged the door open and wheeled herself out, spinning the chair with great expertise. She accelerated sharply along the corridor, the tyres hissing on polished brown linoleum, and she pressed harder with her arms to negotiate the ramps which her husband had had fitted, where previously there'd been a step or two. The lifts had been installed especially for her, two of them, one at each end of the house, so that she had access to every part of the building, even the attic space in the roof. She sped along the corridor, past the library and the staffroom, towards the crowd of parents and boys in the old hall.

The hall was the heart of the school, and now it was full of people. There was a fire burning in the great stone fireplace, and a Christmas tree in the far corner, behind the grand piano. A wide, elegant staircase, usually out of bounds to the boys, curved into the room, but today, for the special occasion of the carol service and the presence of all the parents, some of the boys were using this route to get their trunks downstairs. Dr Kemp was standing in the doorway of his study, a short powerful figure, middle-aged but somehow ageless, the headmaster, the figurehead of Foxwood Manor School. He was talking to some of the parents, taking the opportunity, on this special day at the end of another year, to remind them of the school's motto – 'to strive is to shine' – and encourage them to apply it to the progress of their sons. He turned with a smile as his wife rolled towards him.

I watched from the landing of the staircase, from high up on the top floor of the house.

I was alone in the darkness, still wearing the suit I'd worn under my cassock and surplice for the carol service. I could smell the smoke from the fire; and the resinous pungency of the tree reminded me of my family and home and the Christmases I would never enjoy again. The murmur of many voices rose up the staircase, strangely muted and distorted, but I could still make out the sharp little barks of the headmaster among so many strangers – the parents of all the other boys in the school, who sipped a sherry and warmed the backs of their legs at the fire, who moved awkwardly around the hall and looked at the faces in the faded school photographs, who stared upwards to the honours boards and the names of long-ago pupils of Foxwood Manor who'd progressed to higher and better things.

I leaned on the banister at the top of the stairs and I watched. I saw the knot of people far below, at the foot of the stairs, next to the headmaster's study, move away and out of sight, and I knew that gradually everyone would make for the front door of the hall and go outside.

I moved slowly along the corridor. All the dormitories were empty now, all the lights switched off. I went into my own dorm, and crossed to the window.

Outside it was quite dark. There were still a few cars on the gravelled driveway: a Rover and a couple of Vauxhalls, an Armstrong Siddeley, the bulbous mass of a Mark 10 Jaguar looming in the shadows of the copper beech which overhung the lawn. I watched as boys and parents manhandled their trunks into the boots of the cars and said their final goodbyes to Dr Kemp. Headlamps flicked on, slicing into the darkness of the surrounding woodland. Cars moved off and around the school, their tyres crunching on the gravel, until only three or four were left. Dr Kemp moved among them, in and out of the light, waving away each departing car, then running his hand over and over his grey, oily hair. From my vantage point at the window, I could just see Mrs Kemp's feet in the front door, and I knew she was sitting there in her wheelchair, so charming and somehow so lovely, and so much younger than her pawky, curiously graceless husband.

I eased the window open. Dr Kemp had stopped a boy who'd pushed past him on the driveway, and he was leaning down to talk to him. The man's voice, and the threat in it, cut through the cold, clear air. 'Listen, boy, and remember,' he said. 'On the first day of next term, I want to hear you play for me. I'll know if you haven't been practising. I don't like to be disappointed. Go.'

The boy spun away, and for a second the light from a car's headlamps fell on his cowed and anxious face.

The last car left. It rolled across the gravel, turned the corner of the school house and disappeared. Dr Kemp stood there, alone, his hands hanging loosely by his sides, and he waited and listened, as I did upstairs. The noise of the engine faded, the headlights cut this way and that among the dark trees, and all of a sudden there was silence.

The only light was the light that fell from the front door of the school. The only sound was the ticking of a wren somewhere in the woodland. The air seemed to prickle with cold.

I withdrew my head from the window. As I did so, I banged it on the frame, just hard enough that Dr Kemp glanced up at the sound. For a second, he looked up at me, and he frowned as though he couldn't remember why one of the boys was still in the school. Then he marched to the door and inside. As the door shut, the slab of light which had fallen onto the gravel and across the lawn to the trees beyond was gone. There was nothing but blackness.

After closing the window, I crossed to the door and switched on the light. The dormitory was bare and empty. There was a row of nine beds, each one stripped to the mattress, the blankets and sheets folded neatly, the pillow slips folded on top of the stained, stripy pillows. But in the corner, one of the beds was still made up. On the iron frame, a piece of paper stuck with sticky tape said SCOTT A.

I moved to the bed and sat down. I took a deep breath and prised off my heavy black lace-up shoes without undoing them, and dropped them, *thud thud*, onto the floor. I shuffled to the wardrobe, my stockinged feet silent on the bare linoleum, and opened it. There was a row of wire coat-hangers, all empty except one. It had a tag, SCOTT A., on it, and it was still hung with clothes.

I stripped to my vest and pants, my body thin and mottled white as I shivered and shivered and reached for the corduroy shorts and grey flannel shirt and grey woollen pullover from my coat-hanger, and I dressed as quickly as I could.

I thought that my heart would burst with sadness. Alone in the great rambling house of Foxwood Manor School, alone with Dr and Mrs Kemp. All the other boys had gone, settled into the warm interiors of softly lit saloon cars, breathing the scent of leather upholstery and the familiar perfumes and colognes of their mothers and fathers, cuddling with little brothers and sisters.

I had no brothers and sisters. My mother wasn't coming. My father would never come.

I felt as though my throat would burst with aching. I sniffed very loudly. When I felt for a handkerchief in the pocket of the suit I'd flung onto the bed, I found the tiny transistor radio I'd had in the chapel.

I settled the ear-piece into my ear, cupped the radio in my hand and switched it on. It fizzed and whined. And in the second it took me to adjust the tuning, I caught a movement in the corner of my eye and spun round in horror as the dormitory door creaked slowly open.

I froze, with the ear-piece in my ear and the radio in my hand. The door fell wide open.

But there was no one. An empty blackness, the tunnel of the corridor yawned into the far distance. No one. An icy draught had fingered its way through the school, as though feeling for any residual warmth from all the bodies that had recently vacated it – and, pushing open the door of the dormitory, it had found me, the only living and breathing body left behind.

With a sigh of relief and another glance over my shoulder at the empty doorway, I stuffed the radio under my pillow. I hung my suit in the wardrobe, kicked the black lace-up shoes inside and slipped on my indoor shoes. I clicked off the light in the dormitory and padded from one end of the dark corridor to the other: past one of the lifts, past the other dormitories, past the bathroom and another dormitory and then the other lift, to the landing at the top of the stairs.

Music, I could hear the music before I reached the landing. Someone was playing the piano, down in the great hall. No, not someone. I knew it was Mrs Kemp. Quite different from the ease and swagger of the headmaster's touch, Mrs Kemp played as though the music were a kind of delicate, difficult jigsaw puzzle she was trying to make sense of. She was playing softly to herself, strumming really, the first few lines of 'While Shepherds Watched Their Flocks by Night', and it was beautiful, the sound of Christmas and a feeling that the holidays had come and there was a release from the humdrum business of running a school and the lives of forty-nine small boys. Beautiful, although for me, as I involuntarily cupped a hand behind my right ear, there was a tiny imperfection in the tuning. In spite of that, or maybe because of it, the music eased the sadness in my heart, and, without thinking that I should not, I started down the staircase, down and down towards the hall.

Where I paused. Just as I arrived at the foot of the stairs, as I caught a glimpse of Mrs Kemp's head bent over the keys of the piano, her hair bright in the firelight and the glow from the coloured bulbs on the Christmas tree, Dr Kemp stormed out of his study.

'Stop!' he bellowed. 'Can't you hear it? Stop, for heaven's sake!'

She stopped immediately. He stomped across the hall towards her. 'Can't you hear it?' he hissed. 'Don't you listen?' And as she shunted her chair away from the keyboard, he leaned across her and banged a series of ugly chords.

'There! There! There!' he grunted, with each heavy handprint on the keys. 'If you can't hear how horrid it is, then you've learned nothing after all these years!'

I froze in the shadows. I held my breath and watched as Mrs Kemp put her hand on her husband's hand. Dr Kemp pushed it away and brushed the flopping hair from his forehead, panting a bit.

'Mr huffing and puffing headmaster,' she said very softly. 'I'm not one of your little boys, you know. What are you going to do to me? Swish me with your little cane? Put me in detention? Try to be nice. It's the holiday . . .'

The man pulled himself together. With an odd, embarrassed movement of his shoulders and an awkward hitch of his trousers, he was all of a sudden like a child who'd made a fool of himself in front of a grown-up. Not man enough to apologise, he blustered a bit more. 'The keys,' he said, 'for heaven's sake, where are the keys?' and he reached into the piano stool and took out a wallet of tuning keys, lifted the lid of the piano and started to busy himself inside it, like an irritable surgeon botching an operation. From inside the piano, he produced a few random, plangent notes by lifting and dropping the hammers, peering sideways at his wife and muttering, 'It'll need the tuner, we'll call the tuner, he can come and do all the pianos while he's here.'

'Huff huff, puff puff,' the woman softly said. 'I'll call the piano tuner tomorrow.'

The headmaster emerged from inside the piano, red-faced, his hair flopping again. Again she took hold of his hand, his left hand, where his third and fourth fingers were curled hard into his palm. She brought it to her face and kissed the stiffened joints.

'Your war wound,' she whispered. 'Don't always take it out on the boys, or on me.' She smiled up at his blustery, flustered face. 'And it's the holiday now. They've all gone home.'

At that moment the stair creaked under my feet. They both looked up and saw me standing there. 'Not all of them,' Dr Kemp said. 'Not yet.'

I tiptoed from the foot of the stairs to the corridor leading from the hall. Like a rabbit plunging to the safety of its burrow, I hurried into the darkness. I could hear the tinkle of Mrs Kemp's laughter fading into the distance behind me.

Like a rabbit, but not scared.

I was hurt and angry, and all I wanted to do was to get away from the two people with whom I'd been abandoned. I knew every inch of the building, after nearly five years as a boarder there, and now I padded round corners without slowing at all, up one ramp and down another, past the dark cavern of the library and the forbidden, fuggy den of the staffroom. The school was in darkness, but I needed no light to guide me through the downstairs corridors and into the changing-room at the back of the house. I paused there, struck by the strangeness and emptiness of the place which was usually so noisy and smelly, where sweaty small boys stripped and showered and tumbled and fought, where dozens of pairs of socks and muddy boots were tangled and jumbled together.

Now, in the gloom, all the lockers were empty, and all the pegs were bare – except one, where my own outdoor coat was hanging.

I slipped softly through the changing-room, which had already been swept out and mopped with disinfectant and smelled, to me, so oddly, boylessly clean. I slid back a puny bolt, pushed open the door and stepped outside, into the cobbled stable-yard.

To my surprise, as I crossed the yard I saw a glow of light from inside the furthest stable. I approached as quietly as I could, unable to believe that I could have left a lamp burning the last time I'd been there. The door was ajar. I peered through. There was a man moving slowly in the corner, throwing an enormous black shadow into the rafters. I could smell him too.

'Roly?' I whispered. The man spun round, and I slipped into the stable. 'It's me, it's Scott.'

The man, startled by my unexpected arrival, squinted at me. He was lean and wiry, with the leathery, raddled look of an old jockey: his face reddened by the cold, a flat cap pushed back on a head of thin grey hair. He was wearing green corduroy trousers over a pair of heavy boots, and a waterproof coat which filled the air around him with a whiff of wood smoke and damp soil – not an offensive smell, not to me at least, for it was the smell of the woodland I knew so well, the smell of a wild outdoors and the creatures that lived in it. A double-barrelled shotgun leaned in a corner of the stall. Roly was the gamekeeper, who lived in the woods, in an old caravan a couple of miles from the school.

'Scott,' he said. His smile was quick and weaselly. 'You're still here.'

I crossed the room towards him. I edged past the shotgun, for the dull gleam of it and its fume of oil and burned powder were repugnant to me. I moved into the stall and saw, with a twinge of relief, that the jackdaw was calm, just bobbing a bit and staring to see me come into the circle of lamplight. The bird was calm, but as I stepped up to the man, something wild and strong erupted inside his pungent coat, something kicking and lunging hysterically.

'I came with this,' he said, 'for the bird.'

It was a rabbit. Roly pulled his coat open and expertly grabbed the terrified animal. 'I was going to finish it off,' he said, 'but then I brought it like this, to show you how.' He held the animal out towards me. 'Go on, young man, do you want to do it?'

It had a gunshot in its haunches, a lot of blood where the pellets had blasted it as it weaved and jinked through the undergrowth. And then Roly must have caught up with it as it tried to drag itself away, tromped it under his boot, and he'd stuffed it under his jacket, securing it with his belt so that, paralysed by shock, it was strapped against his body – until, just then, in a trauma of darkness and strangeness and slow suffocation, the rabbit had burst alive again.

I took it, and it kicked and squealed, possessed by an extraordinary strength: every muscle, every tissue expressed defiance and rage in the face of death.

Roly was calm, expert, a good teacher. No fuss, no hurry, he moved behind me and adjusted my hands to the squirming body. I remember the smell of his clothes, his beery breath, the heat in his fingers. He whispered, 'One pull and it's done.'

I pulled. There was a click. I felt the slippage of bone, and the rabbit was limp in my hands.

'Good man,' he said, standing away from me. 'Nice and quick, no pain. Here, use this, you can do the rest yourself.'

He took a knife from his pocket and handed it to me. I lifted the rabbit to the workbench in the stall, and Roly watched approvingly as I started to skin it, as he'd already shown me, slitting and opening and peeling until the flesh of the dead animal, still warm, still twitching here and there like the body of an exhausted athlete, shone in the lamplight.

'I saw all the cars,' Roly was saying. 'Posh, some of them. I can't be doing with all that nonsense. I waited till they'd gone before I came through the wood. What about your folks? Are they coming?'

But all my concentration was on the skinning and cleaning of the rabbit, and the watchful presence of my bird. I was half-listening while Roly went on, 'I don't envy you staying in the big house all on your own, just you and the Kemps, I reckon she's all right but I'm not sure about him . . .' For me, the bird and the warm flesh of the rabbit were all that really mattered, that existed just then.

Indeed, as I sliced the leanest strips of meat from the dead animal and held them to the jackdaw, Roly picked up his gun and made for the door. I was lost in a kind of worship. I didn't see a shabby crow with dusty feathers and a brittle, skeletal frame. To me the bird was an imp, damaged but not beyond repair, delivered into my care by some mischievous spirit of the forest. It took the meat from my fingers with grace and tenderness, obsequious, as though mocking my silly, boyish reverence. I stared deep into its eyes and it stared into mine.

I heard the door creak behind me, heard the heavy step of boots on the cobbles outside. Still I didn't turn from the bird.

'Roly?' I called over my shoulder. 'Thanks, Roly.' I waited, and when I knew that the man had disappeared into the night and left me alone in the stable, I whispered to the bird, 'You're mine, you're mine . . .'

Too late, I realised that Roly had left his knife. I hurried to the door and looked out, but he'd gone. I cleaned the blade with my fingers, flicking the blood onto the stable floor.

THREE

Flint and slate, Foxwood Manor gleamed in the moonlight.

It was eight o'clock that night. The house was a block of blackness, surrounded by deep woodland, and the moon, full and round but embedded in cloud, gave only a milky light – enough to catch a gleam from the walls which were faced with shards of flint and from the slates of the roof. As I crossed the lawn to the front door, there was one light in the building, from the windows of the great hall on the ground floor. Upstairs, the windows of the dormitories on the first and second floors were black. The old house was all but empty. No one moved along the corridors, upstairs or downstairs: no cries or laughter or boyish complaint rang from the changing-rooms or bathrooms; no one was reading in a secret corner of the library; not even a bored and lonely teacher was gawping at the television in the staffroom or drinking beer in his garret.

The light which shone from the hall was the only light for miles and miles. The nearest road – apart from the lane which wound like a worm through the school park – was a twenty-minute drive away, and then the nearest village or pub or telephone box was further still. Maybe, in the darkest corner of the woods, a lamp was lit in Roly's caravan. But that would be all. Foxwood Manor, once the grand and opulent hunting lodge of some reclusive gentry, now a decaying boarding-school, was cut off from the world by acres of deciduous Dorset forest, some of the oldest and densest in England.

An owl hooted. For a moment, the clouds thinned and parted and the moon was bright as daylight. Then the flint and the slate of Foxwood Manor shimmered like diamonds. The dead dry leaves of the ivy which had crawled up the walls and round the windows shivered in a cold wind. The woodland creaked and rattled.

The cloud fogged the moon. Suddenly, at the same time as the house became black again, the bright light in the hall went out.

Dr Kemp was closing the shutters. He moved from window to window and pulled the wooden shutters shut. Then, from outside, the building was in total darkness, as though nobody was inside and it had been abandoned for years.

I went in and sat by the fire with Mrs Kemp and the old dog. It was dismal, the long, oak-panelled room, which had looked and sounded quite festive when all the parents and boys had been bustling there just a few hours before. Now it was revealed in all its shabbiness. It was a poor fire, a few spitting and smouldering spars of fence posts and gnarled timber. The Christmas tree, which almost reached the ceiling in the far corner, was sparsely lit by a few coloured bulbs and draped with tarnished tinsel. Along the walls, the photographs of boys and teachers who had been and gone years ago were faded and fusty, as blurred as the memory of the faces themselves. There was a trophy cupboard, but the cups and shields were nothing much, simply the in-house prizes for tennis or cricket or soccer or shooting contested every year by a dwindling number of Foxwood boys. The honours boards had pride of place, for the school had a history of real achievement under the rigorous instruction of Dr Kemp. There was a roll of names going back through the twenty years he'd been teacher and head-master at Foxwood, boys whom he would never forget, whose talent for music, whose self-discipline and, above all, whose perfect ear had won them scholarships to many different and famous schools.

But the hall was dingy and cold. Worse, somehow, because it was so grand. The size of a tennis court, with an enormous stone fireplace and great tall windows with oak shutters, it had been the warm heart of a lovely country house. With a splendid fire and warm lighting, with the heads of gallant beasts displayed around the walls, with a host of ruddy-faced people, with brave, sweet-smelling dogs asleep on fine rugs, with good wine and hot food and maybe some music, it would still have been the grandest hall in all the county.

But not now. There was a dog, Wagner, an eighteen-year-old black labrador, who was just then snoring sonorously at his mistress's feet: once a fine, strong, handsome beast – his name pronounced the English way in reference to his tail – he was fat, with bad hips, a sagging belly and a malodorous mouth. There would have been music, from the grand piano in the far corner of the room, but not now. There was an excuse for a fire. No laughter, no wine.

As for food, Mrs Kemp said to me, 'Alan, have another biscuit.'

I had a glass of milk in one hand and a chocolate biscuit in the other. On a little table in front of me there was a plate with another chocolate biscuit on it. I sat awkwardly upright on a threadbare sofa. I'd never sat in the hall before – it was out of bounds except during music practice – and I felt uncomfortable and embarrassed. I managed to say through a mouthful of biscuit, 'No thank you, Mrs Kemp.'

Dr Kemp was closing the shutters, with his back to me and his wife, half a tennis court away. But when Mrs Kemp leaned closer to me and whispered, 'Give it to Wagner then', and even as the dog stirred and started to struggle to his feet in anticipation of a treat, the man said loudly, without even glancing over his shoulder, 'No you don't. We've had him all this time and never fed him from the table once. We're not starting now.'

Mrs Kemp raised her eyebrows, winked at me and

back-handed the biscuit to Wagner, who crunched and swallowed it horribly just before Dr Kemp crossed the room towards us.

He stood with his back to the fire, as though he were warming his legs on the flames. As always, he was wearing grey trousers and a chequered tweed jacket, a white shirt and a flannel tie; suede shoes with shiny toes. Fifty-five, he had the build of a man who'd been a sportsman in his youth, stocky and well balanced like a scrum-half, and the disgruntled look of a poor loser. Odd – I remember thinking, although I was only twelve and had known the man for five years and watched him with great caution for all of that time – odd, that a man in such a strong squat body, who looked like he'd been a rugby player or a handy boxer, should be so alive with music. Odd, that someone suffused with a love of music and its beauty should be so testy, so ill at ease with everyone else around him, even with his wife, as irritable as an oyster with a grain of sand pricking and prickling inside it all the time.

Looking at him, I felt a sudden squirming of dislike for the man. And just then Dr Kemp turned such a peevish eye on me that I ducked my mouth to my glass and swallowed long and hard. When I surfaced I had a milky moustache.

'So,' the headmaster said. 'So, Scott, what am I going to do with you?'

I knew I wasn't supposed to answer. It was what Mr Bradfield, my English teacher, called a rhetorical question. But Mrs Kemp, who either didn't recognise the form or had acquired some kind of waiver from years of marriage, said, 'You are not going to do anything with Alan. He's going to spend a couple of nice days with us before his mother comes and takes him home for Christmas.'

'I spoke to his mother on the telephone,' Dr Kemp said. 'She called from Switzerland, said she'd been held up.'

'And you had a letter, didn't you, Alan?' Mrs Kemp put in. 'Did she tell you when she was coming? By the way, could you give me the stamps, for the school album?'

I glanced from one of the faces to the other: from the grey gull's eye of the man to the woman who was trying so hard to be nice. I thought for a moment of the piece of air-mail paper and the crumpled envelope with its bright, Christmassy stamps, lying soiled and sodden somewhere in the woods – of my mother's sweetly childish, loopy handwriting smudged with the damp of the earth and the cold night air.

'Austria,' I said. The word seemed to stick in my throat, with the crumbs of the chocolate biscuit. 'She said the snow was especially good and she might stay another week.'

I saw the look exchanged between the man and the woman, how she tried with a tiny frown to prevent her husband from expressing his exasperation. And quickly, to forestall him, she said, 'Well, you can always take Wagner out with you, for some nice long walks in the woods. And there's the bird, of course. I suppose there's lots for you to do?'

'What about the bird?' the headmaster said. 'What is it, a crow or something?'

It was *my* bird. The idea of describing it, of trying to describe it to Dr Kemp, filled me with a kind of numb, helpless anger. Maybe to Mrs Kemp, I could have told her something – that I'd been out in the woods on a Sunday afternoon in November, when the other boys were doing scouts with Mr Furness or stamps with Mr Newton or raking leaves off the lawns with Miss Hayes and Mr Buxton; that I'd escaped alone to wander the woodland I knew inch by inch after years of exploring, and I'd heard a commotion in the bramble beds – in the tangle of brambles in the deep ditches round the barrows and tumuli now overgrown in the forest. I'd burrowed inside, like a prisoner of war bellying through rolls of rusty barbed wire, snagging and tearing my coat, scratching my face and hands, and found the bird struggling in a straitjacket of thorns.

Nothing but a bit of black rag, waterlogged, spluttering. But to me it had seemed so marvellous in its rage, exquisitely mad, although the struggle had left it exhausted and the tail feathers damaged so badly it would never have flown even if it had managed to tear itself free. Indeed, in its fury, the bird had pecked at its own foot, which had been entwined by the unbreakable bramble wire, and tweaked it off, leaving a raw stump from which the bone protruded. I'd freed the bird, although it jabbed at my hands with its beak, and even when I'd secured it in a firm grip it had pecked and pecked until my wrists were raw. I remember the beat of its little heart between my hands, the heat of it, the force of its life – and I'd carried the shattered, terrified creature back to the stable-yard, where Roly, who'd bump-ed into me by chance on his way back from the woods, had helped me to settle it safely, without panic or commotion, onto the manger in the abandoned stall. Yes, it had trembled and shrieked for a while, so crazed by the trauma of its entanglement and the strangeness of the smells and the alien handling it had experienced that it had flung itself off the perch and dangled by the thong which I'd attached to the intact leg. Upside down, squawking, beating its wet wings until the air of the stable was a whirl of dust and chaff – until I'd eased it back onto the perch and it had stared at me, panting. A wild spirit with wild black eyes.

'A jackdaw, sir, a young one. I found him in the woods.' That was all I said.

The headmaster could hardly suppress a snort of derision. He would have snorted whatever I'd said, this boy who'd been foisted onto him when all the rest of the boys had gone home. 'That's what I said, isn't it? A crow, a jackdaw, what's the difference?'

'A kind of crow, yes, sir. A bit smaller than a carrion crow or a rook and . . .'

'Yes, yes,' the man said. It seemed to annoy him – indeed, it was almost beyond the bounds of possibility – that a twelve-year-old could presume to know something that he didn't. 'Don't you think you should have left it where it was? It'll die, won't it, tied to a perch in a dusty old stable?'

'It would've died in the woods, sir,' I answered, imagining its inevitable end as a sodden, feathery rag enmeshed in thorns. 'I think I can mend it, sir. I've read about it, in one of the books in the library. I can mend its tail feathers and it'll be able to fly again.'

'Well, that's nice, Alan,' Mrs Kemp said, again to forestall her husband, who would have countered in one way or another, unable to defer to a white-faced, red-haired, skinny child sitting in front of him. 'Here, let me take these away from you.' And she reached for my glass and plate, wheeled herself away from the fireside, towards the foot of the staircase at the far end of the hall, and disappeared into the headmaster's study.

Dr Kemp sat on the sofa, so close to me that our knees touched. 'You know, we can turn the situation to your advantage,' he said conspiratorially. 'This is a good opportunity for us to do some work together.' He gestured at the honours boards. 'They all had the gift that you have: Stuttaford, Radcliffe, Pryce, Maundrell, Inkin, Barry-James – a rare gift, the gift of perfect pitch. And that gift conferred on them a duty, a responsibility, which they undertook and fulfilled under my guidance and instruction. When I was a boy a good teacher found the gift in me, and worked me and pushed me and guided me. Unfortunately, I could never fulfil my promise, but now they are yours, the gift, the duty . . .'

And, exactly as I knew and dreaded he would, the man stood up suddenly and said, 'Now, I want to hear you sing. Come along' and he strode away from the fireplace to the piano in the corner.

I felt my whole body, my whole being, go rigid with hatred of the man. Not just hatred, which might have been a manageable, single emotion, but also a colossal crash of boredom: that the man should do and say just what I knew he was going to do and say; and anger at the injustice that I should have been abandoned there, in the gloomy great hall at Foxwood Manor, on that night.

'Please sir. No sir. I . . .'

Mrs Kemp emerged from the study at that moment. She had heard what her husband had just said, and she must have seen the flush of anxiety on my face. 'Oh dear, Alan doesn't want to sing tonight,' she said. 'Of course he doesn't, he's tired and a bit fed up and . . .'

She might as well have slapped her husband in the face.

'What do *you* know?' he blurted at her. 'Of course he doesn't *want* to! None of them *want* to! It's nothing to do with what he *wants*! What do *you* know? When you can't even tell *this* –' and he crashed the nastiest, ugliest dischord on the piano '– from *this*!' and crashed another horrid, ugly chord. 'I mean, what do *you* know?'

There was a long silence. Wagner broke it by struggling to his feet and limping from the fire to the foot of the stairs, where he collapsed in a heap beside the wheelchair with a terrible groan, as though the effort had nearly killed him. Mrs Kemp blinked, speechless for a moment. Then she had the gumption to lean down to the dog, rumple one of his grizzly ears and say, 'Well, Wagner old boy, I know exactly how you feel. Me and you, I guess we're both ready for the scrap-heap.'

Dr Kemp recovered himself quickly. He smoothed back his hair and then wiped his hands down his face, as though washing his anger away. He cleared his throat and inspected his nails carefully, unable to look across the room and meet his wife's eyes or indeed the eyes of the small boy who was sitting on the sofa.

'You're right, of course, my dear,' he said at last. He tried a joke. 'Not that you're ready for the scrap-heap – neither you nor Wagner for that matter. I mean, it's been a long and rather hectic day for all of us, and we're all tired.'

He closed the lid of the piano very gently and crossed towards the fire. 'Go upstairs to your dormitory now, Scott. Get yourself undressed and washed and ready for bed, and I'll be up in five minutes. Go on now.'

I stood up. As I paused at the foot of the staircase, from which I was usually forbidden, Mrs Kemp took a quick, gulping breath and said, 'Perhaps Alan would like to stay with us, in our spare room? It must be awfully dismal, on his own up there in the dorm.'

There was a prickly silence. Dr Kemp swivelled a bilious eye from his wife to me and back again. 'Don't mollycoddle,' he said. 'The boy won't come to any harm. I'll look in from time to time to see that he's all right.'

She sighed, pursed her lips, and said, 'Well, Alan, for a few days, try to think of Foxwood as your home, if you can. Goodnight, sleep tight.'

She smiled so beautifully at me that my heart seemed to rise into my throat. Hoarsely, I said, 'Goodnight, Mrs Kemp,' then trod up and up the stairs and into the darkness.

I stopped on the landing, turned and looked down. Dr Kemp was kneeling in front of his wife's wheelchair. With the same hands which had banged the piano so cruelly a moment before, he removed her shoes with the utmost tenderness and began to massage her feet.

The man bent to his wife's feet and kissed them, as though seeking her love and forgiveness. She placed her hands on his head, loving, forgiving.

It was bitterly cold upstairs. At best, during term-time, the huge iron radiators gave a feeble warmth. Now they were cooling, groaning and sighing like dying beasts. In order to save fuel through the Christmas holiday, the headmaster had turned off the boiler as soon as the boys had all gone home that afternoon. I was in the bathroom, wearing only my blue-and-white-striped pyjama bottoms. Reflected in a tarnished mirror, I looked very thin and small in the big room: skinny white body, tufty red hair, bare feet on bare lino. I leaned over one of the rust-splashed basins – there was a row of fifteen of them, each with its own little mirror in front of it – and brushed my teeth in the icy water. Behind me there were six deep, yellowy enamel baths standing on clawed feet, their taps gleaming in the glare of a single unshaded overhead bulb.

Of course I was alone in the bathroom. In term-time, every night was bath night for one of the dormitories, so that every boy bathed twice a week – and then the room was noisy and steamy, with naked slippery bodies splashing and shouting whenever Miss Hayes allowed them the leeway to do so, or if Mr Buxton was on duty and the boys played up. And sometimes, when Dr Kemp came tip-toeing along the corridors after lights-out and heard the boys whispering when they should have quietened down and gone to sleep, he would burst into a dormitory and demand that whoever was talking should get out of bed, put on slippers and dressing-gown and follow him to the bathroom – where the offender would lean over one of the baths, lift up his dressing-gown, drop his pyjama bottoms and be beaten very crisply with a cane or with the flat of a wooden clothes-brush.

I looked at myself in the mirror and saw the room in the reflection. For a few seconds I remembered with equal vividness the warmth of the comradeship I'd shared there, and the whistle and sting of the cane.

The door swung slowly open.

I watched it in the mirror. A boy stood in the doorway, in pyjama bottoms, barefoot.

It was me, it was my reflection. But then it wasn't me, it was a boy I didn't know. And when I turned he'd gone. There was no one, only the black mouth of the corridor and the wintry breath it exhaled.

Shivering, I turned off the bathroom light and stepped into that darkness. I padded past the empty dorms, past one of the lifts, almost the length of the old house, and came to my own dormitory. It looked even barer and bigger than it had in the afternoon, when I'd sat and watched from the window as the other boys left, because now the curtainless windows were black, just mirrors of my own swift and silent movements around the room.

I had myself for company. No ghosts: although for a moment I wished there had been one, to dispel the utter vacuum in which I was marooned. Again I seemed to catch in the corner of my eye a ghost of myself, a flicker here and a glimmer there of a small boy in stripy pyjamas, a swift, silent figure moving through a row of tall black mirrors.

I pulled back my counterpane and was about to slip into bed when I felt a lump under my pillow, and I took out the little transistor radio.

With a furtive glance over my shoulder, where the door of the dorm was ajar, I adjusted the ear-piece into my ear and switched the radio on. It whistled and crackled and hissed, until I turned the tiny dial with the tip of my finger. And then suddenly – like a signal from another planet far beyond the empty cold room in the empty cold school, light years away from the dark woodland which surrounded the school and stretched for miles and miles into the distance – there was a blast of pop music.

It filled my head – *so here it comes, here comes the night* – it flooded my body. I closed my eyes, shut out the room and the school, and was nowhere.

So I didn't hear the footsteps coming along the corridor towards the dorm, didn't hear them come closer, didn't sense the opening of the door . . .

Dr Kemp came in. He must have seen me standing in the furthest corner and been surprised that I didn't turn to acknowledge his presence; surprised that I ignored him, tapping my foot and twitching my hips in an oddly provocative way.

He crossed the room. Too late to try and hide the radio, I saw his looming bulk reflected in the window.

I froze, unable to choose between a futile attempt to disguise what I was doing or a simple admission of guilt. He stood so close behind me that his breath was hot on my cold wet hair and neck, and he seemed to pause and inhale the scent of my body. And then he heard the tiniest sound: a tinny persistent beat, so faint it could almost have been the flutter of a pulse inside his own head.

He listened. We both held our breath. He saw the wire running from my hand to my ear; he saw the radio. 'Scott!' he barked.

He yanked the wire and the ear-piece popped out. I dropped the radio onto my bed. The music was suddenly loud, and I stared up with horror, to see the man's face so close to mine, to smell his breath and the peppery odour of his body. Dr Kemp barked again – 'What do you think you're doing!' – and grabbed for the radio, picking it up with a look of disgust as though he were handling a toad. He tried to turn it off, but his fingers were too big and clumsy for the dials and the volume went up and up until – 'Damn the horrid thing!' – he banged it onto the floor with sudden impatience.

The music stopped. The silence was very cold.

We both looked down at the little plastic machine on the floor without saying anything. At last Dr Kemp cleared his throat and wiped his face with his hands, and he said, 'I don't suppose it's broken,' in an odd, soft voice which was probably the closest he could come to saying he was sorry for what he'd done. I bent down and picked up the radio. It fizzed in my hands until I switched it off and put it on my bedside locker.

'Time for the prayer,' the man said.

Every night, just before lights-out, Dr Kemp would come to all the dormitories, one after the other, and say the same prayer while the boys stood in their pyjamas by their beds. The same short prayer: I'd heard it several hundred times during my years at Foxwood. And still, each time, I puzzled at the words. Now I put my hands together and closed my eyes.

Dr Kemp said, 'Lighten our darkness, we beseech Thee, O Lord, and by Thy great mercy defend us from all perils and dangers of this night. Amen.'

That was all. I pulled back the counterpane and blanket of my bed and slipped between the sheets. What *perils*? I wondered. What *dangers*? I'd sometimes been miserable at the school, and often I'd felt the almost physical pain of homesickness, a hurt inside my chest and an ache in my throat when I thought of my mother and father and the faraway warmth and familiarity of home. But what were the *perils and dangers* I needed to be defended against? That from time to time a big bullying man would burst into the dormitory and march me down the corridor to the bathroom and beat me on the backside with a clothes-brush? That the same man might sneak up behind me and snatch my radio and throw it on the floor and smash it? If so, the prayer hadn't worked. Now I looked up at Dr Kemp, who had turned towards me and was leaning close.

The man touched me. He'd never done so before, but

this was the first and only time that I had been alone in the dorm with Dr Kemp. With my blanket pulled up to my chin, I watched wide-eyed and afraid as Dr Kemp came closer and the man's right hand came down to touch my head. For a long moment the hand was heavy and still and very hot. Then, as both of us held our breath, as though neither of us knew what was going to happen next and had no way of controlling it, the hand moved very slowly and gently to my cheek and down to the scratch on my neck.

Dr Kemp suddenly straightened up and stepped back. His voice was curiously hoarse, so that again he cleared his throat as he said, 'Your hair, I thought your hair was wet.'

He crossed to the window and stared out: there was nothing but blackness and his own reflection. I watched him without moving my head, because I didn't want the man to look back at me and maybe come looming close again. And, mixed into the dislike I had for the man, I remember I felt the tiniest and oddest twinge of pity for him – perhaps, I wondered, it was strange and sad for the headmaster too, to be alone in the dormitory with just one small boy, now that all the others had gone home and the big old house was all but empty. Another term was gone. Another year was nearly over. Dr Kemp looked older and sadder. From the corner of my eye, I saw how the man appraised himself in the black mirror, saw that his hair needed cutting and his clothes looked a bit too big for him. For a few more moments, the two of us – the man at the window and me sheathed into my narrow, cold bed – held our breath and waited in the stillness of that room, so utterly different from one another, except that we were human beings alive and breathing in that mid-winter night, cut off from the rest of humanity by miles and miles of deep, dark woodland.

He moved to the door, faraway at the other end of the dormitory. He clicked off the light, said, 'Goodnight,' and closed the door. I heard his footsteps soft and slow, down and down the corridor. Then silence.

I lay on my back and stared into the darkness. Not even a streak of light came under the door, because this time the headmaster had flicked off the switch at the far end of the corridor.

The window rattled a little, as a gust of wind stirred the trees of the forest. An owl hooted. Silence.

And just then, the only comfort I could find – for the ache in my throat and the hurt in my chest were almost more than I could bear – was to reach to my bedside locker and feel for the transistor radio. I held it close to my ear, clicked it on and turned the dial. Even this little bit of solace was denied me. There was nothing. A crackle of hope for a split second, a pop and a faint high-pitched whistle – then nothing but a hiss in my ear.

Was there nobody out there? Nobody? Was I alone in all the world with Dr and Mrs Kemp?

I squeezed my eyes shut, and quite deliberately, not in a daydream or a blurry reminiscence, I recalled my father. It was Christmas Day, my birthday, a year before, and my father had given me an air pistol. We were in the hazel copse at the bottom of our garden, and he'd arranged a stack of empty tins – golden syrup, rice pudding, custard powder – to do some target practice. It was a clear, cold morning: no snow but a dusting of frost. My father was wearing brown corduroy trousers and one of his green army pullovers; in the sunlight which fell through the trees his hair was coppery bright, and his eyes shone with the joy of giving his son such a grand present – a Webley & Scott .177 – and showing me how to use it. His hands on the pistol, strong and lean and very white, moulding mine to the matt-black heft of it, teasing one finger to the trigger; his voice, calm and quiet, as I aimed at the tins and fired; the soft, plosive puff of the pistol and the ping of the pellet on the can. We'd practised for an hour, my father and I alone together in the most secret part of the garden, and then, when he stopped for a smoke, I'd slipped down to the stream with the pistol – where, as I waved it carelessly around me, up into the trees and into the undergrowth, for something different to shoot at, I spotted a vole which was plying from one bank of the stream to the other. I sighted on it, as my father had taught me to sight on the tins. I took a breath and held it, as he'd told me to do. I gently squeezed the trigger . . .

'No, Alan, lower the pistol, do not fire.' My father's voice was in my ear, actually inside my head, not shouting, but perfectly firm in the certainty that I would obey him. The vole swam to the bank of the stream and climbed out of the water. It was slick and sleek like a rat, until it shook off a shower of droplets and fluffed up like a cuddly toy. Its eyes were black. Its bead of a nose twitched at me. As I lowered the pistol, the vole turned away and disappeared into a dark tunnel.

My father took the pistol from me and we walked back to the house. I was sickened in my stomach that I'd spoilt the day and dreaded what he might say to my mother. But I remember my heart had swelled and my eyes prickled with tears of love and gratitude when, at the Christmas dinner table, she'd asked if I'd done well with the pistol and he'd smiled and said, 'Alan did very well – he learned a lot this morning.'

Last Christmas: the pistol from my father, the radio from my mother. Now the vision faded and disappeared and I stared into the empty darkness of the dormitory. I pressed the hiss of the radio to my ear, and I wept, with great gulping sobs. As I swallowed, the tears scalded my throat.

Sleep, and the burning in my throat, brought the dream to me again – the faces and the room I didn't know. The music that Kemp had snatched out of my ear suddenly blared again, the lurch and swoop of a familiar, unrecognisable sound, and a gloomy college room strewn with paper whirled around me. This time the faces of the man and woman blurred into view together, locked in a kiss which dissolved in a muddling of pain and tears as though the fusion of their lips had burned them. She was weeping, he was clawing at his throat and choking, and a voice said 'I disgust myself' in a weary monotone. When the lid of a piano slowly opened – and as it did so a pit of the deepest horror seemed to yawn inside my stomach – the reflection of the boy, me at first and then not me, beckoned me close and gestured for me to peer down into the hole. I leaned in. Something like a wire glimmered and snarled towards me and caught my throat and I recoiled with it scalding into my skin . . .

I awoke with a jolt, as if I'd fled to the end of a leash around my neck and been yanked to a bone-breaking standstill.

I lay still, in a quiver of relief that it was over. The radio was still hissing in my ear.

FOUR

Outside on the lawn, a cock pheasant scratched at the hard ground. It was a cold bright day, and the grass was white with frost. It had been a freezing night. Now the sky was silvery grey, the trees bare and black, and the world was a softly creaking, tinkling metallic place. The bird puffed out its feathers, red and gold and iridescent in the thin sunlight. It scratched again, and its little breath was a puff of vapour in the cold air.

Inside the house, I was singing. I'd been singing throughout the morning, and now I was tired of it. It was early afternoon, and we'd only stopped briefly for a lunch of tinned tomato soup and slices of white bread that Mrs Kemp had brought from the kitchen. I sang – *Three kings from Persian lands afar* – while Dr Kemp, employing all his guile as a musician to avoid the few minutely out-of-tune notes which offended him so much, sketched an accompaniment on the grand piano.

Mrs Kemp sat by the hearth. The hall was grey and dismal. There was no fire, so the room was probably not much warmer than it was outside. The lights on the Christmas tree had not been turned on. As I sang, my breath plumed around me. Dr Kemp, in his everyday tweedy jacket, didn't seem to feel the cold, and Mrs Kemp, a prisoner of her wheelchair, was swaddled in a red tartan blanket. She sat by the dead fire, and she brushed and brushed the big black dog, over and over, keeping a kind of rhythm with the music. From time to time she would stop brushing and pick all the hair from the brush and toss it onto the ashes, until there was quite a mat of it lying there.

We reached the end of the carol. Mrs Kemp said, 'That was lovely, Alan,' and she leaned out of her chair to throw another ball of fur into the hearth. I waited for a moment, standing with my hands on the top of the piano, for a word from Dr Kemp.

The word came. 'Again,' he said. 'Let's try to get it right.'

Mrs Kemp was quick to say, 'Well, I thought it was lovely,' and there was a terseness in her voice which I hadn't heard before. 'That's my opinion, for what it's worth. I know we're all "striving to shine" at Foxwood, but sometimes a bit of praise where praise is due might be nice.'

The headmaster looked at her as though she had used a word he had never heard before, a word from a language with which he was not familiar. '*Nice*? We aren't striving to be *nice*.' He made a play of searching the ceiling for inspiration, and then added, with what he thought was withering sarcasm, 'Now there's a good idea for a school motto: '*strive to be nice*'. Yes, let's change the motto for next year and see what a difference it makes to our exam results.'

'You know what I mean, my dear,' she countered, and somehow the tiniest edge of exasperation on her sweet, soft voice was more cutting than his clumsy attempt at irony. 'I know it's a banal sentiment that only silly, mediocre people like me allow themselves, but at Christmas-time it is nice to be nice to one another, or at least to try to. That's what I think.'

Dr Kemp weighed her words carefully. He instinctively felt for the crooked, paralysed fingers on his left hand, and massaged them as if he could bring them back to life again. And he said, with a great effort, 'You're right, my dear. The boy sings beautifully. With work and perseverance he might one day achieve some of the things which I did not. And so, for that reason, let's sing it again. Let's get it right.'

So I sang it again, although my mouth was dry and my lips were chapped after the hot soup. This time Dr Kemp stood up from the piano, gesturing me to continue singing, and he caressed my knuckles with the ivory baton to keep me in time. I sang, and I could smell the man's jacket and his breath and his hair because he loomed so close, sometimes even placing a heavy hand on my stomach to whisper, 'From here, you breathe from here . . .' even as I sang without pause or hesitation. And I reached the end of the carol, unaccompanied, only to wait for the absolute verdict as Dr Kemp leaned to the piano and touched the chord which would signify that my voice was either perfectly in tune or minutely wrong.

The chord hummed in the cold, still room, hung with the motes of dust from the dead fire and the dead tree. I knew I was good, because my ear was true and had always been true, long before Dr Kemp had singled me out. He listened to the notes until they faded to nothing and at last he said, 'Yes, that is good.'

High praise. Mrs Kemp's eyes glistened as she smiled across at me, moved by the beauty of the carol and the unqualified approval of her husband. Only Wagner sounded an off-key note. He groaned long and loud, with a horrible rasping in his throat like a death rattle, so that Mrs Kemp laughed and even the headmaster chuckled at the sound of it.

'Yes, Wagner, time to go out,' she said. 'At long last . . .'

A minute later – the time it took for me to go swerving and skidding through the corridors and into the changing-room for my outdoor coat and shoes and back to the great hall – I followed Wagner as he burst from the front of the school and into the colder air of the outside world. The dog lumbered ahead of me, gathering speed into a lolloping gallop, charging across the lawn and towards the woodland. Another minute, and the two of us were crashing through the dry bracken of the forest, winding through the stands of smooth white birches, in and out of the tall columns of the beech trees.

A grey and steely place, so that, if anyone else had been there to see it, my tuft of red hair would have been the brightest thing in the forest, flickering like a spark through the afternoon shadows. I yelled, my voice a little hoarse from the hours of singing and this sudden exertion – 'Go on, Wagner, go!' – as the heavy black bulk of the dog forced through the undergrowth ahead of me. With a glance over my shoulder I saw that the flinty façade of the school, with its rows of empty black windows, had fallen away and faded, that I'd escaped at last and was dodging and burrowing deeper and deeper into the woods. With another glance, I saw that the dog had startled a pheasant from the bracken, and the bird ran at first, keeping ahead of the dog, until it launched itself into the air and rocketed up, smashing through twigs until it broke clear, a brilliant-hot rocket of a bird which filled the trees with guttural croaks as it made its escape.

'Go on, Wagner, get him, get him!' I shouted, as the dog pressed a hopeful, joyful, futile pursuit. We ran, until at last, as the woodland banked upwards where the lane wound through it, the dog flopped into a nettle bed and lay there heaving, his tongue flopping like an eel and flecked with foam. I threw myself onto the ground and lay by the dog, flat on my back, gathering my breath as I gazed through the tops of the trees to the darkening sky.

A silence grew around us. At first the only sounds were our breathing, slowing and slowing to a steady rhythm, and the sounds of the forest on a late afternoon in midwinter that I knew so well: the cluck of the blackbird, the tick of the wren, the distant staccato of pheasant, and always the sway and creak of the branches. Dusk already. And never a silence, for the woodland was a whispering, living thing, as alive in the depths of winter as it had been in the sappy days of spring and bloom of summer.

I lay there and listened. Stillness, a sense of waiting – waiting for the darkness to fall and the night to come.

But then there was another sound. The dog heard it first. Wagner stopped panting, stopped breathing, and listened. I heard it too. It was the sound of an engine.

It grew louder. A car was coming along the lane, winding through the forest towards us.

I crawled on my belly to the top of the bank, so that I was overlooking the lane from a height of fifteen or twenty feet. The lane was a narrow cutting, barely wide enough for one car, with passing places here and there to allow a flow of traffic. On either side the banks were sheer, ancient hedgerows, much older than Foxwood Manor and the surrounding estate: probably this lane had been a cart track through the forest for hundreds of years. Now, as the dog bellied up beside me to have the same view, I peered into the distance and heard the sound of the engine grow louder. It was a snarling, intermittently roaring sound, the testy, impatient note of a car that was forced to slow and slow and nearly stop for the sharp bends before accelerating briefly along a short straight before slowing again. And I saw the lights: already, only four o'clock in the afternoon, it was dark in the deep tunnels of the lane, where the banks closed in and the trees lowered their bare branches over and across it; so I saw the headlamps cutting towards me, flashing their beams into the forest, now bright, now dimmed, as the car turned this way and that.

The dog growled a deep, throaty, rattling growl. I put one arm around the animal's body and snuggled him close. The car burst into the cutting below us.

An extraordinary sight, at such a time, in such an out of the way, forsaken corner of the English countryside. The car swerved round the bend too fast, headlamps blazing, the engine snarling, and as the rear wheels fishtailed out of control on a patch of frozen mud, it slithered to a standstill with its long nose rammed into the hedgerow, the front wheels mired in a ditch. Long nose, red flanks streaked with mud, the headlamps now blinkered in a tangle of hawthorn and blackthorn and nettles.

I goggled from my vantage point. It was an E-type Jaguar, quite new, something so beautiful and wonderful, so unexpected, that I mouthed an involuntary *wow* and stared, aghast and agog. The car was stuck. The filthiest, loveliest car I'd ever seen, the wheels spun and the engine howled as the driver crunched it into reverse and tried to accelerate backwards. There were two people in the car, a man and a woman, bundled in coats and scarves. I could see them quite clearly – mouthing at each other, their faces white with anger – because, despite the bitter cold and the quickly smothering darkness, the hood was folded down. And now, the deep, narrow lane, which had been so quiet and still a few moments before, was swirling with fumes, loud with the noise of the engine, bright with white and orange light, as though a machine from another planet had suddenly landed.

The driver got out. The engine settled to a rumbling growl as he stood up and slammed the door as hard as he could. He was tall and dark, young – hard to tell in the dusk and with a big black coat pulled up to his ears, a scarf wrapped around his mouth. Now he tugged the scarf from his face, said, 'Fuck,' and marched across the lane so that he was standing just below the spot where the dog and I were lying. He fumbled with his coat and trousers and started to urinate into the hedgerow. A cloud of steam rose into the air. The dog wrinkled his nose at the scent of it. Then the young man zipped himself up and strode back to the car.

'You try,' he said. 'Come on, Sophie, you try, while I push. Just slide across, jam the fucking thing into reverse and let the clutch out.'

The passenger, a girl as dark as the man and just as swaddled in coat and scarf, struggled to move across into the driver's seat, muttering impatiently as she snagged her coat on the gear-stick and hand-brake. 'What the hell are we d-d-doing here?' she stammered. 'I didn't even know you had a b-b-brother till last week.'

'You didn't waste much time then, did you?' the man hissed back. 'Now, clutch down and find reverse – come on . . .'

There was a horrible clang as the girl jerked the car into gear. Once more the air was filled with smoke and a terrible snarling, as she accelerated hard and the wheels spun in the mud. At the same time, the man forced himself into the hedge and heaved with all his weight under the nose of the car. Suddenly, throwing a splatter of mud and ice from its tyres and into the other side of the lane, it lurched sideways and was clear again. The girl just managed to stop before it rammed backwards into the opposite hedgerow.

The man stood with his hands on his hips, his head thrown back, regaining his breath after the effort of pushing. When he crossed to the car, he paused and kicked at the off-side front tyre. 'It's going down, but it'll get us there. Move over.'

With another struggle of big coat and gear-stick, the girl was back into the passenger seat and the man was behind the wheel. A moment later the car throttled forwards, the wheels spinning again as it tried to grip, and it seemed to leap through the cutting and along the lane like some kind of wild animal.

Then it was gone, around the first corner. There was only one place it could have been going to: Foxwood Manor, the only place at the end of the lane. I jumped to my feet, tugging the dog with me. 'Come on, Wagner, let's go!'

I was thrilled to have seen such a car appear in the lane: an E-type, so sleek and slim and smooth, so dirty. My head rang with the sound of it, and I could still smell the fumes of its engine as I hurried to follow the dog through the trees. I was strangely excited by the quick, sudden vision I'd had of the driver and the girl, and the language the man had used: words that I and the other boys at school knew and had even tried ourselves in a clumsy, experimental way, but which I'd never ever heard in real life, from the mouth of a real person. I tried now, as I ran. 'Fuck,' I said, and even in the emptiness and growing darkness of the woodland where no one could see me or hear me, the word felt awkward and ugly in my mouth.

Boy and dog, we stalked the car. Because the lane was so tortuously twisting, winding like a snake around ancient tumuli and barrows of long-ago settlements, negotiating the stream beds and outcrops of rock over which the forest had grown, I knew I could get back to the school almost as quickly as the car would get there – or even quicker – by weaving my way along the tracks I knew so well. So we ran, this time with me going first and the dog huffing and snuffling behind me, and I could see the lights of the car over and away to my left as it spurted and slowed and spurted again through the maze of woodland. On foot the way was direct, and I bent low as I ran, like a hunter trailing a great, snarling wild beast. Sometimes the beast was close by, and I threw myself down or hugged the bole of a beech tree as it shone its eyes in my direction – and then, as the eyes flickered away and the beast moved through the shadows, the mud flecking its flanks and flying behind it, I ran harder, until I could see a light in the school ahead of me.

'Come on, Wagner!' I hissed through my teeth. The daylight was fading fast. The forest was a dark and marvellous place of huge silver trees, frosty undergrowth and the crunch of dead dry leaves underfoot. I knew every step. 'We can get there first! Come on, boy . . .'

At last there was a clear burst across the playing field, across the lawns. I skidded round the side of the school building and into the stable-yard. Just in time, because the lights of the car swept the open space where the dog and I had run just a few seconds before – and as I tumbled into the stable, tugged Wagner inside behind me and pulled the door shut, the car rumbled into the yard and stopped.

I peeped through a crack in the stable door. The noise was even louder, and the impression in the old cobbled yard even greater of an alien machine: because, as well as the roar of the engine, as the car revved so hard that it seemed to heave like an exhausted animal, there was a pounding beat of music which thrilled me even more – *my generation, my generation baby* – a thudding beat against the walls of the stables, which I could feel reverberating in the door itself.

The noise, the lights, the smell and swirl of exhaust fumes – Wagner started to bark. And the jackdaw began to bate. I turned to see its beady black eyes bright in the reflected glare of the car's headlamps, and it was beating its wings so hard that the dust whirled in the air around its head. And as I moved towards it, to try and calm it somehow, I was too late – because the jackdaw flung itself along the perch and beat to the end of its tether. The tether snapped taut. The bird fell upside down and dangled, beating and screeching in a hysterical panic.

Still the engine roared outside, and the beat of the music grew louder. Wagner bellowed from the depths of his barrelled chest. The jackdaw was a blur of wings and claws, a shrieking maddened thing. Just as I timed my grab at it, the engine and the music stopped. I caught hold of the bird's body, through the brittle, thrashing wings, but not before its scaly foot had gripped my hand with needle-sharp claws.

I held the bird close and it fell calm. It heaved in my hands, panting so hard that I felt its little heart would burst. Wagner stopped barking. I put the jackdaw back onto the perch, where it bobbed and ducked like an owl, a manic imp, staring and hissing but settling again.

'All right,' I said. 'And Wagner, good boy.' I crossed to the door again and peered out. I felt a warm trickle on my fingers, and I flicked a few drops of blood onto the stable floor. Taking a firm hold on the dog's collar, I stepped outside, into the yard.

The car's headlamps were still shining. They were yellow on the walls and doors of the stables, a flash of golden light on the windows of the changing-room. The man got out and walked around to the front of the car, so that his shadow was huge and long on the wet cobbles. He was tall, slim, and I caught the flash of a wolfish face under a head of long black hair; coat and scarf, close-fitting black jeans and black boots; a lean dark figure that cast spidery shapes as it moved in and out of the lights.

I knew his face. For a moment, as though by the same kind of neck-snapping jolt I'd felt in my dream, my throat was squeezed shut.

'Get out, Sophie,' the man said. She was slim, even in the bundled coat and scarf: a very white face in the gathering darkness, black, fashionably cropped hair, jeans and high boots. When she tottered on her heels, catching one of them on the uneven surface and reaching out quickly to the door of the car to steady her balance, the dog gave a single, very deep bark.

They both froze and stared in the direction of the sound. The man threw up one arm and shielded his eyes from the lights. 'Wagner?' he said. 'Bloody hell, are you still here?' And as I stepped forwards, he said sharply, 'Who's that? Keep the dog away from me . . .'

'Wagner, sir? You know him?' I tried to say, although my throat was so dry and tight. I managed to shove the dog back into the stable and shut the door. For a moment I puzzled over how this vision from a faraway world should recognise such a homely old creature as Wagner, who'd never in all his years travelled more than a mile or two from the school buildings. I went forwards again, my eyes flicking from the filthy red flanks of the car to the two white startled faces in front of me. I held out my hand, as I'd been trained to do, and said hoarsely, 'I'm Scott, sir. Can I help you, sir?'

The man leaned down and took hold of my hand. He shook it for a moment, then, feeling the warm stickiness of blood on it, let go and inspected his own hand in front of the headlamps. 'Yes,' he said, with a glance across at the girl. 'I guess you can help us. We've come to see Dr and Mrs Kemp.'

I blinked at him, and then at the girl. I nodded dumbly and swallowed hard, unable to speak. They were the faces from my dream.

FIVE

Thinking it was inappropriate to take the visitors into the school through the changing-room, I led the way around the side of the building, across the gravelled drive to the front of the house. Now the late afternoon was utterly dark, as dark as night. There was a glimmer of frost on the lawns. The bare spars of the copper beech were brittle and black against a looming sky. The woodland was a wall of blackness. The shutters in the great hall were already closed and only a gleam of light came through the cracks and under the big front door.

I reached up and rang the bell. The young man said, 'Can't we just go in?' and I instinctively replied, 'No sir, the boys can't, sir,' ducking my head to one side when I saw the exasperation on the visitors' faces. The girl was shivering, pulling her coat tightly around her and hugging herself with her arms. The man had brought a small, soft travelling bag from the car. All three of us glanced up to the sky and saw that a few flakes of snow were floating like moths around our heads. The girl said, 'I'm so c-c-c-cold,' which made the man grin with a quick flash of teeth and softly sing *'hope I die before I get old . . .'* I remember grinning nervously back at him, for I was still buoyed up by the excitement and suddenness of their arrival, and buzzing with the notion that, somewhere in a blurry nightmare, I'd seen them before. The grin froze on my face as the door opened.

Dr Kemp peered into the darkness. He was holding a sheaf of papers in one hand and, with his reading glasses perched on the very end of his nose and his hair flopping over his eyes, he wore a customary look of impatience and irritation.

'Scott?' he said. 'Is that you? What are you doing out there?'

I started to say, 'There's a gentleman, sir, he wanted to . . .' but then the young man pushed forwards, into the light which fell from the doorway, and thrust out his hand to the headmaster.

'Dr Kemp, I . . .' It was all he had time to say. Ignoring the outstretched hand, not bothering to look at the man on the doorstep and not even seeing that there was another person, a girl, standing there as well, Dr Kemp turned back to the house.

'You've come,' he said over his shoulder, hurrying away towards his study at the same time. 'You're late, and it's an odd time to come, but you might as well take a look while you're here.'

The man stepped into the house and the girl followed him. As I came in and pulled the door shut behind me, Dr Kemp half-turned in the doorway of his study, threw a quizzical look over the top of his glasses, and then disappeared from sight.

'It's the grand, over there in the corner,' his voice came barking out. 'I've done what I can, but it's practically un-playable. I'd be obliged if you could take a look. And since you've come all this way, you could look at the others, in the chapel and the music rooms. Scott'll show you.'

That was it. The headmaster had returned to his study and the muddle of end-of-term paperwork on his desk. The young man and the girl stood at the door. They stared into the gloomy cavern of the great hall, where at least the fire was flickering in the hearth and the lights of the Christmas tree threw splashes of colour on the photographs and trophy cupboards and honours boards on the walls. 'What is this, Martin?' the girl whispered, but he silenced her by lifting a finger to his lips. He took her by the wrist and led her into the hall, in the direction of the piano.

'Let's have a bit of fun,' he said.

I moved off towards the corridor, which, lightless, led off the hall like a tunnel. Although I was intrigued by the two visitors and the extraordinary way in which they'd arrived at Foxwood, I knew from my years of training at the school that I should keep out of the way: I was only a boy and they were grown-ups who had business which did not concern me at all. In any case, I was wearing my outdoor coat and scarf and shoes, all bespattered with mud from the chase through the forest, so I thought I should hurry along to the changing-room and take them off and get back into my indoor shoes. I plunged into the tunnel, feeling with my feet for the ramps, touching with my cold fingers the door of the library, the staffroom, the gun-room, through every twist and corner of the pitch-black corridor.

But then I stopped in the darkness and listened. Indeed, at that moment, three people inside the building stopped what they were doing and listened to the sounds of the piano which were coming from the far corner of the great hall.

Dr Kemp was in his study. He must have heard the notes from the piano, and of course he knew it was the stranger who'd just arrived at his front door who was playing. I stood at the further end of the downstairs corridor and listened, and I too knew that the young man who'd burst into my unhappy world was playing the piano. Mrs Kemp, just then coming down in one of the lifts, heard someone playing the piano in the hall, and she could tell it wasn't her husband. She knew that, unexpectedly, someone else was in the house, and she didn't know who it was.

It was the way the music changed in just the first minute of playing that made the three of us cock our ears so curiously.

The pianist had started with a few stately chords, then a scale embroidered into an elegant arpeggio. Clearly he was a competent musician, whose style at the keyboard was easy and unhurried. He essayed the style of the piano tuner for whom he'd been mistaken. He sat in the shadows of the corner of the hall, having stationed the girl behind him so that she was lost in the darkness, and he caressed the keys with a lover's touch. And then, slowly, so gradually that it was impossible to say where or when it was happening, the sound altered – a blurry chord here, a stealthy syncopation there – and the piano tuner's respectful appraisal of a tired and neglected instrument became the dirty sound of the blues.

I turned back towards the hall. I heard in front of me one of the lift doors clanging open and I saw Mrs Kemp propelling herself out backwards. Without bothering to close the door, she spun the wheels of her chair and accelerated as hard as she could ahead of me, towards the hall, from where, now, there came a kind of music that the house had never heard before. The sleazy blues had become a full-blown boogie-woogie, with a rollicking bass and a hammering right hand and even the ridiculous, random scrubbing of the pianist's elbow.

Dr Kemp and Mrs Kemp burst into the hall at exactly the same time, myself a second later. The headmaster, who'd listened approvingly to the first minute of playing, had leaped from his desk with such anger at the progression of the music that he had shoved a pile of paperwork onto the floor. Now he exploded from the door of his study. Mrs Kemp whirled into the hall at the same moment, and I slithered to a standstill behind her.

'What *is* that noise?' Dr Kemp shouted.

In the same breath as her husband, Mrs Kemp's high little voice said, 'Who *is* that?'

The playing stopped. Not immediately. The fingers on the keyboard could not resist an insolent coda, like the signature of a bluesman finishing a late-night set in a smoky club. Then there was silence.

It was broken when the two indignant voices started again – 'What *are* you doing?' from Dr Kemp and the same 'Who *is* that?' from a querulous Mrs Kemp.

The dark figure at the piano stood up and came forwards. The man seemed to lope across the hall. He was, somehow, a part of the shadows cast by the tower of the Christmas tree and the flickering light of the fire.

He approached Mrs Kemp first. With a beautiful smile, he leaned down to her, took her hand in a graceful, swooping movement and kissed it. 'Mrs Kemp,' he said, 'you're as lovely as ever . . .' and as she flushed and stared up at him, for the way he loomed was so overwhelming that it seemed to preclude the presence of her husband a few feet away, he added, 'It's Pryce. Surely you remember me?'

I watched the wonderful transformation of the head-master's face. All of the anger, the exasperation, the hostility, seemed to slip away from Dr Kemp. He actually looked younger, suddenly, in that second. With a look of real affection and a sincere welcome in his voice, he stepped forwards with his hand outstretched and said, 'Jeremy Pryce? Well, how marvellous . . .'

'No.' It was Mrs Kemp who interrupted. She turned her face up to her husband. She was still flushed from the young man's kiss, and her beautiful hair caught the light of the fire. 'No,' she said, and her voice was slightly hoarse, 'it isn't Jeremy, it's Martin. It's Martin Pryce.'

Another transformation of Dr Kemp's face. His out-stretched hand seemed to freeze in mid-air. His face froze too. His smile set, taut and cold. He took hold of the man's hand and shook it, briefly.

'Martin Pryce,' he said, and added with an enormous effort, 'welcome back to Foxwood Manor.'

Night fell. It fell on the woodlands and all of the creatures that sniffed and scurried and swerved through the darkness. The treetops creaked and the dry leaves rustled. There was no moonlight. The stars were smothered in cloud. Cold.

The night gathered around the old house and the people inside it. In the great hall, Mrs Kemp sat at the fire with the two visitors, Martin Pryce and his friend Sophie. Oddly unnerved by their presence, I'd found an excuse to get away and just watch what was happening from the shadows. Mrs Kemp leaned towards them and refilled their glasses with sherry.

Dr Kemp was in the furthest, most shadowy corner of the hall. He'd opened the top of the piano and was leaning deep inside with a torch and a set of tuning keys. From time to time, as the voices at the fireside murmured politely in deference to the almost holy ritual that the headmaster was performing, he would emerge from inside the piano, his hair flopping and his glasses slipping off the end of his nose, and he would strike a bass note.

The sounds were oddly plangent in the big room, with a hollow reverberation from the oak panels and high ceiling as though the hall were another corner of the forest outside.

Mrs Kemp was trying to make some conversation, volunteering a few reminiscences of Martin's days as a boy at the school and attempting to draw out the stammering Sophie, but it was halting, desultory, with the headmaster huffing and puffing in the corner, with the melancholy notes of the piano hanging in the air like the hum of a bell. In any case, she could see that Pryce was content to sit back and drink, swallowing several glasses of their good sherry in unnecessarily big gulps until his teeth and lips gleamed in the firelight and his eyes shone.

Suddenly, Dr Kemp straightened up and then sat himself at the keyboard. He launched into a Chopin sonata, playing with a panache, a verve which seemed a bit put on, a false and inappropriate bravado. To me, it just sounded wrong. The three at the fireside raised their eyebrows at each other and smiled with relief, for the music was bright and vigorous, altering the mood in an instant. 'That's better,' Mrs Kemp mouthed silently at the young people beside her, raising her glass in a kind of toast.

Not for long. The headmaster stopped in mid-phrase, tried the same phrase again, stood up and slammed down the lid of the piano. He knew it was wrong too. He stomped across the room towards the fire. As he reached to the mantelpiece and picked up his own glass of sherry, Pryce glanced at Mrs Kemp and said, 'Oh dear, it sounded all right to me.'

The headmaster sighed. 'It may have sounded *all right* to you,' he said. He stood with the backs of his legs close to the flames. The fire was burning low; the logs had collapsed, exhausted, into a smouldering heap and there were only a few coils of ivy waiting on the hearth as fuel. He took a swig from his glass and said, with a mixture of contempt and pity in his voice, 'I expect it sounded *all right* to Mrs Kemp and to your friend, er, Sophie, is it? It would have sounded *all right* to most people. But there are two people in this room to whom it didn't sound *all right* at all.'

Pryce and Sophie and Mrs Kemp looked round to see who the other person might have been. I stepped into the hall, from the long dark corridor where I'd been hiding, and I stood there, too shy at first to approach the grown-ups. I was holding an armful of logs.

'Come in, Scott, come in,' Dr Kemp said. As I came forwards, the headmaster continued, directing his words to Pryce. 'This boy has perfect pitch. For him and me, the music was painfully off-key, as indeed it would've been for your brother Jeremy . . .'

Two things happened to interrupt the headmaster's grumpy speech. I caught my foot on the edge of the threadbare rug in front of the fire and dropped the logs onto the floorboards with a rumble like a roll of drums. At the same moment the girl stood up, spluttering and choking on a mouthful of sherry, and she hurried off to the darkness of the Christmas tree, where she carried on choking and spluttering into a handkerchief.

It all stopped Dr Kemp in mid-sentence. He leaned down and helped me to stack the logs at the side of the hearth, while Pryce, with a wolfish grin of amusement on his face, said to a concerned Mrs Kemp, 'Sophie's OK, don't worry. It just went down the wrong way. I should tell you that she hasn't got perfect pitch either – in fact I reckon she's tone-deaf. But that's one of the things I like about Sophie: she isn't perfect, by any means.'

'Where's Wagner?' Mrs Kemp put in, trying to smooth over the little moment of confusion.

As Sophie returned to her seat, dabbing her eyes and mouth and throwing a snarly sidelong look at Pryce, I said, 'I left him outside, Mrs Kemp, inside the stable. The gentleman doesn't like him.'

It was the first time I'd really seen the visitors, although I'd watched their arrival in the shadows of the stable-yard and escorted them through twilight to the front door. They'd taken off their big coats. Pryce was wearing a black round-neck pullover, black brushed-denim jeans and black elastic-sided boots. He was lean and angular, with bony wrists and a pronounced Adam's apple, long black hair and strong, beaky features; so that, as I met the mocking, sardonic look in the young man's eye, I thought of the cormorant I'd seen on the lake, far off in a part of the woods that only I explored. Like the cormorant – sleek in the water, and then, drying its wings in the sunlight, a sinister, croaking sea-crow – he seemed like a visitor from another world. The girl was a pretty little urchin in a black pullover like the man's, jeans and high boots; she had an electric-blue silk scarf knotted loosely around her throat. And the flash of blue, her startled eyes and the tuft of hair like a crest on her head, reminded me of a fledgling jay I'd found last spring: Roly had shot down the nest and hung both the parents on his gibbet, alongside the corpses of stoats and weasels. The fledgling, peppered with pellets, had died in my hands.

Again it came to me: a jolting flash of the dream I'd had, and their presence in it.

Dr Kemp snapped at me, 'The dog lives here, in this house, not in the stable. Go and get him.'

I'd placed a couple of the logs onto the fire and coaxed the flames alive again with holly twigs, but then I stood up and dusted my hands over the hearth. Glad to get away again, I stepped gingerly past the young man's outstretched legs and boots and away towards the darkness and security of the corridor.

I heard the voices of the grown-ups behind me. It was Sophie, the gawky, flustered girl who was probably eighteen years old but looked like a child, who was covering her embarrassment by broaching a different line of conversation. I hesitated, eavesdropping, as she said, 'W-w-where are all the boys, M-m-mrs Kemp? The school seems very q-q-quiet . . .'

'It's the Christmas holiday, Sophie,' Pryce explained with mock weariness. 'That's one of the reasons we thought it would be a good time to call by, remember?' He said to Mrs Kemp, 'We were passing, not far away, driving down to my parents for Christmas, and I couldn't resist a little detour to drop in and say hello.'

'So who's the b-b-boy?' Sophie persisted. I'd turned out of the hall and was hidden from the adults. Peeking round the corner, I paused to catch Mrs Kemp's reply.

She said, 'His name's Alan Scott. Sometimes it happens at the beginning of a holiday, or at half-term. For some reason or other the parents can't come – maybe they're overseas, in the services, or, unfortunately, wrangling through a divorce or something – and then, once in a while, we're left with a little waif or stray for a few days.'

'Well, here's wishing him a very happy Christmas,' Pryce said, draining his glass and replacing it expectantly on the table in front of Mrs Kemp.

'In Alan's case,' she went on, ignoring the glass, 'there was a tragedy. It happened this summer. His father was an army officer serving in Northern Ireland. He came home on leave to England and . . .'

At that point, I bolted. I turned and ran into the blackness of the corridor. I just wanted to be swallowed in the darkness, to blot out the words I was hearing, to hear nothing and see nothing and feel nothing. To remember nothing. To be nothing.

But as I ran, I could feel the nightmare coming back to me, as it had so many times in the months of that summer and autumn. I tried to run from it, as though it were a terrifying black shadow pursuing me through the tunnel. I skidded and swerved down the corridor, so fast I seemed to fly, my fingertips brushing the familiar reference points of doors and door handles, my feet swift on the smooth lino and polished ramps. As I turned and saw the deeper darkness of a door in front of my face, I skidded to a halt and saw my own hand, a glimmer of white, reach out and push. I pushed the door open and went through.

There, in the changing-room, my own coat was the only coat. It looked like the figure of a man in black, looming in the shadows and waiting for me.

The room altered. For a dazzling moment the nightmare was real.

My living-room at home. A man was standing in front of me, in black trousers, a black vest and black balaclava. His eyes were cold and hard as they swivelled towards me. He was holding a short, stubby, double-barrelled shotgun. My father was kneeling on the floor, and the muzzles of the gun were pressed to the back of his head.

His face angled up and the words came out in hoarse, horrid slow-motion. 'Get away, Alan! Get away! Your mother . . .!'

An explosion like the end of the world. Such a noise that I felt my head might have burst with it. But it wasn't my head that burst. When the man in black pulled the triggers, my father exploded. His head burst open, in a welter of blood and smoke.

I ran. Past my coat, which had become a coat again. Through the room which had become a changing-room again. I stumbled out of the door at the back of the school and into the stable-yard.

The air was delicious. Cold and clean, it woke me instantly from the nightmare and returned me to the present moment. So I pattered across the cobbles, hardly glancing at the long red car which was parked there, and I fumbled with the latch of the stable door where I'd left the dog.

I fell inside. I could hear the stirring of the bird and feel the soft, warm nuzzling of the dog as I scrabbled for the matches on the shelf. I struck and struck a match and at last it flared into life. Applying it to the wick of a paraffin lamp, I saw how the flame threw a flickering light and fluttering shadows around the familiar room.

The jackdaw blinked at me and stared. But this time it was the dog I'd come for. I sank to the floor and hugged him with all my strength. In all my lonely, empty world, the big old dog was everything I wanted.

The nightmare had faded and gone, although I knew that the reality from which it had spawned would never change. Right now, in the safe, secret place I'd found for myself, with only a cranky crippled bird and a slobbery labrador for company, I buried my face into the animal's neck.

'Wagner,' I remember whispering, overcome with relief, 'good boy, good boy . . .'

I held tightly to the dog's collar and Wagner tugged me like a chuffing locomotive, back through the changing-room and along the corridors. At the further end I could see the light of the hall, and as we came closer I could hear the grown-ups' voices grow louder and louder. Reluctant to rejoin them, I paused at the entrance to the hall, peeked and listened.

Pryce was by the Christmas tree, leaning towards the rows of old school photographs. Dr Kemp had settled at the fireside with his sherry and his wife. Pryce was saying, as though the conversation had continued seamlessly since I'd fled from the room, 'But usually the damage is done over a period of time, over months and years, rather than by a single traumatic incident. I mean, just look at these sad little faces. I wonder what's become of all of them . . .'

He glanced back to the Kemps and shrugged when neither of them rose to his bait. He peered at another photograph, rubbing at the dust with his fingers, and said excitedly, 'This one, for example, take a look at this, Sophie.' And as she got up and joined him, he smudged at the photo and said, 'Do you recognise this darling little angel, Sophie? I must have been eight or nine years old at the time.'

The girl peered so close she almost touched the glass with her nose. After a moment she said, 'I recognise him b-b-better than you do, Martin. It isn't you, it's Jeremy.'

Wagner had been peering short-sightedly into the hall, leaning with all his weight on his collar, and when he spotted the tall figure of the young man against the lights of the Christmas tree, he lunged forwards with a horrid, strangulated growl. I tried to restrain him, but the dog gained a few yards with the suddenness of his movement and dragged me almost to the hearth before I could check him. Pryce and Sophie turned in alarm. Dr Kemp reached for the dog's head and grabbed the collar.

'Well, *you* recognise me, don't you, Wagner?' Pryce said. 'Remember this?' And as the dog made another futile, gurgling lunge forwards, Pryce held his right hand towards the brightness of the fire, to show a neat white scar in the fleshy part of his palm. 'Yes, Wagner, that was you, remember? I'm scarred for life. If you aren't damaged when you come to Foxwood Manor, you are by the time you leave . . .'

The words hung in the air. Mrs Kemp shifted in her wheelchair, flushed and lowered her head, so that her face was covered by the soft swing of her hair. Pryce had the grace, at least, to say, 'I'm sorry, Mrs Kemp, I didn't mean . . .' before she gestured at him with an odd flapping of her hands, as though his words were no more annoying than midges on a summer's evening. On impulse, Sophie sat down beside the woman and took one of her hands in her own.

'It's all right, dear, thank you,' Mrs Kemp said to the girl. 'I came to Foxwood as the riding mistress, many years ago, when Dr Kemp was a young music teacher here. Not long after we were married, I had an accident, so that . . .'

The headmaster tried to stop her with the lift of his eyebrow. But she continued, with a nod towards a photograph on the mantelpiece, a fading picture of a smiling, beautiful young woman on a big grey horse. 'My lovely Dapple, the love of my life, so handsome and fine. And a miracle, the shades, the subtlety of his marking. *'Glory be to God for dappled things . . .'*

Sophie took up the line – *'for skies of couple-colour as a brinded cow, for something-something on trout that swim . . .'* so that Mrs Kemp laughed brightly, like the girl she'd been when the photograph was taken.

'He was an ill-tempered brute,' the headmaster put in.

'He didn't like you,' she said, 'because he could tell you

were frightened of him. With me, he was sometimes a bit awkward, a challenge maybe, but marvellous . . .'

'He was downright dangerous.' Dr Kemp made a tiny off-hand gesture at her wheelchair, like a lawyer resting his case.

She pursed her lips, then said softly to the girl, 'We fell in the woods, me and Dapple. I gave him his head and he wouldn't stop. We fell and we were both hurt, me like this, and Dapple too – sadly, there was nothing to be done for him.'

A gust of wood smoke blew down the chimney and roiled from the mouth of the fireplace. There was a long silence.

At last the headmaster said to me, 'Well, Scott, it's your bedtime. Thank you for bringing the logs, and for taking care of Wagner. I know you're very fond of him. Go up now, and I'll be there in a few minutes.'

Sophie seized the moment, or tried to. She let go of Mrs Kemp's hand and leaned towards Pryce, taking his hand instead. She made a cute play of finding the scar and kissing it better. 'Poor little b-b-boy. It's t-t-time for us to go, isn't it? Come on now . . .'

He prised her fingers off him. He smiled too, but it was a cold smile he made with his fine white teeth. His eyes were not smiling as he leaned to the fireside table, picked up Sophie's glass and drained the sherry in a single gulp.

'I've been drinking,' he said. 'Better not drive.' He flashed a look at Dr Kemp. 'All right if we stay?'

In the boys' bathroom at the top of the house, I was brushing my teeth. I stood at the sink, in just my stripy pyjama-bottoms, and I shivered, barefoot, reflected in the mirrors of a big cold room. When I heard the footsteps and voices along the corridor, I had a bewildering mixture of feelings which I tried, in a second or two, to sort out before the grown-ups came tromping past. Without turning, I watched in the mirror as the young man and his girlfriend went past the bathroom door, followed by Dr Kemp. Of the three of them, only Dr Kemp glanced in and saw me, and I caught a glimmer of hopelessness in the headmaster's eye which added another, even stranger ingredient to my stew of feelings. Because I, who'd been so resentful of my abandonment with the Kemps for the Christmas holiday, who'd been so thrilled and unnerved by the sudden, swaggering arrival of the strangers, now felt a twinge of resentment that they were marching along my corridor and peering into every empty dorm. More than that, I felt the tiniest creeping of fear in my neck and down my spine, and in the prickling of my palms.

I spat into the sink. My mouthful of water and toothpaste swirled in the brown-stained enamel and slithered down the plug hole. I frowned at myself in the mirror. Confusing – I couldn't work out if I was glad or annoyed that the young people had come.

I put my head out of the bathroom door and watched them. I heard Sophie protesting that *she* could drive, that she'd had only one glass of sherry and *she* could drive. I heard Pryce replying that there were dozens of empty beds and surely they could stay one night and they'd be gone first thing in the morning – and I heard Dr Kemp say, with all the civility he could muster at being steam-rollered so thoroughly in his own house, 'Of course, of course, there's plenty of room. It isn't a hotel, but there are clean sheets and plenty of blankets and . . .'

Pryce paused at one of the dormitory doors, flicked on the light and looked inside.

'No, I don't think so.' He flicked off the light and proceeded further. At the next door he stopped and flicked on the light and peered in. 'No, not this one.' With a resigned Sophie and an uncharacteristically browbeaten Dr Kemp trailing behind him, and me following like an eavesdropping shadow, he paused at the dormitory next to mine. 'Ah,' he said, 'let's see . . .'

Pryce flicked on the light and looked in. He saw a row of fifteen iron beds, all stripped to their bare mattresses, a bare brown linoleum floor, bare white walls and two curtainless windows as black and cold as the night outside. Not a hotel. But he smiled strangely and drifted into the room, past bed after bed, touching each one as he went by as though it were a familiar pet. And at last, when he came to the one in the furthest corner, he stopped. There was a funny, altered twist of a smile on his mouth and a wistful gleam in his eye, as he stroked the icy-cold frame of the bed. He turned to the man and the girl who'd waited at the doorway for him to speak.

'This one,' he said. 'Can I, Dr Kemp? *My* old bed . . .'

At midnight the house was dark and silent.

In the great hall Wagner slept by the hearth, snoring gently, as close as he could get to the glow of the dying embers. He'd slept there all the nights of his life, through sultry, airless summers and the aching cold of winter. It was his place. Now he sighed in his sleep and felt the last warmth of the fire in his old bones.

It was silent along all the corridors of the house. No, not quite silent. From time to time the panelling creaked as the temperature dropped, and sometimes the wind which swayed in the forest and rustled the ivy on the walls outside made the windows rattle in the empty dormitories. So dark, so cold – the house seemed to groan and shift like a bear in deep hibernation, slowing its breathing, slowing its heart, sleeping a dead sleep.

I was half-asleep, restive, alone in my dormitory, aware of the gleam of winter on my face. The hiss in my ear was not the hiss of the wind in the trees: it was the sound of my transistor radio, which I'd left switched on, on my pillow, for the last ounce of comfort it could provide me. No music, since the headmaster had banged it on the floor, but only a whisper, as though it were exhaling a long, last breath before it gave up completely.

But then there was another sound from somewhere in the building. I rubbed my eyes and blinked, and I felt for the radio and turned it off. Suddenly alert, I lifted my head and listened as hard as I could, to try and catch the sound that had woken me.

Voices? In and out of the silence, I thought I heard a muffled cry, or a shout, or a muttered exclamation. It came to me again, so that I slipped out of bed and padded barefoot to the door of the dormitory. I opened the door and peered into the corridor.

Voices – and in the distance, the faintest flicker of light on the floor of the corridor, coming from beneath a closed door. Not a dormitory, but on the opposite side, perhaps from one of the lifts. I squinted into the darkness, thinking that Mrs Kemp was coming down in the lift for some reason, that perhaps she'd left something she needed in the hall and was going to fetch it. I stepped forwards and my feet were silent on the bare lino. As I continued on and on, I saw that the light was coming from inside the bathroom.

The cries too. I stood outside the door and the light played on my feet, for it was moving, fluttering – not the glare of the overhead bulb, but the living light of a flame. I heard the high, suddenly muted cry of a woman, and the strangely rhythmic grunts of a man.

I pushed the door open. A candle was burning, a stub of wax on one of the sinks, and the single flame was reflected again and again in the row of mirrors. Pryce and Sophie were standing naked, their bodies locked together. He was forcing her backwards against the wall and ramming himself deep inside her.

I'd never seen such a thing before. Now I saw it in multiple, moving reflections, the whole length of the room, in mirror after mirror. The candle guttered, the room darkened, the flame recovered and stood up again, and still the man thrust himself into the girl. She cried out, although one of his hands was partly covering her mouth, 'You're hurting me – Martin, Martin . . .' and he squeezed his eyes shut and grunted and pushed so hard that her feet were lifted right off the floor.

His back and buttocks were shining. Her face, wet with tears, twisted away from his and she opened her eyes wide. She saw me and cried out, 'Martin! The boy! Martin!'

Pryce did not slow his steady, quickening movement. Perhaps he could not. He turned to look at me, the little boy who stood in the doorway. He leered, his tongue wet, his teeth silver in the light of the candle, and he thrust with exaggerated vigour at the girl. He silenced her by kissing her long and deeply – and at last, when they drew apart, her face was muddled with fear and pain as though the fusion of their lips had burned her.

I spun out of the room, banging the door behind me. I ran back along the corridor, across my dorm, and buried myself deep in my bed.

SIX

I n the morning, the world was quite altered.
All night the snow had fallen, steadily, heavily, settling in deep silence. Now the woodland was muffled in snow and every sharp, cold edge of the house was softly blurred.

Dr Kemp stood in the stable-yard with Pryce and Sophie. It was a miraculous day of bright sunshine and a clear blue sky. The three of them were staring at the car. I had thought it looked so marvellously cruel the evening before, like a bloody, muddy beast of prey, but now it was asleep under a thick white blanket. The snow had drifted deeply around the spoked wheels. And the inside of the car was full of snow, because it had been left all night without the hood.

I'd gone out early, thrilled to see the world so wonderfully changed, and now I watched the grown-ups from inside the stable where I kept the bird: Pryce and Sophie, wrapped in the coats and scarves they'd arrived in; the headmaster, wearing his familiar brown anorak and a brown trilby. Dr Kemp bent to the car and scuffed away the snow with his foot. The off-side front tyre was completely flat.

'You'll need to change the wheel,' he said.

Pryce shrugged. 'There's no spare. Anyway, I don't think she'll start, even if we manage to dig her out.'

Dr Kemp, his face reddening with the cold, did not add anything. His exasperation at the carelessness of the young man, who was travelling in mid-winter without a spare wheel, unprepared for even a puncture, who could have moved the car into one of the empty stables instead of leaving it outside all night, was apparent in every twitch of his mouth and stamp of his feet. His crooked fingers were aching, as he'd told me they always ached in winter, because I saw how he rubbed them hard to ease the throbbing pain: his war wound, as his wife called it, and now, as though to fuel the testiness he felt at the idiocy of these unexpected, unwanted visitors, he must have thought of the stupid accident which had so miserably disabled him.

War wound. He'd told me the story, in the privacy of one of my singing lessons; he saved it, he'd said, for only the best of his pupils, and I'd been one of them. Soon after the outbreak of war he'd been conscripted and presented himself at Aldershot barracks, where by chance the recruiting officer had recognised him as a young musician who'd already made a mark as a concert cellist.

Deliberately to protect him from harm, the officer had kept him as his personal driver, the safest of all wartime postings, snug and warm in a big black Humber. The following week, his fingers had been irreparably crushed as he struggled to change a wheel.

Now I watched him from the stable doorway, as he stared at the flat tyre on Pryce's car, as he rubbed at his crippled hand. He flicked his eyes impatiently into the sky, where the rooks were clacking softly around their nests at the top of the beech trees, and higher still a buzzard was wheeling and mewing. It was a delicious day, the kind of day he must have looked forward to at the beginning of the Christmas holiday, which he and his wife could savour alone without boys or teachers or visitors. He sighed and chafed his hands together. He caught a movement at the other end of the yard and saw me, peering out of the stable.

'Let's give it a try,' Pryce said.

He yanked open the driver's door. He dug away the snow on the seat until the upholstery showed through and he climbed inside the car. He inserted the ignition key and turned it, and we could all hear the whir and click of the petrol pump as the engine primed. And suddenly, deafeningly, the crashing chords of 'My Generation' which he didn't bother to turn off before he pressed the starter button.

The engine churned and churned. The music blasted out. And as the engine churned slower and slower, as a couple of bangs like shotgun blasts exploded from the exhaust pipes and the air was filled with the stink of oil smoke, so the music churned slower as well, grotesquely distorted, *'my generation – my generation baby . . .'* just as loud but even more dangerously ugly.

'You could turn that off!' Dr Kemp was shouting. 'Turn it off!'

But Pryce cupped his hand to his ear and grimaced as though he couldn't make out what the man was saying. And still he pressed and pressed at the starter button, pumping at the throttle with his foot so that the exhaust pipes banged again.

The battery died. The music slowed to a grinding standstill. As the smoke drifted and thinned, as the rooks whirled in sudden confusion, at last there was silence and stillness again in the snow-filled yard. Pryce essayed a couple more jabs at the button. There was nothing.

He got out of the car and banged the door shut. 'She's dead,' he said.

Sophie looked hopelessly from Dr Kemp to Pryce and back to the headmaster. 'Isn't there s-s-somebody . . .?' she started to say. 'I mean, c-c-can't you telephone someone and maybe . . . ?'

'The phone is dead,' Dr Kemp put in, pointedly echoing what Pryce had said. 'The lines are down. It happens out here if there's a heavy fall of snow. And the snow-plough can't come because the lane's too narrow. Mrs Kemp and I can be cut off for days, or even a week at Christmas and New Year. We don't usually mind . . .'

Pryce took a deep breath. He held it for a second, then blew out a silvery plume, like a man enjoying the best and most expensive cigar in the world. He flashed a glittering smile at the headmaster.

'It's so beautiful,' he said. 'And you've got company this time.'

I was singing. '*In the bleak mid-winter, frosty wind made moan – earth stood hard as iron, water like a stone . . .*'

I stood with my hands on top of the piano, as Dr Kemp accompanied me, and it was a timeless scene in the grand, shabby hall, where now the light from the snow outside fell on every cobwebby crack in the oak panelling, on every smear of dust on the photographs and the honours boards, on the dry needles of the Christmas tree and the mottled tarnish of the tin cups in the trophy cabinets. The light was perfect, too perfect, because it showed every imperfection of the neglected room. Mrs Kemp sat at the hearth, and although the fire was burning briskly, spitting and crackling, the glow of it was quenched by the gleam of snow. The light showed how lovely she was, a fragile, broken creature swaddled in her wheelchair, her stockinged feet resting on the body of the sleeping dog.

I sang until, thump, a snowball hit the window nearest to the piano, stuck for a moment and slid slowly down. I hesitated in mid-phrase, so that Dr Kemp stopped playing. At the same time, Wagner struggled to his feet and started barking in the vague direction of the thump, although he had no idea what had caused it or what it meant. His voice was hoarse and booming, after the precision and clarity of the carol.

'Thank you, Wagner, that will do . . .' the headmaster cried out above the noise, so that the dog slumped down again, still wondering where the thud had come from. 'Now, Scott, try to concentrate. Where were we? *Earth stood hard as iron . . .*'

I took a breath and continued to sing. There was another thump, harder than the first, and this time Pryce's face appeared in the blur where the snowball had struck the window. Wagner was on his feet again, bellowing, big and brave and ready for battle. Dr Kemp sighed heavily, and in a little space between the barks he mouthed at the young man outside, 'Yes, Pryce, that will do, thank you very much,' in more or less the same weary way he'd addressed the dog.

The difference was that the young man didn't respond with the automatic deference that Wagner had shown. He affected misunderstanding, frowning and cupping his hand to his ear as he'd done in the stable-yard.

'Go,' the headmaster intoned loudly. 'Go elsewhere, please.'

The face disappeared, although a hand made a final swipe at the snow on the window so that a long smear remained. Wagner collapsed onto the floor with a terrible groan, breathing hard.

'Yes, old boy,' Mrs Kemp said to him, 'it is a pity for you to be indoors on a day like this, isn't it? Perhaps you'll be able to go out soon?' The question mark in her voice hung in mid-air, like a chime.

Dr Kemp relented. 'Well then. The last verse, one more

time, and that'll do for this morning. *Snow had fallen, snow on snow . . .*'

I burst out of the front door. Wagner forced past me so violently, mad to get out, that he almost knocked me headlong. Boy and dog, together we flung ourselves onto the lawn and ran and ran, for the joy of the sparkling whiteness of the snow, the snapping cold of the air and the perfect blue heavens above.

I shouted and whooped, the dog bellowed from the depths of his barrel chest – until we both stopped and listened, oddly abashed by the deadened echo of our voices.

A flock of crows rose from the trees and whirled like cinders, black and smutty and strangely silent. As old and as wise as the woods, they did not cry out. They only folded and unfolded, alerted by the cries but not alarmed. Indeed, even before we reached the middle of the lawn, beneath the bare boughs of the copper beech, the crows had returned to their roost, shuffling their wings, watching and waiting.

'Hey, Scott!'

A snowball thudded on the back of my head, an explosion of ice on my red hair. And there was Pryce, already armed with another snowball and ready to launch it: a big grinning boy a few years older than me, hurling the snow and then bending for more. I bent to the ground, scooped a handful of snow so crisp and crunchy and easy to compact that, in one single movement, I'd packed a missile and thrown it. It smacked on the side of the young man's head. Nothing could be better, more perfect, than to be boys in snow on a sparkling morning – so we joined in battle, we shouted and dodged and scooped and ran and hurled, until at last we closed in hand-to-hand combat, smothering handfuls of snow into each other's faces and necks and laughing and spluttering.

We rolled apart. For a second, gasping for breath, as I blinked at the infinite sky through kaleidoscopic eyelashes, I was suffused with love – yes, it felt like love, the warmth of companionship with this miraculous man who'd arrived at Foxwood in a snarling, filthy red chariot with a stam-mering elf as his companion, who'd spoken such rare, forbidden words, and who later, in the fluttering candlelight, had performed an act of such startling bestiality that I'd surely never forget it – who, overnight, had transformed my lonely world into a glitter of snow and sunlight.

Then, 'Fuck!' Wagner came for Pryce.

Sophie had been watching, as disinterested as the crows, crouching in the snow with her arms around the old dog's neck; it seemed that she'd found a friend in Wagner. Myopic, he'd sensed from her touch and her voice that she was someone he would never dream of biting. But as he watched the blur of snowballing and fighting, and when he knew that his true friend, me, was in battle with a tall dark figure he'd never liked and indeed had learned to hate so many years ago, he wrenched himself from the grasp of the girl and came rollicking forwards, burly, black and all but blind.

The dog hit Pryce's shoulder with a breathtaking shock. Wagner rolled him over, and he shoved his grey, slobbering muzzle into his enemy's throat. For a mad moment, Wagner had the young man pinned into the snow. Only the scarf and the collar of Pryce's coat prevented the dog's teeth from meeting bare flesh.

The teeth tore at the young man's ear. Pryce squealed, 'Fuck!' again as I manhandled the dog away.

Pryce sat up and squeezed the lobe of his ear. He said the word once more when he saw blood on his fingers, and he flicked a spatter of it into the snow. In the bright sunlight the blood was black at first, then red, and almost at once it fused into the ice, the loveliest pink. I hugged the dog, who was panting so hard that his fat old body was hot and huffing like a boiler. Sophie stared and gaped, as if half-afraid, half-thrilled by the conflict, and a funny, fake smile played on her face.

I tugged Wagner across the lawn, our feet crunching where the snow was still perfectly unmarked. I spotted something under the boughs of the copper beech, and bent to pick up the frozen capsule of an owl's pellet: sometime in the night, since the snow had stopped falling, a tawny owl must have perched in the branches and regurgitated this pellet of indigestible matter. I broke it apart with numb, clumsy fingers, and found, among the chitinous remains of many beetles, the skull and bones and matted fur of a shrew that the owl had swallowed whole. I glanced upwards to see where the owl had gripped the tree with its talons, and I tried to imagine how the bird had sat there, its feathers puffed out, its swivelling head hunched into its shoulders, through the cold, dark hours before dawn broke, while I'd been fast asleep in bed. I saw also that Sophie had crossed towards Pryce and knelt beside him.

The girl winced as Pryce took hold of her arm and pulled her closer. 'You're hurting me,' she said. 'You hurt me last night . . .'

He tried to kiss her, but she squirmed like a child and averted her face, flicking his lips with her hair.

'Hey relax, Sophie,' he said, and he caressed her cheek with the snowflakes on his fingers. 'No one knows we're here. No one knows anything. Look, we're in the middle of nowhere.' And he gestured around him, at the encircling woodland and the tall, cold sky.

But the girl glanced over her shoulder towards the house. There was a movement in one of the upstairs windows. They both saw that Mrs Kemp was watching them.

'Don't worry about her,' Pryce said. 'We'll do what we came to do. There are a few loose ends I need to tie up, then we'll get out of here. Trust me.'

He looked up again at Mrs Kemp.

'Revenge is a dish best served cold,' he muttered, 'and it doesn't get much colder than this.' The woman withdrew from the window.

He tried again to pull the girl close, and this time she relented, quite wooden as he folded her into his arms. I watched him closely, and the momentary joy I'd experienced in the snowball fight dissolved into a shudder of anxiety. I held my breath as they kissed, and, without realising I was doing it, I clenched my fingers so tightly that the skull of the shrew popped in my fist. For a second, Pryce turned his eyes and stared at me.

Dusting the remains of the pellet into the snow, I led the dog across the lawn and back to the house.

Dr Kemp was working in his study. Mrs Kemp was there too, keeping him company with tea and fig rolls which I'd helped her to bring from the kitchen. While he was shuffling accounts, deciding which bills it was best to pay and which could be put aside a little longer, she leafed through a riding magazine she'd already read many times before. Wagner lay sleeping at her feet. The study was a fine, tall room with panelled walls and a corniced ceiling. There were books everywhere, and stacks of sheet music on the mantelpiece of a grand fireplace. The hearth itself was heaped with papers. The formidable faces of the past headmasters of Foxwood Manor peered gloomily down from a row of oil paintings.

Sunlight fell through a high window, reflected from the snow outside. I was moping in a corner, nibbling a biscuit. The only sounds were the steady rhythm of the dog's breathing, the scratching of the headmaster's fountain pen and the flick-flick-flick of Mrs Kemp's fingers on familiar pages.

They both glanced up at the tromping of footsteps in the corridor above their heads. Wagner cocked an ear without opening his eyes. A heavy tread and a lighter, softer footfall: the movement of other people elsewhere in the house was strangely unsettling for Dr and Mrs

Kemp. He sighed with exasperation and cleared his throat to say something, but she quickly put in, with a smile in her voice to try and keep him sweet, 'He's revisiting his childhood, that's all. There's no harm in it.' Then, when they heard the rattle of a door and the clank of the pulleys as one of the lifts started to move, as Dr Kemp tutted and puffed to himself, she added, 'It says "No boys to use the lifts". Martin Pryce is not a boy, and nor is the sweet little Sophie. Try to ignore them, dear, they'll be gone in a day or two.'

'How will they be gone?' he snorted. 'The lane is blocked, the telephone is out of order, his swanky car has a flat tyre and a flat battery. How will they be gone?' He made a great play of tossing a sheaf of bills into the air, so that they fell back onto the desk in an untidy heap. 'I had the lifts installed for you, and for nobody else.'

'Please, dear, try not to get worked up,' she said, and she reached to him and squeezed his hand. She turned to me, a bit embarrassed that I should hear them wrangling, and said, 'We must remember it's Alan's Christmas holiday too. We should let him try to enjoy himself a bit.'

Pryce had been touring the school, revisiting the half-remembered corners of his childhood. He had Sophie in tow; with nowhere else to go, she was a helpless satellite. And I too had been in his thrall, following him from dorm to dorm, where he'd trailed his fingers along the frames of bed after bed and recited the names of the boys who'd slept there, a list of half-forgotten names like the mumbled words of a prayer. For a while, I'd tagged along as he mooched through the bathrooms, watched him lie down in one of the baths – in all his clothes, of course, so that he looked like a corpse in a deep, white coffin – and do a clownish reminiscence of long-ago matrons and masters-on-duty. At the further end of the top corridor, he'd pulled open a tiny door and peered up a narrow staircase to the attic in the roof of the house – a mysterious place traditionally out of bounds to the boys on pain of dreadful punishment, but which, according to Foxwood legend, had once or twice been visited in the dead of night by the daring and foolhardy.

I'd said I'd never been up there. Pryce said that *he* had, but shrugged and looked away when Sophie scoffed.

Now, from the headmaster's study, we heard them come down in one of the lifts. Mrs Kemp signalled to me with a little smile that I was excused, so I picked up another fig-roll and hurried along the bottom corridor – to rejoin the tour, for something to do, to be with anyone else for a change from the Kemps. The three of us veered in and out of the classrooms, where Pryce went opening and slamming all the desks before he found the crude carving of his own initials. He rattled the door of the gun-room, which was always locked, and recited the sign in a pompous, headmasterly voice – NO BOYS TO ENTER WITHOUT A MEMBER OF STAFF. We went through the changing-room, where Sophie grim-aced at the residual smells of wet socks and muddy boys, past the door to the stable-yard and into the chapel.

Pryce paused as soon as he stepped inside. It was as though, somehow, the room sucked all of the bombast and truculence from him and pulled him back, really back, to the days when he'd been a choirboy at Foxwood Manor. He fell silent. He gazed at the rows of pews where generations of boys and teachers had sat, at the stained-glass windows with the crest and motto of the school frostily lit by a gleam of snow, at the cassocks hanging on pegs at the vestry door. A small private chapel, built into the house long before it became a school, it might have seated fifty or sixty at most – the family and estate workers and a few parishioners from scattered hamlets – a place of worship and music and close-togetherness in such an isolated location. Now, quietened by the stillness of the room and the feeling that so little had changed within it for scores or even hundreds of years, Pryce walked up the aisle to the choir-stalls. He found the place where he used to sit, the very spot where he'd rested his hymn book and his psalter and the anthems and carols he'd sung, and he touched the polished oak with reverent fingers.

So much dust. He ran his thumb through it, the specks of skin and hair of all the people who'd sat there: even, as he examined the powder on the tip of his nail, even of himself, the minutest remains of himself as a boy at Foxwood Manor.

A cobweb drifted past us. It wafted through the air, dislodged from a dark corner by the sudden intervention of three warm and breathing bodies into the room. And, for an oddly holy moment, I thought of the generations of spiders which had lived their lives in the chapel, their lineage as long and as noble as any of the gentry who had passed this way and whispered their futile prayers.

Pryce was quiet, as though entranced. Until his eyes lit on the piano.

'I'll play,' he said. 'And Scott, you can accompany me.'

As Sophie sulked in another corner of the chapel, scuffing her boots at a dapple of red and blue sunlight on the floor, Pryce sat at the piano and flung open the lid. He blew a cloud of dust from the keys. Very softly and beautifully, he started to play 'While Shepherds Watched Their Flocks by Night'. No mockery, no tomfoolery: he played the carol with grace and simplicity, so that Sophie sat down in the back row of the pews and I stood silently in the aisle. It was lovely. It somehow made the room complete, suffused with a holiness beyond the ken of a million spiders.

At the end of the verse, Pryce stopped and left the final chord humming in mid-air. Then he looked archly at me. 'I thought you were going to accompany me. What's up?'

'You mean . . .?' Confused and embarrassed at the thought of singing for the visitors, I stepped towards the piano and cleared my throat.

'No, I don't mean your precious fucking tonsils,' Pryce said. 'I mean . . .,' and he gestured into the shadows where the cassocks were hanging, by the open door of the vestry 'I mean the fucking bell. Give it a few tugs, in time with the music.'

I turned and hesitated. I could see the bell rope hanging like a noose inside the vestry. I'd rung it many times, whenever my turn came to ring it for the beginning of Sunday morning service. Now I glanced from Pryce's wolfish smile to Sophie's bleak, ashen face.

'Go on, Alan,' Pryce said, and he started to play again. 'Dr Kemp won't mind. I'm playing a Christmas carol, that's all.'

So I stepped into the vestry and took hold of the rope. Pryce was playing another verse, with perfect reverence. I essayed an experimental tug and the bell in the roof of the chapel sounded a single muffled note. It was soft, it was pure, it was in keeping with the carol, on a sparkling snowy afternoon a few days before Christmas. I tugged again, and again, and Pryce played up.

The sound of the piano carried through the building. The tolling of the bell, clear in the cold air, carried there too. Where Dr Kemp would hear it in his study.

I knew what would happen: the headmaster would lumber from his desk and down the corridor, and his wife would try, unsuccessfully, to soothe him, to stop him – and I knew that, by tugging the rope the very first time and sounding a single note, I had aligned myself with Pryce and now it was too late, impossible, to stop and realign myself with Kemp.

There was a shift in the music. Pryce's playing was changing, blurring, and I tolled faster to keep up with the beat. Somehow, with skill and stealth and sleight of hand, Pryce was transposing 'While Shepherds Watched . . .' into the doomy dirge of 'Paint it Black'. I recognised it, it was always on my transistor radio, or had been until the headmaster had broken it. My stomach turned over at the sudden realisation of what he was doing. But by now the bell was tolling a regular, faster beat which I couldn't stop, and Pryce was playing louder and louder, with a deadly insistence, repeating the same menacing monotone over and over . . . *I see a red door and I want it painted black – no colours any more I want them all turned black* . . .

Dr Kemp burst into the chapel.

Too late, Pryce shifted in a split second back to the carol. It made it worse. By the time the headmaster was halfway up the aisle, Pryce was smiling like an angel and playing with utter loveliness. Dr Kemp was unstoppable. He bore down onto Pryce, his face purple, his hair flopping, his lips flecked with spittle, and he shoved him right off the piano stool onto the floor.

The bell rang three more times. I was powerless to stop it. Pryce scrambled to his feet and thrust his face into Kemp's.

'Don't you touch me!' he yelled. 'I'm not one of your little boys!'

'How dare you?' the headmaster bellowed. 'Here, in this place! In my house!'

They stood chin to chin, panting: a handsome boy of twenty, his smooth complexion flushed with anger; a florid, middle-aged schoolteacher, the veins popping in his temples. The only sound in the chapel was their breathing, because the final notes from the piano had faded to nothing, the bell was silent, and the girl and I were holding our breath.

Dr Kemp found something to say. Struggling to control himself, he took a step backwards. 'You are a guest in my house,' he said very slowly. 'I'd be obliged if you would forbear . . .' His sentence dried up, shrivelled and died.

Pryce stepped back too. Theatrical, he ran a hand through his hair. 'Forbear?' he said. He pondered the word, as though he'd never heard it before. 'Of course, Dr Kemp, we're grateful for your hospitality.'

He turned back to the piano and closed the lid. He made a tiny, courtly nod of his head, the closest he could come to an apology, and proffered his hand. Dr Kemp ignored it. So he moved past the headmaster, towards the back of the chapel.

'And Scott, as for you . . .' Dr Kemp let the words hang in the air. I came out of the vestry. Behind me, the rope was still swinging. 'As for you, I'm disappointed, and you know what that means.'

Sophie spoke up. She'd watched the confrontation, speechless, aghast, but now her voice, despite the stammer, cut clearly through the room. 'It wasn't h-h-his f-f-f-fault – he only d-d-did what M-m-m-Martin . . .'

'Please don't interfere,' the headmaster said. 'At least you could allow me jurisdiction over my own house.' He signalled to me with a lift of his eyebrow and marched out of the chapel. I followed him.

It was twilight at four o'clock. I was in the stable; I'd lit the lantern and was bending close to the flame, to see what I was doing. The rest of the room was in darkness. In the far corner, the jackdaw hopped from one end of its perch to the other, with a rhythmic rattle and click of its claws. I didn't look up to watch, and in any case, the task in which I was so deeply engrossed would shortly take me back to the bird. As ever, Wagner was in the stable with me. He'd wolfed the remains of the rabbit which I'd fed to the jackdaw, and now he was dozing on the cobbled floor.

I was whittling the tip of a feather with Roly's knife. The feather was from the bird itself, one of its tail feathers which had been bent almost ninety degrees when it was tangled in the brambles. I'd carefully cut it off, just below the fatal kink, and now I was whittling the tip into as sharp a point as I could.

I held the feather close to the lamp and flicked the dust from it. Perfect. I thought for a moment how good it would be to keep it and use it as a quill, to dip the point into an ink-well and write with the magical blue-black feather of an imp I'd rescued from the forest. I held it like a pen and wrote my name in the air.

I winced, put the feather down and blew on the palms of my hands, one after the other. There were three welts on each palm, red and very sore. Not the quickly fading signs of a nightmare I'd had, but harsh and painful reality: the marks of the headmaster's cane.

Anointing the point of the feather with glue, I took it, and the lantern, across the stable to the jackdaw. To quieten the bird, all I did was blow gently on its whiskery face. And it settled immediately, angling its head this way and that for the waft and warmth of my breath, blinking at the lamplight. Without the slightest fuss, finding my tiny target first time, I imped the newly sharpened quill straight into the round socket left after the removal of the damaged feather. I held it a second, made a minute adjustment and stood back.

'There,' I said. 'Soon you can fly.'

I blew little kisses of air into the bird's face, and it bristled at me, shivering its wings around its body like a cloak. Then it swivelled its head and started to rearrange the tail feathers the way it liked them. I looked on intently, concerned that my handiwork would be undone. And I was watching, unconsciously blowing on the palms of my stinging hands, when I heard a sound outside in the stable-yard.

Wagner heard it too, and started a long, low growl. He stopped when I bent and touched his muzzle. There were footsteps and voices. Turning down the wick of the lamp until it was snuffed in a plume of smoke, I peered over the door into the yard.

The sky was dark. Big flakes of snow were whirling like a million moths. The moon, round and faint behind a smothering cloud, threw a feeble light – enough for me to see Pryce and Sophie crossing the yard towards the car. Their footsteps crunched to a standstill.

Pryce made a desultory swipe at the bonnet. The snow had frozen hard. He rubbed his hands and looked around. Sophie was shivering in her coat and scarf, wobbling on her high heels.

'She'll go in one of the stables,' he said. 'They're all empty, I think.'

'So s-s-s-sad,' she said. Her shivering made her stammer worse. 'The whole p-p-place is so empty . . .'

'There hasn't been a horse here since Mrs Kemp had her accident,' Pryce said. He made a pistol shape with his fingers, fired an imaginary shot and blew away the smoke. 'Not since Dapple got his *coup de grâce*. Here, let's try this one.'

He went to one of the stables and tried to pull the door open. The snow had banked against it so he kicked it clear with his boot. He kicked and kicked, because the snow had crusted into ice, until at last when he wrenched at the door it grated ajar. It was a wide, double door, and over years of neglect and lack of use the hinges had rusted and sagged. Cursing, straining, Pryce had to lift the door and swing it clear of the snow, so that it yawned open and revealed the dark space inside.

'All right.' He was breathing hard. 'Now help me, Sophie. We can do it together!'

He leaned into the car and released the hand-brake. They both bent to the bonnet and strained with all their weight, to try and push the car backwards. It didn't budge. The flattened tyre seemed to be frozen to the ground. Again they shoved, their boots slithering hopelessly, until at last there was a splintering of ice and the wheels broke clear. They stood up, heaving, their breath billowing around them.

'For fuck's sake, Sophie, are you pushing or just sticking your fat arse up into the air? You've got to help me!'

'I'm p-p-pushing the stupid thing!' she retorted. 'It's not my f-f-f-fault we're here and . . .'

'It *is* your fucking fault! If you hadn't been screwing around with Jeremy . . .'

'That's what you w-w-wanted me to do!' she spat at him. 'That's why you t-t-took me to see him! It was all your idea! I did what you w-w-wanted me to do, and then you went c-c-crazy . . .'

'You were the fucking final straw!' he hissed at her.

Maddened, she stood away from the car and hissed back. 'You couldn't s-s-stand it, could you? Seeing him happy! You had to go and t-t-tease him with me, you had to remind him of all the sh-sh-shit you'd given him! Now there's no chance for him, and no chance for us, just this m-m-mess, this bloody mess!'

He lunged at her, grabbed her shoulders and shook her to silence. He blew the words into her face, a fume of steam in the freezing air. 'Listen, Sophie. Right now, at this moment, you're here with me. Here, now, with me. That's all there is, nothing else. Now push!'

I'd steeled myself to go out of the stable and help them, but at the angry exchange I hid behind the door. I watched as they bent and pushed again, and every inch they won was an exhausting effort, for the snow in the yard was deep and hard. At last they shifted the car back and back until its nose was angled towards the door of the stable that Pryce had opened.

Sophie squatted with her head between her knees, as though she would retch. Pryce, with his hands on his hips and head thrown back, lurched into the stable and clattered around inside, emerging a moment later with a spade.

'N-n-n-nice timing,' she wheezed. 'We move the sodding car and then you f-find the sodding shovel.'

He attacked the snow in front of the door and around the wheels of the car. He flung the spade with an enormous clang back into the stable and they rested another minute. I watched, and all this time Wagner leaned his hot, heavy head against my thigh, his body rumbling and ready to go. Pryce and Sophie braced themselves for the final awkward manoeuvre. He grappled the steering wheel and shoved at the same time, wrestling the car as though it were a reluctant steer, while she applied her puny weight to the rear bumper. The flat tyre flapped and squelched. And that forbidden word, which I'd thought so rare the day before, was hissed and stuttered and grunted so often in one fraught minute that it was just a meaningless noise of fluster and frustration.

The car rolled into the stable. The two people who'd fought so hard to get it there stood and stared at it with resentment in their eyes. A long slab of snow slid off its nose and onto the stable floor. And once more, as I peered from my hiding place, the car was an animal, shivering the ice from its pelt, revealing its reddish, filthy flanks.

Pryce came out with the spade. He made a few tentative raking movements at the mess of footprints and tyre marks, then looked up at the sky. The snow was falling heavily.

'No need,' he said. 'In a few hours there won't be a sign that anyone's been here. It'll give us time. Here, Sophie. Help me, the last thing . . .'

Together they lifted and closed the door of the stable. Without speaking, with hardly the breath to speak, they crossed the yard and went back into the school.

SEVEN

D r Kemp bent to the walnut cabinet, opened the lid
and put a record on the turntable. No one spoke as
he set it turning and gently placed the needle on it. There
was a crackle and a hiss, and we all waited for the music
to begin.

It was nine o'clock in the evening. Mrs Kemp was
sitting by the fire in the great hall, with Martin Pryce and
Sophie and me; and Wagner, of course. Despite the fact
that the humans were eating bacon sandwiches from a
tray balanced precariously on a table I'd been ordered
to fetch from the headmaster's study, the dog lay very
still and kept his eyes closed. He'd been trained from
puppyhood not to beg for food, indeed, to avoid eye
contact with humans who were eating. So now,
although the smell of the bacon was tantalisingly good,

he feigned sleep at his mistress's feet. I could tell, however, from the twitch of an ear at every word that was spoken, that the dog was wide awake and hoping for a treat.

The fire spat a spark onto the hearth rug. Dr Kemp rubbed it out with the sole of his shoe. In the far corner of the hall the lights on the Christmas tree were flickering – not by design, but probably because one or two of the bulbs were loose. We all listened to the hiss of the needle on the record and waited.

'No prizes for guessing,' Pryce said, one beat before the music started.

Smooth, swirling strings, a sweet melody and a surge of muscle. The lazy power of an orchestra filled the room. Sophie nodded her head and raised her eyebrows at Mrs Kemp. 'I think I know this – what is it?'

Before she could speak, the headmaster gestured towards me, to indicate that I should answer the question. 'It's Fauré's Requiem, sir,' I said. A bit of salt from the sandwiches had got onto the palm of my right hand, the grains burrowing into the welts. In a free world I could have leaned over to the dog and let him salve the irritation with his tongue. But I sat as still as the dog and endured the stinging by clenching my fist.

'Like I said, no prizes for guessing,' Pryce put in. 'I think I heard this every night of my years at Foxwood.' He directed himself to Sophie. 'Every night, after Dr Kemp had been round the dorms and said the prayer and turned all the lights out, he'd come downstairs and put on this record. We'd hear the music creeping up the stairs, crawling along the corridors, slithering under the doors and under our beds and . . .'

'That sounds horrible,' Mrs Kemp said. 'We used to play it often, we still do. But I didn't know that the boys could hear it upstairs in the dormitories.'

Pryce pulled a teasing, doubtful face at her. 'That was the whole idea, wasn't it? Wasn't it, Dr Kemp?'

The headmaster had taken his ivory baton from the mantelpiece and was conducting as the record played. 'A requiem is for the repose of the dead,' he said, 'not a lullaby.'

'I know that,' Pryce persisted. 'I mean, you intended it to be part of our schooling. Even at night, you were dinning the music into our heads.'

'Dinning?' the headmaster said. He closed his eyes as he swished the baton up and down, from side to side. 'I teach music at Foxwood Manor. I instill music, and the love of music, into the boys. I have music in my head all the time, waking and sleeping . . .'

'And you make sure the boys do too.' Pryce leaned back, smiled, and conducted airily with a bacon sandwich. 'These days, teenagers like a different kind of music.'

Mrs Kemp countered, seeing that her husband had deliberately shut his eyes and ears from Pryce's playful provocation. With a charming smile at him and Sophie, she said, 'Well, the boys at Foxwood aren't teenagers. So, in the meantime they listen to the music we . . .'

'How old are you, Alan?' Pryce's question was so abrupt that it stopped her in mid-sentence. It surprised me too, having assumed I was excluded from the grown-ups' conversation.

'Twelve,' I said. Before Mrs Kemp could butt in and make her point, I added, 'I'll be thirteen on Christmas Day.'

Honours were even. Pryce and Mrs Kemp held each other's eyes and held their smiles. In a final thrust she shrugged and said, 'Twelve or thirteen, it makes no difference.'

He parried with, 'He'll be a teenager, like Sophie, and that makes all the difference.'

Sophie was drawn into the conversation by the use of her name. She asked Mrs Kemp if she was a musician too, like her husband, and the woman replied that Dr Kemp had tried his best to teach her, but without much success – not, of course, because of any limitations in his ability as a teacher, but because of the paltriness of her talent. The music swelled around us, moody and moving and somehow tremendous, and Dr Kemp swayed with it, as though mesmerised. It was odd, as I'd remarked before, to see someone who looked so everyday, so ordinary, so commonplace, absorbed so utterly by the music. The headmaster was a part of it, he was lost in it.

With a nod in his direction, as he continued to conduct with his eyes closed, Mrs Kemp whispered to Sophie, 'Music is the life-blood of the school. It runs through the building.'

Pryce had heard her say it before. He must have done, it was a kind of mantra at Foxwood Manor. He sighed and let it go by, unworthy of comment. Mrs Kemp saw the disdain on his face, and she suddenly looked enormously, almost unbearably tired, as if she could have wept with tiredness. Her eyes prickled with tears as she looked at her husband, whom she loved so much despite the suddenness of his moods, who cared so much for the music and for the boys he taught.

She turned to me, and I could see the gleam of her tears. And she could tell from my face that I understood her, how Pryce's unconcealed contempt made her heart ache for the man she loved and honoured despite all his shortcomings.

To disguise her feelings from Pryce, she whispered, 'Alan, my dear, would you do something for me, please, before you turn into a teenager and get too grown up to pay attention to an old thing like me? The lights on the Christmas tree, you could tighten the bulbs and stop them from flickering . . .'

Glad to oblige, to have any excuse to leave the fireside and the bickering adults, I got up and moved into the shadows in the corner of the hall. Dr Kemp must have sensed my passing, because he opened his eyes, emerging as though from a trance. He put down the magic wand of his baton, exchanging it for the mundane reality of a bacon sandwich.

As though he'd never been away, he said to Pryce, 'Did you really mind? I mean, did you mind listening to this up in the dorm at night?'

'It's too late to mind,' Pryce said. 'The music is in my head.' He held up his hand, as he'd done once before. 'It's like the scar I got from Wagner, I've got it for life whether I mind or not.'

I was having no success with the Christmas tree. In fact, after I'd tried all the bulbs and tightened them one after the other, they were flickering more spasmodically than before and fizzing in their sockets. But the look I got from Mrs Kemp, when I glanced to her for advice or help, warned me to stay where I was and say nothing: a look that said in an instant that sometimes it was better to seek out the shadows and the safety of darkness.

'It's c-c-c-creepy,' Sophie said. 'A bedtime requiem. "*Grant them, O Lord, eternal rest.*" Do the boys know what it m-m-means?'

Pryce ignored her. He said disarmingly, as the music from the record player soared and his greasy-bacon fingers moved with the rhythm, 'The strange thing is, I really don't know if I love it or hate it.'

Dr Kemp acknowledged the remark with a graceful smile, as though he too were prepared to give ground, and he said warmly, 'My boy, how could you hate this? Just listen . . .'

So we all listened together, Pryce and Sophie, Dr and Mrs Kemp, Wagner aquiver for a lick of fat or a sliver of rind, and me, furtively at work on the festive lights. The longer we listened and said nothing, after the ugly confrontation of the morning and the ensuing punishment that the headmaster had meted out to me, the more likely it would be that we could spend a civil evening together. Mrs Kemp was counting the seconds. The music was lovely, a kind of healing.

But then Pryce glanced across the hall to me. Unaware that anyone was watching me, I'd been licking the palm of my right hand and then blowing on it. I looked up and met his eyes. Mrs Kemp saw that Pryce was looking, and she saw what I was doing. And in the grey coldness of the man's eyes, she must have known that the time for healing had run out.

'It's my turn.' Pryce's words were so sudden, so unexpected, so out of context, that they seemed louder than they actually were. The other grown-ups frowned quizzically at him, as he knew they would do, and he said again, 'It's my turn,' in the tone of voice a teacher might use with a simpleton.

The headmaster leaned to the record player and turned down the volume, in order to elicit some sense from what Pryce had said.

Given the floor, the young man said, 'No one's asked me what I do or where I work, although we've been here a couple of days already, but I'll tell you anyway.' He was charming, the firelight gleaming in his eyes. 'Funnily enough I'm in the music business too. A bit like you, Dr Kemp, but different.' He paused and waited for the headmaster to raise a questioning eyebrow. 'Like you, I instill a love of music. I work for a record company. The more sales I generate, the more records I shift, the more I'm appreciated by the company and the more money I get. You saw the car? Not bad for a twenty-year-old . . .'

'That's marvellous, Martin,' Mrs Kemp said. 'So what do you mean, it's your turn? Do you mean you just wanted to tell us that? I'm so sorry we didn't ask you. We get a bit absorbed with our own little life out here.'

'No, I mean it's my turn to play a bit of music. The kind of music I like, and Sophie likes, and Alan likes. The kind that millions of young people like. I've got some upstairs. Shall I go and get it?'

Dr Kemp shuddered. 'Please no, not if it's anything like the dreadful racket that was blaring out of your car this morning.'

'Thank you, Martin, but I think it would jar a bit,' said Mrs Kemp, attempting the difficult task of supporting her husband and mollifying Pryce at the same time. 'In an old-fashioned place like this, with a couple of fuddy-duddies like us . . .'

'Thank you, but no thank you,' the headmaster put in.

'*You* would like it, Mrs Kemp, you're still young,' Pryce insisted, leaning towards the woman with sudden enthusiasm. 'It has energy. You'd feel the heat in it. I'll go and get some.'

He jumped to his feet. At the same moment, Kemp lunged to the record player and turned the volume as high as it would go. The music blasted out, rattling the speakers. He shouted, 'Remember this, Pryce? Remember? You'll never forget it!' and he swished his arms up and down, from side to side, conducting with exaggerated passion.

The noise was deafening. They were face to face, jutting their chins together. Straight away, Wagner was up and ready for action. The dog wrinkled his muzzle into a horrible mask, teeth bared, eyes wild, and went for Pryce.

'Jesus!' Pryce lashed out with his boot. The table crashed to the floor. Wagner did a canine double-take, saw the scattered sandwiches, and decided in an instant that bacon was a higher priority than protecting his master. He swerved away from Pryce's boot and snaffled a sandwich as fast as he could.

Mrs Kemp laughed brightly, and Dr Kemp turned down the volume to make a sarcastic remark about Wagner's dubious allegiance. As I set the table upright, Pryce salvaged the last of the sandwiches from the floor and took a big bite out of it, more to thwart the dog than because he wanted it himself.

Only the girl was not amused. Pryce said, 'Not funny, Sophie?' because she was staring at him, incredulous, as though nothing in her life would ever be funny again.

She tried to echo the word, 'F-f-f-' but it stuck in her throat. She hunched her shoulders and heaved, like a cat struggling to cough up a ball of fur, until at last she regained her breath and wiped her mouth and eyes, catlike, with the back of her hands.

I returned to the fireside, knelt and hugged the dog, which was breathless from the exertion and slobbering at the taste of bacon. Mrs Kemp seemed determined to keep the mood light. 'Martin, could you have a go?' she said. 'Alan's been trying to fix the Christmas tree lights – could you?'

Pryce smiled gracefully and drifted away from the hearth, to the cool shadows at the end of the hall. The music was softer now, and there was a perceptible lifting of tension as he left the rest of us grouped around the fire. He must have known that was why she'd asked him so sweetly to do this unnecessary task: to make a little space, to have a little peace without him. So, obligingly, he wandered past the school photographs, paused, took another bite at his sandwich and studied the rows of serious faces. I watched him smear the glass with a greasy fingertip as he moved to the Christmas tree.

From where I was kneeling, I saw him bend to the skirting board, where the floor was carpeted with pine needles. In the socket there was an adapter overloaded with plugs, and the flex for the lights was so frayed that some of the wires were bare.

He put down his sandwich and jiggled the adapter. The Christmas tree lights went off and the music slurred almost to silence. Another jiggle and the lights came on; the music lurched and picked up again. 'Sorry,' he called out, crouched on the floor behind the bole of the tree. 'It isn't the bulbs, it's the plug. The connections are loose.'

He knelt, disappearing into the darkness. Mrs Kemp started quizzing Sophie, drawing her out a bit. The girl had recovered from her coughing fit. She was saying that she'd left school in the summer, had had such disastrous A-level results that her parents had hit the roof, that she'd packed a bag and run off to London and taken the first job she could get, in the record company that Martin worked for, 'not really working, just looking cute and b-b-brainless at the front desk . . .' I was listening, and aware that Pryce was listening too, because once or twice his face popped up as though he were ready to butt in and stop the girl if she said too much.

The music continued, so marvellous, so much a part of Foxwood Manor. It swooped and lurched again. 'Sorry,

sorry,' I heard Pryce mumbling through a mouthful of bread and bacon, and I knew he'd jiggled the wires on purpose: because, in the prickling of my palms which was suddenly more than just the salt in my wounds but a flash of the dream I'd had and the faces in it, I knew that the music was as maddeningly familiar to him as it was for me.

The lights stopped flickering. Pryce stood up and stuffed the last of his sandwich into his mouth. He looked round for somewhere to wipe the bacon grease from his hands, ducked out of sight again.

At last he wandered back to the fireside. Dr Kemp was conducting again, more relaxed now, allowing himself a little nod of thanks as Pryce sat down. I was holding Wagner's collar, and I tightened my grip as he leaned towards Pryce.

'It's all right,' Pryce said softly, 'I think he's getting used to me.' I warily let go of the collar and Wagner sniffed at Pryce's fingers. After a moment, the dog lifted his head, peered blearily around him, and limped away. He disappeared into the shadows. 'He's hot,' Pryce said.

The music was reaching a surging climax. '*Quando coeli movendi sunt, quando coeli movendi sunt, in dia illa tremenda . . .*'

There was a sharp bang at the other end of the hall. A flash, a cloud of smoke. The music groaned and died. And there was a dreadful, snarling commotion by the Christmas tree.

Everyone – except Mrs Kemp – jumped to their feet. The tree groaned and leaned and fell to the floor with an enormous crash. The lights exploded like a crackle of gunfire. The snarling continued for another second, became a horrid gurgling growl, and stopped.

We gathered around to see what had happened. It took Mrs Kemp a few frantic seconds to manoeuvre her wheel-chair from the fireside to the wreckage of the Christmas tree.

Wagner's teeth were clenched on the bare wires. His eyes bulged red, and his legs twitched as though he were asleep and dreaming of rabbits. He was smouldering. A haze of blue smoke rose from his fur.

EIGHT

The spade cut through the snow and the encrusted blades of grass, then banged to a jarring halt. The impact sent a shock through Dr Kemp's wrist and right up to his elbow. The ground was frozen hard. It might as well have been rock.

He and Mrs Kemp were on the lawn, under the branches of their favourite copper beech. I was there too; I'd been trying to help.

It was another glorious morning. In the night it had been snowing again, so all the world was gleaming, a pristine, immaculate world from which all things less than perfect had been expunged. The sky was blue, the sun was shining. Indeed, there was a glow of sweat on the headmaster's brow as he struck again and again with the spade. Mrs Kemp sat beside him in her wheelchair, wrapped in her coat and scarf, with the tartan rug around her legs. Wagner's body lay on the dazzling snow.

'It's no good.' Kemp stopped and wiped his face with the palm of his hand. He was breathing heavily. He loosened the scarf around his throat and glanced back to the house. After fifteen frustrating minutes he'd made hardly a dint in the surface of the lawn. Before that, he and I had struggled to get the unwieldy corpse out of the house. The only way, after we'd tried and failed to carry it in our arms for more than a yard or two, had been to use his wife's wheelchair. Kemp had taken her into his study, leaving her sitting at his desk with the door shut, and then I'd helped him to manhandle the dog on board. A bizarre sight, if there'd been anyone else to see it, as we'd emerged from the front door and crunched the chair through the deep snow, not with the headmaster's beloved wife but the stiffening body of a dead labrador. And there, in the spot he'd decided on, we'd attempted to lift the dog and rest it gently on the snow, but its bulk and unusual rigidity had proved so awkward that at last there was no choice but to tip it unceremoniously onto the ground. It had lain there on its back, its legs sticking into the air, until Kemp rolled it onto one side.

Now, having returned to the house to bring out his wife, he was clanging at the unyielding ground with a spade. No good, no good, no good. Mrs Kemp began to sob. He hurled the spade into the snow and stood there, heaving for breath, with tears of rage and sorrow pricking in his eyes. He panted at me testily, 'There's no need for you to be here, Scott, for heaven's sake go indoors.'

Pryce and Sophie were watching from the great hall. 'Come on, old man,' Pryce whispered, 'we need a good, big hole.'

He strolled to the piano, where the tree lay bristling and black, where fragments of glass from the exploded bulbs crunched under his boots. He sat down, and with one finger he played the first lines of 'In the Deep Mid-winter', so spare, so cold, every note an icicle. He stopped, affecting the headmaster's look of puzzlement and exasperation, and reached for the leather wallet of tuning keys that lay on top of the piano. He stood up, lifted the lid of the instrument and propped it open.

'What are you d-d-d-doing?' Sophie asked, unnecessarily. He was leaning into the piano and randomly loosening string after string. 'Don't you think . . .?'

'The piano tuner never made it. I'll have a go. Now, which way do you turn these things?'

Unseen, unheard, I'd come into the hall from the long corridor. I'd been watching them, hesitating, dazed from the exertion and misery of helping the headmaster with the dog. When Pryce opened the piano and I saw my reflection in the shine of the lid, I stepped forwards, as though in a dream, to meet the figure of the boy who was walking towards me.

With a feeling of horror in my stomach, I peered into the dark hole. Before either Pryce or Sophie had time to acknowledge that I was there, I saw what he'd been doing and I said sharply, 'Please don't, sir, I got into enough trouble yesterday.'

'The b-b-boy'll get the blame,' Sophie blurted. 'Kemp's already mad about the d-d-d-dog . . .'

'The dog had it coming. So has Kemp.'

Pryce pushed me out of the way and submerged himself again in the piano. He turned a key with one hand, while his other arm snaked out and felt blindly for the keyboard, and the notes he struck were strangely plangent, quite different from the chilly air he'd conjured from the carol.

Sophie gestured hopelessly at me, seeing the despair on my face. Pryce glanced up from the piano and saw the little exchange. 'Hey Alan,' he started, 'are you with me or Kemp? Do you want a bit of fun with us, or a cosy threesome with the old farts?'

'Watch out!' Sophie hissed without a hint of a stammer.

Through the window we saw that the Kemps were approaching the house. We heard the crunch of the wheel-chair on the snow, the hiss of its tyres as it ran up the ramp to the front door. And as the handle turned and the door creaked open, Pryce said, 'Alan, here!' and tossed the wallet of tuning keys through the air.

I had no choice but to catch it and stuff it into my pocket, just as Kemp propelled the wheelchair into the hall.

Without looking at me or Pryce or Sophie, the headmaster manoeuvred the chair to the fire. His face was set, as though frozen, but ruddy from the cold and the effort of pushing. His breathing was hoarse. Mrs Kemp's face was hidden behind the fall of her hair. She was dabbing her eyes and nose with a white handkerchief.

'You shouldn't have come out,' he said to her. 'It's much too cold. You should've stayed indoors.'

'I wanted to be there,' she said, controlling her voice with difficulty. 'And now we've left him lying in the snow . . .'

Kemp swivelled furiously towards Pryce. 'I don't suppose you could've helped at all, instead of just standing there grinning like a fool.'

Pryce demurred, affecting the manners of a perfect gentleman. 'I'm so sorry. I didn't want to intrude at the graveside.'

'There is no grave,' the headmaster retorted, 'so, by definition, there is no graveside.' This provoked an outburst of sobbing from his wife. He bent to her and put his arm around her shoulders.

'Oh dear,' Pryce said. 'Perhaps we should make some coffee, to warm you up a bit. Come on, Sophie.' He led the girl out of the hall and into the corridor.

I stood there, as though nailed to the floorboards. My whole body ached with the unfairness of the situation. My head groaned with it. It was mean, just mean, that I was standing in that place, at that moment, with an enormous nail of obligation driven through each foot. The effortlessness of Pryce's exit made it worse. I was on my own. And the question that Pryce had tossed to me just before the Kemps came in, as casual and yet as weighted as the keys he'd tossed through the air a moment later, whirled in my mind.

It wasn't the first time I'd considered it. I'd lain awake the previous night and weighed it one way and the other, the same question, my eyes staring into the darkness of the dormitory. On the one hand, I was a twelve-year-old choirboy, blessed with a perfect ear and imbued with a genuine love of church music; on the other, I was an incipient teenager, my ear glued to the rock'n'roll on my transistor radio. On the one hand, I was a prefect at Foxwood Manor, infused with a grudging respect for my headmaster and a real affection for the headmaster's wife; on the other, I was a defiant adolescent thrilled by the arrival of Martin Pryce. Who was I? And when I glimpsed the reflection of a small boy in the polished blackness of the piano, it wasn't me, but a different boy who folded and vanished as I turned my head towards him.

'You've let the fire go out.' Dr Kemp's words cut through the room. 'While you're here with us, Scott, you could do something to earn your keep, couldn't you? This is supposed to be *our* holiday as well, you know.'

I bent to the hearth immediately, trying to set aside the thought of what would happen next, or soon: in either case, the appalling inevitability of it. I picked up some of the holly twigs and branches I'd collected from the woods a few days before, which I'd carried into the hall and stacked neatly so that they'd be dry and ready for burning. I laid them onto the neglected embers, knelt close and blew softly. There was a sudden glow and a little blue flame stood up. It licked around the fuel that I'd put there. With a crackle and spit, the fire was alive again.

Dr Kemp was kneeling too. He'd taken off his scarf and coat and was helping his wife with hers. He slipped off her shoes and started to rub her feet gently; they were white as marble between his reddened hands. 'We all loved the old boy,' he was saying. 'Was he seventeen, eighteen? And this was his place, right here, in front of the fire . . .'

Mrs Kemp wept again. As I stood away from the hearth and saw her shoulders shuddering as she sobbed and sobbed, my heart ached to see her crying, and a lump came into my throat. The headmaster squeezed her feet, then looked up and saw the sadness in my eyes.

'Oh yes,' he said, 'the boys were fond of him too, years and years of Foxwood boys. What a character, what a dog . . .'

And then he stood up. He held my eyes as though there were a special bond between us, something only we could understand: a bond which excluded his wife and the love he felt for her and was far beyond the comprehension of Pryce and Sophie. I read his thoughts – I wished I could not. It was a nightmare, to know what the man was about to say, and to be powerless, utterly powerless to forestall it.

'Music,' he said. 'At a time like this, people like us, we have our music.'

It was hopeless to protest. I gaped at him, stammered, 'Please sir, please sir, no sir', but the headmaster was too much for me. Evincing an avuncular kindliness which he must have thought appropriate to the occasion, Dr Kemp was overwhelming. He'd seen in my eyes how much the death of the dog had moved me, and now he reached for my hand and eased me across the room towards the piano. He even, feeling me wince from his touch, folded open my palm to appraise the three red stripes on it, and he pursed his lips to express sympathy tinged with regret.

He said gently, 'It's your gift, it's your duty. Sing for me and Mrs Kemp. Sing for Wagner.'

I held my breath as Kemp sat at the piano. My heart had stopped beating.

The headmaster played an arpeggio. With a yell, flapping his hands as though he had dipped them in boiling oil, he leaped to his feet.

'What's this?' he roared. 'Who has done this?' He banged a chord, a mess of noise. He whirled at me. 'Where are they? You know what I mean! Don't just stand there gawping like an idiot! Where are they?'

For a blinding second, thinking he meant Pryce and Sophie, I gestured feebly towards the corridor. He shoved past me, snarling, knocked over the table that had been knocked over the night before, and stormed to the hearth. His wife blinked at him through bleary eyes.

'*You* know where they are!' he shouted. 'I left them on the mantelpiece! I put them on the piano! I was *using them*! The keys! Where *are* they?'

'Anyone for coffee?'

Pryce emerged from the corridor, with Sophie behind him. He was carrying a tray with five steaming mugs and a plate of mince pies. He frowned at the overturned table. 'Oh dear, where can I put this?'

'It's unplayable!' the headmaster shouted. 'The piano is

unplayable! It might as well be chopped into pieces and burned on the fire! That's all it's good for!'

Pryce put the tray on the hearth, gave a mug of coffee to Mrs Kemp and took one for himself. 'What happened to the piano tuner you were expecting? I suppose he's stuck in the snow somewhere.'

'I'm looking for the tuning keys!' the headmaster hissed at him, barely controlling his anger. 'They were here, on top of the piano, and now they're gone. Have you seen them?'

'Search me,' he said, like an innocent caught in the crossfire. 'Alan? Any idea?'

They all stared at me. I saw a flicker of a smirk on Pryce's face and felt the cold grey eyes run down to the bulge in my pocket. I licked my lips, for my mouth was very dry, and said, 'No sir, no idea, sir.'

Pryce moved to the piano. 'Don't touch it,' the headmaster said softly. 'I cannot stand the noise.' Pryce ignored him. He set his mug down on the end of the keyboard, right next to the highest note. The headmaster repeated himself, as softly as before. 'Do *not* touch the piano.'

Pryce sat on the stool. 'Unplayable? I like a challenge.'

As he laid his hands on the keyboard, the headmaster stormed towards him. Pryce had one second to bang out the first excruciating line of 'Ding Dong Merrily on High' before Dr Kemp reached the piano.

Pryce withdrew his fingers just in time. Bellowing, 'Are you deaf?' the headmaster slammed the lid shut with all his might. The mug splintered into smithereens. The coffee splashed onto Pryce's hands and face.

There was a lull. The only sound was the drip-drip-drip of coffee from the piano to the floor. We all looked at each other, as though waiting – waiting for a familiar sound to fill the silence. But there was no gurgling growl. No booming bark. Nothing to punctuate the moment with a resounding exclamation mark.

It was an uncomfortable silence. It pronounced the unalterable fact that Wagner had gone for ever.

'Be careful, Dr Kemp,' Pryce said at last. 'Be very careful.' His voice was gentle, as soft as silk. 'I'm not deaf, although you've told me many times that my ear is not as good as yours. That's one thing you instilled in me at Foxwood.'

Mrs Kemp was crying very quietly. The fire collapsed and settled, consuming itself. The coffee dripped and dripped and stopped dripping.

Outside, in the treetops, the carrion crows were calling.

Dr Kemp ordered me along to the practice room at the other end of the school, near the kitchens and dining-room. I had no choice but to obey his abrupt command, although I took a couple of seconds and the opportunity – in the sullen activity which followed the confrontation, as Sophie mopped the spilt coffee and put the table upright, as Pryce picked up the shards of the broken mug, as Dr Kemp tried once more to console his wife – to slip the wallet of tuning keys out of my pocket and down the side of an armchair, where I thought I could pretend to discover it later. Then I hurried to the practice room and waited for the headmaster to come.

The room was tiny, not much more than a walk-in cupboard with an upright piano and a stool in it. The floor was piled with sheet music, there was a shelf stacked with old hymn books and psalters, and there were books of graded pieces on top of the piano itself. The light came from a bare overhead bulb and a ventilation panel near the ceiling.

I'd spent many hours in there over the five years I'd been at Foxwood Manor, on my own, with the door shut, working on scales and fingering exercises and the pieces I practised for Dr Kemp. More recently, since the death of my father, the room had been a place where I could escape from the dull routines and enforced matiness of prep-school life, find a quiet, peaceful corner among the nightmares which filled my head; where sometimes I thought of a hymn we often sang in chapel – *'speak through the earthquake, wind and fire, o still small voice of calm . . .'* – and I tried to conjure the calm, loving voice of my father.

But now I was squeezed into the little space with the headmaster. Dr Kemp sat at the piano and I stood beside him. With the door closed, the air grew stale and stuffy.

'Again.' Dr Kemp kept repeating the word, and so, dutifully, I repeated the phrase I was singing. The pitch rose, the tension too, and the testiness in the headmaster's voice increased in the way he said those two dry syllables. He banged a note. 'Listen! Can't you *hear* it? If you can't *hear* it, if you don't *listen*, if you don't use your *ear* and *listen*, then you're no better than all – than all – than all the rest of them!'

I wetted my lips and sang the phrase again. I knew the tuning was perfect, but the tone was woody, my voice deadened in the dead stale air of the cupboard – as though I'd been locked inside the suffocating darkness of my own school trunk and was shouting, hopelessly, to be let out.

'Again.' The headmaster played the same phrase a semitone higher. This time he jumped from the stool. He pressed his body right against mine, from behind, put his arms around me and put his hands on my belly – 'From here! You breathe from here!' – and his hands were big and hot, burning through the material of my shirt, burning my skin as I breathed deeply and sang. 'Again!' the headmaster cried out, holding himself hard against me, so close that the odour of his breath and his body were suddenly strong in the airless room. 'No, no good, no good!'

With an expression of utter weariness, almost defeat, he thrust me aside and stood there, panting like a wounded bear. 'Go. Just go away. I've had enough.'

Quite miserable, I dragged my feet along the corridor. I didn't know where to go or what to do. For the first time, even the prospect of communing with my bird or searching out Roly in the woods seemed pointless: what a choice of company on a dreary winter's afternoon, a crow with a brain the size of a pea, or a weasly old hermit. Trying to shake the meanness of these thoughts from my head, I found myself close to the entrance to the hall and saw Mrs Kemp still sitting by the fire.

*   *   *

She'd stayed there, alone, since her husband's row with Pryce. From the other end of the school she must have heard the muted sound of the piano in the practice room and our repeated, fruitless exercises, the same futile arpeggio. Now she was staring into the fire, where the flames were blue from the sap as the holly twigs fizzled and spat. Her eyes fell miserably on the spot on the worn carpet where Wagner used to sleep, where he'd been sleeping only twelve hours before. She stared into space.

Suddenly, there was a movement at the window. I caught it from where I'd paused to watch her, and she turned her head to see what it was. The sunlight was dazzling, but there was a flutter of black against the blanket of snow. Again, a similar movement, a bit of blackness, as though someone had tossed a rag from an upstairs window, a rag or an old glove, and then again, bigger, past the window and onto the snow.

Crows. She wheeled herself quickly across the room, to the further end of the hall near the piano. I tiptoed to another window and looked out too. I heard her gasp at the sight of what the crows were doing.

The birds were dropping from the treetops. They'd stopped calling. And in their silent, uncanny communion, there was a terrible purpose. They fell to the body of the dog.

'Oh no, please . . .' She leaned towards the glass and banged on it with the heel of her hand. The crows, six or eight of them, sprang from the dog and wafted into the air. They dropped, and they hopped through the snow on their black, muscular legs. She banged again, and again they recoiled from the dog, cloaking their bodies with half-open wings. Then the boldest bird flapped and flapped and beat through the air, lifting a cloud of sunlit powdery snow like a miraculous halo, and it landed on top of the dog. It pecked. But the beak, a black dagger, jarred on the stiffened, freezing body. So the bird sprang to the dog's head. And it pecked. Another bird slunk through the snow to the other end of the dog. Where it pecked.

'Oh please God no . . .' Mrs Kemp rapped and rapped on the window. She banged with all her strength, but her fists were weak and white and the glass was like ice.

Instinctively, I moved to help her: to reach for the front door and open it wide, to step outside and clap the crows away. But as I started forwards, a hand closed onto the collar of my shirt. It wrenched me back with a breath-taking jolt.

Pryce. A second later, with my shirt wrung so tight against my throat that I thought I was strangling, he'd lugged me into the corridor, back-heeled open the door of the staffroom and pulled me inside.

He pinioned me there. And he hissed into my ear, with both of our faces close to the crack in the door, forcing me to peer out with him, 'Let her work it out for herself, she thinks she's so fucking perfect.'

She was shouting, 'Dr Kemp! Headmaster!' but her voice was feeble from sitting too long in the freezing air, from the smoke of the fireside, from weeping. She took as big a breath as her lungs could hold, and she shouted,

'No! No!' thumping the window at the same time. 'Dr Kemp! Please! Please!'

The crows were on the dog. They were hungry. The night had been bitter and long: a long night to be hunched in a cloak of wings, muffled in a coat of feathers, shivering in the treetops while the forest creaked and groaned through the hardest frost of winter. Hungry, they were on the dog, plying their beaks in the softest places.

We watched her. I couldn't speak, I could hardly breathe, as Pryce screwed my collar tighter and his face bent close to mine. We saw her spin her chair and thrust with all her weight towards the headmaster's study. There was a look of steel on her face, as cold as the glass on which she had bruised her hands. She had neither the time nor the inclination to go wheeling the whole length of the school for the assistance of her husband, who, as far as she knew, was preoccupied with venting his unhappiness in a misguidedly punitive singing lesson, so she sped to his desk, pulled open a drawer and rummaged among a mess of papers until she found the bunch of keys she was looking for.

In moments she was accelerating along the smooth lino of the corridor, so close to our faces that I caught a waft of her perfume; and almost directly opposite us, she skidded to a halt at the door which was her destination: NO BOYS TO ENTER WITHOUT A MEMBER OF STAFF.

Still we could hear her hissing, 'Dr Kemp, headmaster . . .' but the words were all but smothered by the hoarseness of her breathing. 'No no, please God no . . .'

It was only a noise she made to drive herself faster to get what she needed. We watched her as she found the key, as she fitted it into the keyhole with speed and accuracy and a well-oiled snugness, and she rolled inside the room, unlocked the big black iron safe and tugged the door wide open.

A row of guns: half a dozen single-shot, Martini-action .22 rifles.

She snatched one of them from the rack, pulled the lever and opened the chamber. She ripped open a box of cartridges and thumbed one into the chamber. The smell of the gun was strong, a dark oily smell which did not allow for cobwebs and fustiness. She snapped it shut. She was in and out of the room in less than thirty seconds and thrusting back along the corridor, towards the hall again, with the gun balanced on the arms of her chair and the box of cartridges in her lap.

Pryce manhandled me across the staffroom. I'd never set foot in there before, only glimpsing inside whenever I'd had to knock on the door and ask for one of the teachers. Now I had a second to glance around me as I was whirled from the door and over to the window. Threadbare armchairs, a table littered with sherry glasses, left-over Christmas cake and overflowing ash-trays. A noticeboard stuck with duty lists, newspaper cuttings; the calendar for December 1966, a red-faced Santa with a bikini-girl snuggling on his lap. Bizarrely, a glass case with a stuffed badger inside it.

No air. A fume of stale smoke and stale middle-aged men.

Pryce had me at the window just in time. He sniggered, tightening his grip at my throat, as Mrs Kemp burst out of the front door of the house. The brightness was intense, after the gloom of the hall, and she hurtled the chair down the ramp so hard and so blindly that it crunched into the snow and tipped over. She was flung right out of it and landed headlong, with such a thump that all the air was driven from her body.

The crows were startled by her sudden appearance, but they did not relinquish their prize. As she sprawled in the snow, winded so badly that she gaped like somebody drowning, they bent their beady eyes towards her.

We watched from the window of the staffroom.

Mrs Kemp dragged herself over the snow on her belly and reached for the rifle. Lying in the snow like a backwoodsman, she splayed her legs, steadied her breathing and squinted down the barrel, just as I'd learned to do in the school's rifle range. She fired. But still her chest was heaving, so the first shot missed her target and thudded into the swollen body of the dog. The birds scattered, alarmed by the sudden report and its repercussions in the woodland; the way the dog groaned as a blast of gas escaped from the bullet hole in its belly. But one of them was reluctant to let go of the dog's tongue, which it had pierced and tugged out like a slice of veal. The woman ejected the spent cartridge, scrabbled for the box which lay nearby, reloaded and fired again, and her second shot sent the crow cartwheeling through the air and onto the lawn, an explosion of black feathers on the sparkling snow.

Dr Kemp appeared at the front door. He'd heard the shots and come running. In a blink he took in the extraordinary scene.

The wheelchair was capsized at the foot of the ramp. His wife lay flat on her belly, retching for breath, a rifle flung to one side. Under the copper beech, the dead dog was deflating. A crow was sculling around it, beating the lawn with shattered wings.

Pryce let go of me. I squirmed away from him, across the room and into the corridor. I was right behind Kemp at the front door of the house, as he ran forwards and bent to his wife, turned her over and felt her fragile body gasping.

'My dear, my dear,' he panted, 'what on earth are you doing?' and he tried to lift her from the ground. He glanced up and saw me at the door, staring, so astonished that I couldn't move. 'Help me, Scott!' he called out. 'Bring the chair, the chair . . .'

I was galvanised into action – or would have been. About to run down the ramp and right the chair, I felt a hand on my shoulder. Pryce was beside me, and the weight of the hand stopped me dead. He squeezed my shoulder hard enough to show that he meant me to stay where I was, and then he let go, brought his hands together and started to clap.

Slow, sarcastic clapping. Kemp, cradling his exhausted wife, goggled back at him. Pryce stood at the top of the ramp, and he clapped. 'Bravo,' he said. 'Good shooting, Mrs Kemp.'

And then, before the headmaster could express one jot of the outrage he felt, Pryce strode swiftly onto the lawn.

He was superb, a gentleman come to the rescue of a distressed lady. In one effortless movement, he bent to her, swept her into his arms and stood up. She gazed up at him, a limp, swooning figure. He blew softly into her face. 'You have snow on your eyelashes,' he whispered.

I hurried to the chair and set it upright. In another moment, Pryce was wheeling the woman up the ramp and into the house.

Dr Kemp struggled to his feet. He was negated, he was a negligible man. He dusted the snow from his trouser legs, picked up the rifle and the box of ammunition, stomped to the front door and disappeared inside.

I watched the stricken crow. It had slowed down and stopped, but it was still alive. I crunched across the lawn towards it. The bird lay on its breast, its eyes wild, its breath hissing through whiskery nostrils. Both wings were outstretched, spread-eagled, and as I came close it tried with all its failing strength to row away from me. It pulled at the ground with its beak and claws, crawling like a grotesque clockwork toy.

So I bent to the bird. It flopped against my foot, quite submissive, as though it knew what I was going to do and wanted it done quickly. It allowed my hands on its head and neck, a kind of blessing. I pulled very suddenly and the bird went limp.

Disinterested, the other crows watched from the woodland. Even before I'd walked off the lawn and around the side of the house, they dropped from the trees, in silence, to the body of the dog.

It was evening. In the stable, in the lamplight, I held the dead crow close to the flame and plucked the feathers from its breast. I'd nearly finished. The bird had been so brazen a few hours before, gleaming on the sunlit snow; now it was little, skinny, nude. It still had a head, but the weight and heft of the beak were out of proportion to the naked body. The legs and claws, strong and black, almost saurian, were quite incongruous. I swung the bird by its feet, and it weighed nothing. I took it across the room to my living, impish jackdaw.

'Dinner,' I said, and I draped the crow onto its perch. The jackdaw angled its head this way and that, from me to the odd prize I'd brought. I didn't know whether it would find my gift appealing or offensively inappropriate. But at last, after a moment's comical deliberation, it sprang to the crow, stood on it with all the weight of its one puny remaining leg, and mantled it with its wings. Like a hawk, it made a claim. It applied its beak to the bare flesh.

An owl hooted in the woodland.

The sound made me feel very lonely. I examined my hands, from which the stripes of the headmaster's cane were fading. With them, I'd saved the life of the jackdaw I'd found in the woods; with them, I'd blessed the crow, its cousin, with a quick death; and my fingers had been intimate with the workings of the owl's stomach. But now, as the jackdaw tore at the crow, as the owl quavered in the frozen forest, I knew that, for them, I did not exist. I'd never really touched them. Owl, jackdaw, crow: there was a kind of triangle, and I stood outside it.

I felt cold in the stable. There was no big black dog to warm me. I blew out the lamp, stood in the darkness for a few moments, and then I went outside and closed the door.

NINE

By ten o'clock the building was in darkness. No one had felt like sitting cosily around the fire. Indeed, the fire had burned down and gone out and no one had bothered to relight it. Its little residual warmth seeped out of the school and no one did anything to stop it.

No fire, no piano, no Christmas tree. No conversation. No appetite for the cheese sandwiches that Sophie had made in the school kitchen and offered to Dr and Mrs Kemp and me.

By nine o'clock the headmaster had sent me to my dormitory, and, for the first time in all my years at Foxwood, I undressed and washed and put myself to bed without a sign of Dr Kemp, without the prayer. I turned my own light out. I heard Pryce and Sophie go to their own dormitory soon after that, and heard the clanking of the lift as the Kemps went up to their apartment.

The house creaked. No footsteps, no voices. Not a groan or a whisper or even a flutter of snoring. A still night. A silent night. An unholy night.

Fast asleep, I dreamed that I was outside.

Barefoot, in my stripy pyjamas, I was crossing the snow-covered lawn. There was bright moonlight and I could see the dead dog beneath the copper beech, shining like a pool of oil. I called softly, 'Wagner, good boy', and the dog stood up and came to me. I bent to stroke him. He seemed bigger than usual, his body oddly stiff and swollen, and his tongue lolled so heavily that it almost brushed the snow. Together we went into the woodland, where the birches were gleaming, the beeches were silvery columns, where the moon threw marvellous shadows. We were walking and walking, and I was looking for something. In the dream I didn't know what I was looking for, not yet, not yet. But I felt no fear, no anxiety, nor did I feel the cold, because I knew that Wagner was there and he was helping me. 'Go on, boy, go on . . .' The dog moved stiffly ahead of me, now a big black shape in the moonlight, now a piece of the deepest shadow.

And then, in my dream, I found what I was searching for.

I saw Wagner nosing in the snowy leaves and nuzzling the dark soil of the forest, I knelt to the ground to gather the scattered scraps of blue air-mail paper – and I sensed that someone was moving towards me. Someone was in the woods with me, unseen, unheard, coming closer and closer, so that I froze and held my breath and stared around and listened as hard as I could for a footfall or a

whispered breath – somebody coming, closer and closer
. . .

I awoke. The door of my dormitory swung open.

Wide awake immediately, without moving at all, I
flicked my eyes towards the blank space, where the
corridor looked black and empty. I lay perfectly still,
without even blinking.

At first there was nothing, nobody. Perhaps it had been
the wind again, a shudder of cold air blowing from one
end of the building to another.

Then the floorboards creaked, and a figure came into
the room.

It tiptoed to the bed nearest to the door, and touched
the frame. I stared, frozen still and holding my breath,
and I heard the hiss of whispering. The figure moved to
the next bed and touched it, leaned down as though
peering for someone, and it whispered again. The figure
came slowly closer and closer, from bed to bed, touching,
looking, whispering.

Until I could stay silent no longer. I licked my lips and
said, 'Dr Kemp?'

With an odd cast of its head, the figure seemed to
glance in my direction. It moved another bed closer,
leaned down and felt at the bare mattress. 'Jeremy?' it
whispered. 'Are you there?'

And then the figure loomed at my bedside. This time it
could sense there was really someone in the bed. 'Jeremy,
are you awake?' it hissed, and as it bent so close that I
could feel its breath on my face, I squirmed out and
pressed myself, terrified, to the cold wall.

It was Pryce. He stared down at my bed. For a moment I thought he would lean down and feel at the dint on the pillow where my head had been, touch the warm outline where my body had been lying.

But there was no dint, no outline. There was a boy, lying where I'd been lying.

I saw him, and so did Pryce. The boy was asleep, his face white, his eyes closed, his black hair gleaming on my pillow.

And Pryce was hissing, 'Jeremy!' with a pleading, an urgency in his voice. 'Jeremy, wake up!'

The boy's eyes flicked open, from Pryce to me. And then he was gone.

I froze against the wall. Pryce touched the dint in my pillow, found it empty, straightened up and blinked around the dormitory. He was a man emerging from a strange dream.

At last he peered at me, as though he'd never seen me before in all his life, and he said, 'Where *is* everybody? Where *is* he?'

He turned and walked silently out of the room, leaving the door wide open behind him.

Pryce went deeper and deeper into the corridor, like a vole slipping into a damp, dark tunnel. He moved past the other dormitories and the lifts and as far as the bathroom, paused and opened the door and went inside. As he turned on the light, the bulb shining in the row of mirrors and all the sinks and baths threw an odd, fragmented gleam from the room and into the corridor.

I followed where he'd gone. I was afraid to get back into my bed, where the boy had been lying. Shaken out of the dream I'd shared with Pryce, I tiptoed after him and peered into the bathroom.

He'd torn open his shirt and flung himself to his knees beside one of the baths. After turning the taps on full he doused his head in the icy water, until his long hair was dripping and his shirt was wet through, and again and again he dunked his head, gagging and spitting, as if to lose himself in the noise and the drumming pressure.

He didn't hear what I heard: the clank of the lift, the opening of the lift door and the unmistakable hiss of the tyres of Mrs Kemp's wheelchair as she came along the corridor. I heard it all, and I had time to take one step backwards into the empty dormitory opposite the bathroom, to stand in the darkness as she wheeled right past me.

She looked into the bathroom, frowned and hesitated, and then rolled herself inside.

Pryce was groping for the tap, to turn it off while he still held his head under the gushing water, when he felt her gentle touch on his shoulder.

'Sophie,' I heard him say, without looking up. 'Jesus, Sophie . . .' and I saw him feeling for the hand that was touching him.

Straightaway he knew it wasn't the girl. He blinked through the water and his tousled hair and saw Mrs Kemp. She'd wheeled her chair right up to him: she was wearing a nightdress, her hair loose and soft, her eyes sleepy.

'I heard you,' she said. 'I heard the water. Are you ill?'

Still kneeling, he gripped her hand. 'A dream,' he said. 'I had a horrible dream.' With his other hand he swept back his hair and wiped the water from his face. Like a frightened child, he lowered his forehead onto her knee. 'I'm so sorry I woke you.'

'A bad dream,' she said. 'It's coming back here. Why did you come back? Upsetting yourself, upsetting us . . .'

She tried to extricate her hand from his, but she couldn't. With the other she reached for the tap and turned it off, and then she put her hand on the top of his head. 'You're soaked. You're cold. Why did you come back?'

She couldn't see his face, which was pressed onto the soft material of her nightdress. But I could see it, from where I stood at the door of the bathroom. She didn't see how he squeezed his eyes shut and held his breath as he felt the heat of her leg against his cheek and the touch of her hand on his hair.

'To see you,' he whispered. 'And now that I'm here, I can't leave.'

'Silly,' she said. She held her breath too, acutely aware of the weight of his body as he leaned against her. 'After all this time, why would you want to see me?'

He lifted his head, still holding one hand, and he caught her other hand too, while her fingers were still entangled in his hair. Her nightdress was wet where his cheek had pressed on her knee. On his knees at her feet, gripping both her hands, he stared up at her. 'It's this place.'

'Of course,' she put in, 'after all the years you spent at Foxwood . . .'

'No, no, I don't mean Foxwood.' With a movement of his head he gestured around the bathroom. 'I mean *here*, in *this* place. Don't you remember? Look.'

He let go of one of her hands, long enough for him to reach for the plug and drop it into the plug hole. He turned on the tap again.

'What are you doing . . .?' she started, but her voice was drowned by the roar of the water.

He caught her hand again. 'You remember,' he said urgently. Up on his knees, his chest and belly bare right down to the belt of his trousers, he was suddenly a gleaming, powerful figure. The water was running hot now, hotter and louder, and as the bath was filling a cloud of steam came roiling out, fogging the entire room, misting the mirrors, hazing the light bulbs in silvery haloes. She licked her lips, and the glimpse of her tongue brought a quick, crooked smile to his face. 'Yes, you remember,' he said. 'I can see you remember.'

'Don't be silly, Martin,' she said, and I heard a quaver of panic in her voice. 'Childhood memories play tricks on all of us. Now, go back to bed and . . .'

Before she could try to resist, to try and match his strength with her puny arms, he pulled one of her hands forwards and pressed it, palm open and flat, against his chest. The other he pressed to the side of his neck.

'The first time!' he hissed. 'Here, in this bath!' He tugged her closer to him, her face towards his. 'You were washing my hair, and you touched me like this, and for the first time . . .' He rubbed the palm of her hand down his chest and the smooth hot skin of his belly and he closed his eyes in a kind of swoon. 'Here,' he said, and he held her hand to his groin. 'I was hard, like this, for the first time.' He snapped his eyes open again. 'Remember? Here, in this place . . .'

She snatched her hand away. 'I never touched you! Get away from me!'

He was on his feet. The room was a blur of steam and the bath seemed to thrum a deeper, rumbling note as the water rose higher. For the second time that day, I saw him pick her up, as though she weighed nothing. She cried feebly, 'No, no! Please, no!' and when she glimpsed through the fog that I was watching from the doorway she raised the pitch of her voice and called out, 'Alan, tell Dr Kemp! Tell him!'

Pryce swung her over the bath. 'In the water you'll be weightless,' he whispered, his mouth pressed to her throat.

I stepped into the room, as she moaned and writhed, as he lowered her to the surface. She twisted her head to the doorway again and cried, 'No Alan, don't tell him don't tell him please never please don't . . .'

Pryce smothered her words with his mouth, kissing her deeply. 'In the water you'll be free,' he murmured to the woman, and he laid her deep into the bath. 'In the water you are whole, you are perfect . . .'

Her nightdress swirled around her; she gasped at the sudden heat. He slipped out of his clothes and stepped into the bath. She stared up at him as he lowered his body to hers.

'You knew I'd come back,' he said. 'You wanted me to
. . .'

He threw me a triumphant sidelong glance, and I spun
away into the darkness of the corridor.

TEN

Pryce struck the ground with the spade, winced at the jarring in his wrists and struck again. He'd taken off his coat and rolled up the sleeves of his shirt, and now he was working hard. Dr Kemp and Sophie and I watched.

It was a cold, grey morning. Unlike the previous mornings, the sun had not pierced the cloud and broken through, so the icy breath of night still hung in the woodland. The sky lowered on a strangely silent world. A silvery mist drifted and swirled in the treetops.

After a while, Pryce stood back and wiped his brow. He'd managed to make a considerable hole; having forced a way into the rock-hard earth at the surface, he'd hit a seam of softer soil and was cutting deeper with every blow. We were underneath the copper beech. The dog lay nearby. Kemp had draped the body with a sheet, for decorousness, to protect it from the crows, and to smother the smell.

Kemp stamped his feet and blew on his fingers. He looked older, I remember thinking as I glanced at the headmaster; in a matter of days he seemed to have bowed and shrunk, so that the brown jacket hung loosely on his frame and his trilby was almost ridiculous, a size too big. His eyes were watery. His nostrils were chapped and blue; his nose dripped and he did nothing to stop it. His skin was mottled grey, as though the blood had drained from it. Like the sunless, lifeless morning, the pallor of winter was on him.

Or maybe it was the contrast he made with Pryce. The young man was burning with energy. Hot, strong, plying the spade quite easily now that he'd broken through the crust and into the yielding mulch that lay beneath, he'd hit a steady swinging rhythm. His youth gleamed on him and around him, the aura of his maleness. He tossed back his hair, swept us three shivering spectators with a glittering smile, and attacked the ground again.

'It doesn't have to be too deep,' the headmaster said. 'I think you've done enough already.'

'We don't want anyone to find him,' Pryce said. His breath smoked. 'I mean, with a winter as hard as this, maybe a fox or a badger will get the scent and try to dig him out.'

He looked into the mist, and we all followed his eyes. In the forest, where the smooth whiteness of the lawn petered into tangled undergrowth, the crows were perched high up, watching. They made not a sound. They gripped and swayed with the creaking movement of the branches, but they themselves were motionless, like pieces of iron welded to the gantry of the trees.

'They're hungry,' he said. 'It's best if he goes good and deep.'

A shot rang out. The birds beat into the air and flapped away, over the roof of the school and into the distance. Pryce jumped and stared around. 'Who's that?' he blurted, unusually startled. 'Who's out there?'

'It's the gamekeeper,' Kemp said. 'He . . .'

'A gamekeeper?' Pryce said. 'There was never a game-keeper!'

Kemp stared at him queerly. I looked at him sideways; still numb after the scene I'd witnessed the previous night, quite unable to meet Pryce's eyes, I was nevertheless surprised to see how discomfited he was. Pryce glared at me, and I ducked my head. Sophie, who'd stood frozen and mute ever since we'd all trooped onto the lawn, started to say, 'A gamek-k-keeper? Maybe he c-c-can . . .'

Pryce cut her off. 'No, Sophie . . .'

'There is a gamekeeper,' the headmaster said firmly. It was uncanny to see how quickly he asserted a shred of his authority the instant he saw that Pryce was rattled. 'His name's Roly, he works for one of the farmers.'

'Has he got a t-t-tractor or something?' the girl tried again. 'Maybe he c-c-can . . .'

'No, Sophie.' Pryce stared her out. Then, more gently, 'Sophie my love, we don't need anyone.'

Kemp shrugged. 'Whether we need anyone or not, it's no good asking Roly. He's a surly old fellow, just banging around the woods with a shotgun or festering in his caravan. He wouldn't put himself out for anybody.'

Another shot. The sound echoed in the icy forest and faded to nothing. 'He's further away this time,' Pryce said. 'Good.'

There was a longer silence. Pryce rubbed the palms of his hands together and turned to the hole he was making. The blade of the spade sliced deeply, keenly, into brown earth.

Kemp pulled the sheet off the dog's body. He tried to do it in a dignified and respectful way, but it snagged on one of the hind legs, which had stiffened at an odd, unlifelike angle. With his hand to his mouth, he bent close and freed the sheet and took it right off. He snapped the sheet open and laid it into the hole.

'Would you help me?'

Pryce nodded, and together they lifted the dog from the ground and lowered it onto the sheet. There was only a faint whiff of decay. The body was frozen hard, locked in rigor mortis. The dog stared obliquely at the sky, its mouth set into a twisted snarl; the tongue had stiffened into a long grey blade. Pryce stood back.

The headmaster knelt to the grave. He stroked the dog's head. He took hold of one of its paws and squeezed it hard, in the way that only a loving owner would do, who knew every ridge and whorl of the pads, every notch in the blunted claws, and could read in them all the miles and years of walking they'd done together. Still holding the foot, reluctant to let go, he gazed around the lawn and into the forest, into the branches of the copper beech.

At last he whispered, 'This is a good place for you, Wagner, it's your place.' He stood up with some difficulty, for the cold was in his knees and his hips. 'It's our place.'

He looked at Pryce and tried to lighten the moment. 'It's a mighty big hole you've made. Big enough for me as well, when the time comes.' He glanced back to the school, where his wife moved dimly in one of the upstairs windows. 'For both of us.'

He read not a glimmer of warmth in the young man's eyes. With a lift of his brows and a movement of his hand to the spade, Pryce merely asked if he should start to close the grave. Dr Kemp pursed his lips, and his mottled face set in a look of determination. 'I'll do it,' he said. 'I wish I could have dug the hole myself. I'll fill it in even if it kills me.'

He took the spade from Pryce. 'Don't judge us too harshly,' he said. 'We've always done our best for all the boys who've been at Foxwood. That includes you.'

Still Pryce said nothing. He reached for Sophie's hand, as though to lead her away from the grave and back to the house. But she recoiled, and, in a quick, instinctive movement, she stepped to the headmaster, folded her arms around him and hugged him.

His body seemed to sag, all of a sudden, as though the warmth of her embrace had thawed the aches and pains from his bones. His eyes filled with tears. To cover his embarrassment, he eased the girl away from him and wiped his face. 'Thank you, thank you,' he murmured. He pulled out a handkerchief and blew his nose, then peered blearily into the treetops for something to say. As a clumsy non-sequitur, he added, 'It'll snow again. It's Christmas.'

Pryce and Sophie trudged across the lawn. Kemp leaned into the grave and folded the sides of the sheet over the dog, shrouding it completely. I waited a moment for the headmaster to say that he needed help or give me permission to go, but he seemed to have forgotten that I was there. I moved away as quietly as I could.

When I reached the corner of the building, I paused and looked back. Dr Kemp had taken off his jacket and thrown his hat onto the ground and was shovelling the earth into the hole – a small, dark figure against the silvery woodland, under the spreading boughs of the tree, beneath a leaden sky.

Sophie moved along the downstairs corridor. She'd come down the boys' staircase, on her own. It was only five o'clock in the afternoon, but it could have been midnight, the house was so dark. She must have thought the Kemps were in their apartment at the top of the building, and that I was moping upstairs or in the yard.

Utterly dismal, the silence and the chill, the musty gloom. She padded up and down the unfamiliar ramps, she slithered on the worn lino; she tiptoed past closed wooden doors, past the iron grilles of the two lifts. She hurried past doors which were ajar and whose shadows exhaled a whiff of stale cigarette smoke, the dust of a neglected library, the lingering smell of little boys.

I'd been skulking in the library. I heard her come down the stairs and go by.

When she reached the great hall the only light was the glow of the embers in the hearth. I watched her as she felt for the switch on the wall, found it, but then decided not to turn on the lights. Instead she crossed to the fire, fumbled and fumbled for something beside the walnut cabinet of the record player, until at last her hand fell on the telephone.

With a furtive glance around her and back to the grand staircase, thinking she was quite alone, she picked up the receiver and put it to her ear. I could hear the faint humming from where I was hiding. She pressed down the receiver bar and released it, but there was only a humming, no dialling tone. She dialled a number, waited, listened. She jiggled the bar impatiently, hissing *come on come on*, and still there was nothing but a hum, worse and more infuriating than silence: it was the sound of somewhere faraway and out of reach.

'It still isn't working . . .'

Sophie whirled around at the sudden voice. She dropped the receiver so hard that it banged on top of the record player and fell towards the floor. Mrs Kemp wheeled silently towards her. 'Still not working,' the woman said, 'but I don't blame you for trying.'

Mrs Kemp pushed her way to the hearth. I knew she'd been sitting at the window earlier in the afternoon, in the far corner behind the great black bulk of the piano, watching the grave of the dog: keeping a kind of vigil. She must have stayed there into the evening, through all the hours I'd been lurking in the library. From time to time, I'd been drawn to the window too – no more snow, not yet, although the sky had bulged with snow clouds and threatened throughout the short hours of daylight – until, in the sullen glimmer of dusk, the heap of earth was the only mark on the lawn. It looked as though the dog were still lying where we'd left it the day before. Yet I'd seen the headmaster filling the hole and patting it smooth with the flat of his spade, so I knew that Wagner was safely sleeping where nothing and no one could disturb him.

Alone in the lightless hall, Mrs Kemp had been sitting and watching his grave.

'I'm sorry I frightened you,' she said to the girl. 'I was sitting and thinking.' In the glow of the embers, her face was thin and lined. Her fine hair looked dry. Her fingers twitched at something in her lap, picking and unpicking. She had the dog's brush in her hands and she was teasing out a ball of hair.

She reached to the girl and took her by the wrist. 'I don't blame you for trying,' she said urgently. 'For trying to get out of here. I know you said your mother and father were angry with you and you'd run away from home, but it's Christmas, you should be with your family and . . .'

'How can I? There's no phone, no car, no . . .' Sophie winced at the strength of the woman's grip.

'Are you hurt?' the woman hissed. 'Is Martin hurting you? You must get away from him! He's a bad bad man . . .'

'How can I? I can't get out and I can't go home! It's too late! We're both bad! It makes me sick to think about it!'

She suddenly knelt onto the floor and, taking hold of both Mrs Kemp's hands, leaned forwards and pressed them to her face in a sad, impulsive gesture, as if they were the only comfort she could find in such a wretched place.

'I thought Martin loved me,' she started, and then the words came sobbing, spilling from her. 'At first he was nice to me, he was nice and funny and – and then last week, he took me to see his brother in his college rooms. I didn't want to go but he made me, and it was horrible, he . . .'

'Tell me, Sophie, go on, tell me,' the woman whispered to her. 'Did he hurt you?'

'We drank a lot, we drank too much, the three of us – until it was late and Martin crashed out somewhere and left us on our own, me and Jeremy – and we were kissing and it was nice and I thought it was OK and it was what Martin wanted me to do . . .' She took a big gulping breath, looked up at the woman and said, 'I thought it was why he'd taken me to see Jeremy, to go with him for the first time 'cos he'd never had a girl before, and so we . . .'

She kissed the palms of the woman's hands. She was confessing, she was begging forgiveness. Having gone so far and said so much, she wanted – she needed – to go on.

'But then Martin woke up. He came in and saw us together, me and Jeremy, and he – he just went crazy, I couldn't stop him – it makes me sick . . .'

'Ah, there you are.' Pryce's voice cut through the darkness, from the foot of the staircase. He crossed the hall to the hearth, and he smiled at the woman and the girl, as he saw Sophie let go of Mrs Kemp's hands and get up from her knees. The light from the dying fire gleamed on his teeth and the whites of his eyes. 'So, what's this? A cosy chat? Not talking about me, I hope?'

Mrs Kemp flinched from him, ducking her head, and her fingers worked fast and feverishly at the dog's brush. Sophie said nothing, just smearing at her eyes with the backs of her hands. The quiet was so intense that even a fall of needles from the Christmas tree seemed suddenly loud: so quiet that Pryce heard a very faint humming from the fireside.

He saw the receiver of the telephone dangling on its flex. His smile somehow froze, as charming as ever but oddly crooked. 'Any luck with the phone? What's the matter, Sophie? Don't you like it here?'

'Dr Kemp thought it might be rec-c-c-connected soon,' she said. 'I just tried . . .'

Pryce reached for the receiver and put it to his ear. 'Hello?' he said. He cooed into the mouthpiece, *'Is there anybody out there?'* He replaced it gently on its cradle. There was a click, then dead silence. 'No good,' he said. 'Good.'

He took Sophie by the wrist and, the tiniest bit harder than he needed to, squeezed on the bone. She squirmed and grimaced, but he didn't let go. 'Come on, Sophie, you've been talking too much. I want you to help me with something.'

He led her out of the hall. Before they were swallowed into the darkness of the corridor, Sophie cast a look over her shoulder. Mrs Kemp had wheeled herself as close as she could get to the hearth. She tossed the ball of hair into the embers.

It sizzled and burst into flame. For the briefest moment it lit the pain and the fear on her face, and then it went out.

ELEVEN

T he school kitchen, a scene of catastrophic disorder
. . .

Every pan, every utensil, had been used and left
heaped, unrinsed, unwashed, in the sink. The stove was
splashed with gravy. The oven door swung open, billowing a breath of residual warmth into the air. On the
work-table, there were loops of potato peelings, onion
skins, the wrinkly outer leaves of sprouts.

The room was empty and dark, but a mouse had
crossed the floor and shimmied up the table leg and onto
the top to investigate the scraps. With its whiskers it
tested the edge of a meat tray, decided it had cooled
down enough to negotiate, and hopped inside to nibble
the sweetness of a roasted parsnip that had been left
behind. The silver of stainless steel shone in its eyes. It

moved from corner to corner of the tray, leaving tiny footprints in the congealing fat.

I'd been sent to the kitchen a few times, to run an errand, to fetch this and that. Now, back in the great hall, the fire was blazing. It was the best fire since Pryce and Sophie had arrived. I'd carried armfuls of logs and stacked them neatly on the hearth, careful to be sure that neither a toad nor a bat were sleeping there, rebuilding and reviving the fire from the embers which had all but died earlier in the evening. Pryce had told me to do it. And throughout the evening I'd watched the fire and kept it ablaze.

It had been the only successful part of the proceedings. When the Kemps had come down in the lift, along the corridor and into the hall, they'd found a table set for all of us. An hour later, it was strewn with the remains of a cheerless Christmas dinner: the carcase of a capon, picked to the bone; a tureen of bland, over-cooked vegetables; a solitary bottle of wine beside a candelabra whose flames had dripped wax onto the table cloth and finally sputtered out; the crumbs of a few mince pies – the paltriest trappings of a slapdash dinner, not enough, and not a scrap of festive spirit.

In the corner, the tree had been propped against the wall. The flex and its shattered bulbs dangled haphazardly from the branches.

The fire threw a ball of heat into the room. Mrs Kemp sat close to the hearth; once, the flames had driven her back when my carefully constructed pyre had collapsed in a shower of sparks and spilled towards her feet: the liveliest moment of the evening. She had not come to the table. Morose, deeply wounded in a way that her husband could not have imagined, she hardly spoke. She'd hardly eaten. Dr Kemp finished his wine, set down the empty glass, got up and joined her at the fireside.

'Not exactly a banquet,' Pryce said. 'But it was the best we could do. We used up everything we could find in the kitchen.'

'Yes, everything,' the headmaster said sourly. 'And no, not a banquet. We didn't think there'd be five of us. There would've been plenty for me and Mrs Kemp, for the dinner we traditionally have together on Christmas Day.'

Pryce shrugged. 'We thought it would be a nice surprise for you. It's Christmas Eve. Sophie and I wanted to show our appreciation of your hospitality.' He raised his glass, still half-full, and waved it in the air. 'Thank you for having us.'

'I don't know what we'll eat tomorrow,' Kemp said.

'The snow'll clear soon,' Pryce went on. 'I'll get the car started, get the tyre blown up just enough for us to get going, and we'll limp away. Sophie and I'll be gone.' He turned to me, as I knelt on the rug where Wagner used to lie. 'What about you, Alan? Have you heard from your mother?'

Kemp harrumphed. 'He might as well stay until the beginning of next term. There's no word . . .'

'She couldn't come anyway, could she?' My voice was unusually forceful, louder than I'd meant it to be. Flushing from the heat of the fire, I blinked at the adults' surprised faces. 'I mean, even if she's back in England, the road's blocked and the phone isn't working. It's not her fault.'

Mrs Kemp reached to me and put her hand on my head. 'No, it isn't, Alan. And it isn't your fault either. I'm so sorry you're having a horrid time . . .'

'Did you w-w-w-want anything, Mrs Kemp? A glass of w-w-w-wine, before Martin drinks the lot?'

The woman shook her head. Before she could speak, her husband said, 'My wife has a chill. I told her not to come outside with me yesterday. And then she was lying in the snow for goodness knows how long.'

'A hot bath,' Pryce said. 'Best thing for a chill. Let the heat get deep inside you.'

The woman stared at him. She fixed her eyes on his, unflinching. Then she swivelled her eyes onto me. And she read on my puzzled, frightened face that it was as extra-ordinary for me as it was for her, to think of what Pryce had done to her the night before: so nearly unbelievable that it had left us both numb, that it must have been a dream, that surely we'd had the same dream and now we could read it on each other's face. Then she turned back to Pryce, and she stared at him so hard and so coldly that it was he, at last, who looked away.

She felt for her husband's hand and squeezed it – the crotchety, moody man to whom she'd been married for the past twenty years – and I felt her despair at the realisation that *he* didn't know what had happened to her during the night, that he would never know, that for all he knew she was glum because the dog was dead.

How odd. *I* knew, a little boy of twelve, and her husband did not. And it would be like this forever.

Pryce said, 'Good shooting, Mrs Kemp. I mean, yesterday. I was impressed. And I say that as a bit of an expert myself.'

How odd, that he could look at her, that he could speak to her, that he was not dumb with shame . . . I remember these thoughts running through my head, I remember opening my mouth to speak them. But my mouth opened and closed, my tongue was still, and I just stared at him while the ideas trickled away and left my head empty.

Sophie snorted. 'You aren't an exp-p-p-pert on anything, Martin. What do you know?'

He got up from the table and strolled across the hall. He peered into the trophy cabinets, found the one he was looking for and opened it. He took out a little tin cup, tarnished and dented, which looked as though it hadn't been cleaned in years. He blew into it and a cloud of dust flew out. 'School shooting champion, under-11,' he said. 'It's got my name on it.' He rubbed it up and down his sleeve.

'It's p-p-pathetic,' Sophie said. 'You're pathetic.'

'I'm inclined to agree.' Dr Kemp leaned to the fire and put another log on it. He did it in a somehow proprietorial way, as if to assert that it was his fire, in his house, where he should have been enjoying Christmas with his wife. He sat back in his armchair, assuming an air of magnanimity. 'Really, Pryce, I don't want to disparage your prowess as a marksman. I meant it yesterday when I said that my wife and I do all we can for all the boys in our care. But you wouldn't scoff so much if you'd made any significant achievement at Foxwood.' He waved his empty wine glass towards the honours boards on the walls. 'These are the boys who took a pride in the gifts that God gave them. I don't see your name, although your brother's is there. Of course you were a valued member of the school and, like it or not, you'll always have a love of music that we fostered in you. But your brother had a perfect ear, and he had self-discipline. Scott, your name will be up there too, if you . . .'

'Well, I'm proud of this.' Pryce interrupted the head-master with an elaborate show of polishing the cup, breathing on it, rubbing it, holding it to the light as though it were a priceless antique. 'Apart from my initials carved into an old desk, it's the only sign that I was ever here.'

'And what about your brother?' All of a sudden, Mrs Kemp's voice rang clear and strong. 'Tell us about Jeremy.'

Pryce hesitated, taken aback by her intervention. He tried a little swagger, a laconic smile. 'Why do you want to talk about Jeremy, when you've got *me* here?'

'He went to Oxford, didn't he? He won a choral scholarship.' She made the points and pressed them home. 'Come along, Martin, we've acknowledged the sum of your achievements: at school you were the under-11 shooting champion, and now you're a salesman with a big car. How's Jeremy getting on?'

Turning to the girl, who'd swung her head so low that her fringe of hair completely covered her face, she added,

'Jeremy was a favourite of ours, Sophie, one of our brightest and best. You were telling me you'd met him a few days ago . . .'

'Yes, as a matter of fact Sophie *has* met Jeremy,' Pryce put in quickly. 'I introduced her to him in his college rooms last week. They got on rather well – didn't you, Sophie?' She didn't look up. His voice was very soft, but something in the way he spoke made a curious pause, an uneven beat in the pulse of the conversation – as though everyone in the room had stopped breathing. 'But we'll deal with Jeremy later. He's on the agenda.'

'What do you mean?' Mrs Kemp said. 'What agenda?'

Sophie was crying. She made not a sound, but her shoulders heaved and shuddered in a strange, silent convulsion. The Kemps stared at her. I stared at Pryce.

Slowly, with great deliberation, Pryce ticked the items on his fingers. 'There was the dog, there was Mrs Kemp, there's Jeremy, and there's Dr Kemp. All in good time.'

A longer silence. The flutter of the fire. A little gasping sob from the girl.

Mrs Kemp whispered, 'What do you want with us?'

'I don't understand,' the headmaster blustered. 'What are you talking about?'

Pryce moved to the hearth, reached up and put the tin cup on the mantelpiece. He stepped back and appraised it. Then he turned to us, and he licked his lips with a flickering, snakelike tongue. His eyes were cold and empty.

'It's Christmas,' he whispered. 'Let's have a game.'

* * *

'Get the keys,' he said to me. 'There's a good boy.'

I blinked. For a paralysing moment I thought of the piano tuning keys I'd stuffed down the side of the armchair that Dr Kemp was sitting on. Pryce saw the terror in my eyes, and said, 'No, Alan, the keys in the study. You know where they are . . .'

The relief, for a split second only, was so marvellous that, without hesitating, I got up from the hearth and turned towards the door of the study. I stopped dead when the headmaster said, 'What the devil's going on? Scott, you know you never go into my study unless . . .'

And I was held there, hovering between the fireplace and the study. Pryce was saying, 'Get them, Alan, Mrs Kemp has belittled my expertise . . .' and the headmaster repeated, 'I've told you, Scott, you don't go in there except . . .' so that I just stood there gaping, swivelling my face from one to the other as they both spoke to me at the same time.

'The keys, Alan, from the headmaster's desk.'

'Sit down, Scott, he has no right to tell you to . . .'

'Just get them, Alan, the bunch of keys.'

'For heaven's sake, Scott, just do as I say and . . .'

I took a step towards the open door of the study. Mrs Kemp's voice cut through, unusually shrill, the ugliest sound I'd ever heard her make. 'Listen to me, Alan! Keep out of there!'

It produced a startling response from Pryce. 'Shut up!' he yelled into her face. 'You got what you were waiting for! I've dealt with you!'

Kemp was on his feet, bristling and limber like a bear.

'How dare you?' He lunged at Pryce with all his weight, his arms stiff, his fists clenched.

But Pryce was too quick and strong for him. Quite easily, his height and youth too much for the huffing, purple-faced headmaster, he held him off. Kemp tried to speak, but his anger was so great, his body quivering with rage, that the words refused to come. Mrs Kemp was pressing her hands to reddened cheeks. Sophie had stopped crying and had looped her arm around the woman's shoulders. When Pryce spoke, his voice was no more than a whisper.

'Everyone jumps for the headmaster of Foxwood Manor School. The boys jump, the teachers jump, his wife jumps – well, she would if she could. It's time for a change. You don't bully me any more, Dr Kemp.'

He propelled the man backwards and sat him into his armchair as though he were a helpless geriatric.

He turned to me, where I stood frozen at the door of the study. 'Get me a gun.'

My mind went blank. Reacting in fear, almost an automaton, I was in and out of the study in a matter of seconds. I grabbed the bunch of keys from their customary place in the top drawer of the headmaster's desk, flew out of the room and out of the hall and into the darkness of the downstairs corridor. My heart thudding, I just wanted to get away from the scene, a scene of ugliness and violence almost to match the extraordinary things I'd witnessed in the upstairs bathroom, the things that Pryce had done with Sophie the first night and with Mrs Kemp just the night before.

I skidded through the shadows, jangling the heavy bundle of twenty or thirty keys – the keys for every room and cupboard in the school, on a single ring that the headmaster jangled with him wherever he went. The keys were the symbol of Dr Kemp's authority: his ownership of the school and everything in it. Now it was me, Alan Scott, a skinny, red-haired, twelve-year-old boy, who was holding them.

I slithered to a halt, fumbled for the right one and inserted it into the lock. It snicked and turned.

NO BOYS TO ENTER THIS ROOM WITHOUT A MEMBER OF STAFF. Inside the gun-room, where the single bulb festooned with cobwebs threw a yellowy light, I unlocked the safe. At the sight of the guns, I recoiled and squeezed my eyes shut, swallowing a bubble of nausea at the images that came to me: at home again, in summer, a man in black with a black balaclava and a thick, stubby gun, my father kneeling; my father twisting his head and shouting *Run, Alan! Run!* and an explosion of smoke and blood . . .

Now I reached into the cupboard, with my eyes still shut, and my fingers found the long, smooth barrel of a .22. My other hand felt for a box of cartridges. As I backed away and slammed the cupboard shut, as I turned the key and switched off the light, as I fell out of the gun-room and into the corridor and fumbled to close the door again, it was as though I were shutting the door on my nightmare and locking it up. All of a sudden the image was gone. Except that I was holding in my hands a real reminder of my dream, a dream that wasn't a dream but a piece of my life that had really happened, that would never change, that could never be completely shut away.

I trod along the corridor, towards the point of light at the further end that was the great hall.

A game, Pryce had said, *a game for Christmas*. The rifle was heavy and cold. I knew I could still change my mind. So far I'd done what Pryce had told me to do, but I could still change my mind and put the gun back in the cupboard and lock it away. Then I could drop the whole bunch of keys behind the dustiest books on the highest, darkest shelf in the library, or stuff them deep inside a burst leather sofa in the staffroom where no one could find them, and go back to the hall and realign myself with Dr and Mrs Kemp.

But I kept on walking, with the gun in one hand, the box of cartridges in my pocket, the keys in my other hand.

Because, because – the words were the shuffle of my feet on the smooth lino – because it was only a game and no harm would come of it, because I was big and brave and nearly a teenager and more akin to the devilment of Martin Pryce than the stuffiness of Dr and Mrs Kemp; because I'd have some mind-boggling tales to tell my friends when they came back to school in the New Year.

These were the reasons, the excuses, I ran through my head as I walked the length of the corridor and saw the light at the end grow bigger and bigger. But when I stepped into the hall and all the grown-ups turned and stared, I knew in my heart that I'd opted for Pryce and I was doing what Pryce had said because I was afraid of him.

Crack! The tin cup flew into the air and landed, miraculously, upside down. Eject, reload, and *crack!* again. The cup leaped off the mantelpiece and clanged onto the hearth.

Pryce had immediately relieved me of the rifle and the cartridges. While the headmaster had tutted and puffed, slumped as deep into his armchair as he could go, while Mrs Kemp and Sophie sat bravely upright, white-faced, with their arms around each other, Pryce had loaded the gun, stepped away to the opposite side of the hall and taken aim at his cup. Now it bounced into the fireplace, dented by the bullets that had struck it.

'For Christ's s-s-s-sake, Martin . . .'

'I've lost none of my skills,' he crowed. 'I'm still the dead-eye I was when I was ten.'

He reloaded and fired at the cup again, where it had landed by Mrs Kemp's feet. It jumped a foot into the air. The bullet ricocheted off the hearth, fizzed across the room and embedded itself in the side of the piano.

'You bloody fool!' the headmaster blurted. 'It won't be so funny if somebody . . .'

He stopped in mid-sentence, as Pryce reloaded and trained the gun at him and past him.

'It's a game, headmaster, it's Christmas,' Pryce said, and he levelled the gun just over the man's head and fired into the trophy cabinet he'd left open. Ejecting and reloading every time, the spent cartridges jumping from the chamber and smoking on the carpet, he fired and fired. The cups clanged and jumped. Cups that hadn't moved for years were suddenly loud and hot, and the bullets lodged in the ancient oak panelling behind them.

'Alan, your turn.'

I'd stayed by the headmaster's study, well away from the shooting. Maybe I thought that by running the errand and bringing the gun, I'd done all that was required of me. Now Pryce took hold of my wrist and tugged me centre-stage.

'Come on, Alan, have a go. When I was your age I was already a champion, my name engraved for posterity – is that the right expression, Dr Kemp? – on a magnificent trophy. Here, just try it.'

He thrust the gun at me. I recoiled from the heat of it, the smell of it.

Mrs Kemp stepped in. To me, she was a beautiful, classical heroine: her fine blonde hair was aflame in the firelight, her perfect complexion was flushed from the heat of the blaze. 'It's not fair. I told you about Alan. Leave him out of this.'

Pryce paused, as though to let it sink in. He seemed to weigh what she'd said. 'Thank you for that, Mrs Kemp. Yes, you told me the story, but I'm the teacher now. We know what the problem is, so let's deal with it. Alan, come on . . .'

He held me close, pulling me hard against his body, and pushed the gun into my hands. 'Trust me, Alan. I know you're afraid of guns, and I know why. You were afraid of Dr Kemp but you're not any more, thanks to me. So let's do it with the gun, come on.'

I squirmed like a fish. Pryce shouted through clenched teeth, 'Do it!' and pulled the trigger. With one arm he encircled me, with the other he pointed the gun randomly into the air and fired into the ceiling. A cloud of plaster showered down.

'For fuck's sake, Martin! You're f-f-f-fucking crazy!'

Pryce shoved me away. 'Jesus, Sophie, of course I'm crazy. I'm an old boy of Foxwood Manor School, you wouldn't expect me to be sane, would you? I mean, look at Alan, the poor snivelling little sod, and look . . .' He reloaded and trained the gun across the honours boards and the school photographs. 'Look, hundreds of crazy people, and just think of the ones you've met – me and Jeremy, both of us fucking crazy . . .'

The girl took a breath, very deliberate, determined to slow things down. She made a flagging gesture with both hands, as if to calm a runaway horse. She said very quietly, 'Don't tell them, Martin. If you don't tell them, we can still get out of this.'

He put the gun on top of the piano. He crossed to Sophie and took her head in both his hands. It was a curious gesture. His hands were big and powerful, cupped around her small, round head. They could have been lover's hands, and he might have leaned down and kissed her; or they could have been the hands of a killer, strong enough to break her neck with a single twist. He just held her head and swayed it from side to side, as though it were a ball, or a bowl full of water.

He said to her with particular politeness, although some of the words were ugly, 'We can never get out of this, Sophie. It's like Fauré's fucking Requiem. It goes back too far. What happened last week to you and me and Jeremy started here, at Foxwood, fourteen fucking years ago.'

He let go of her head and stood back. He had the rapt attention of everyone in the room. He said to Mrs Kemp, 'You wanted to hear about Jeremy. Well, it's Jeremy I've come to talk about. It's why we're here.'

TWELVE

P ryce sent me outside for more firewood.

It was snowing heavily. An odd expression, wrong really, because the snowflakes were as light as moths. There was no wind, but as the snow fell from the heavens and came to earth, on some mad impulse it whirled in the trees and danced in the cold air until it floated to the ground. In a glimmer of moonlight, it was pretty, it was a picture: the vast, silent woodland, the big old house with just a faint gleam of gold from its shutters, the snow so soft on the lawn with not a footprint of man or beast.

Christmas Eve. It looked like a Christmas card; or a Christmas ornament, a globe filled with water and artificial snowflakes, shaken to make a perfect winter scene.

Not quite a silent woodland. The trees groaned as they moved together, very old and very cold; not dead, although their branches were so black and so bare, but ancient living things which felt the ache of the ice in their bones. I heard the yelp of a fox as it limped through the derelict bracken. I listened and watched as an owl beat through the air and landed in the copper beech. It gripped with its talons and shuffled its feathers, and it heaved and heaved until it retched a shining black pellet which fell to the ground and steamed a little. A minute later, the owl had wafted into the forest, and the pellet was hidden under gently deepening snow.

I went around the house to the yard. The owl hooted. I peered into the stable, where the jackdaw heard the sound and stared into the darkness. As it sprang from one end of its perch to the other, as far as the leather jesses would allow, the silvery bells tinkled softly. The bird hissed, as though in answer to the owl. It could hear the snow falling in the stable yard, and the whisper of the wind in the trees.

In the great hall, when I returned with an armful of logs, Pryce was talking. He was sitting in one of the fireside chairs. He'd picked up the gun again and was cradling it in his arms.

He was calm, his voice tinged with nostalgia.

'My dear little brother, my little Jeremy – it's funny, but before he came to Foxwood, I seem to remember that Dr Kemp thought I was quite a good singer, with quite a good ear. But then Jeremy arrived, and he had perfect pitch, which made all the difference. Like Alan here, he was born with a gift from God. He was angelic, brilliant, perfect Jeremy Pryce, and from then on, I was just not good enough.'

He pointed the gun at the honours boards, training it up and down until he found his brother's name.

'Yes, Jeremy went up to Oxford this autumn, with a scholarship. But these were the formative years, at Foxwood Manor. Jeremy was the headmaster's darling, a quiet, sensitive thing – always in the study with Dr Kemp, always in the music room or the chapel with Dr Kemp, always behind closed doors. So that some of us – not me of course, because I was his protective, loving older brother – some of the other boys wondered what else was going on in there, apart from the music, the headmaster and Jeremy locked away so long and so often. You know how they giggle, horrid smutty boys, how they tittle and tattle. Somebody coined a name for Jeremy: he was Dolly Boy, the headmaster's little Dolly Boy . . .'

The headmaster sighed noisily and rolled his eyes at the ceiling.

'Yes, it sounds so silly, doesn't it?' Pryce went on. 'Petty, prep-school stories. But Jeremy was afraid. He told me. He was afraid of the other boys. And worse, he was afraid of Dr Kemp.'

'It's preposterous,' the man said. 'I don't know why we're sitting here listening . . .'

'Afraid of Dr Kemp. He told me. He was ten years old, a long way from home, and often alone with Dr Kemp, who . . .'

'I won't hear any more of this . . .'

'Who would sometimes sit on the edge of Jeremy's bath and watch him, and sit on the side of his bed at lights-out and sometimes touch . . .'

'I never touched him, I would never . . .'

'And sometimes touch him or else just look and look – so that the other boys saw what was happening and made life a misery and a torment for Jeremy Pryce, the headmaster's little Dolly Boy . . .'

'None of the boys are unhappy here. It just isn't true.'

Pryce levelled the gun at the school photographs. 'Look at the faces. Lost and lonely little boys, bullied and abused by Dr Kemp . . .'

'That's enough!' The headmaster struggled to pull himself out of his chair. 'I won't have any more . . .'

Pryce pulled the trigger. A bullet shattered the glass of one of the photos. Sophie and Mrs Kemp squealed. He reloaded and fired again, and another photo exploded into smithereens. Kemp collapsed back into his chair.

'Jeremy was afraid and unhappy at Foxwood.' Pryce's voice was unnervingly matter-of-fact. 'It all started here, and it didn't stop when he left. When he went to public school, when the two of us were at public school in our teens, the rumours went with him. There were other boys who'd been at Foxwood, and they kept the Dolly Boy nickname going – not just the nickname, but the reputation too. Jeremy was pale and shy and pretty, small for his age. Some of the senior boys, and even one of the masters, took advantage of him . . .'

'I just don't believe it,' the headmaster said.

'They took advantage of his prettiness and shyness. They used him for sex. He told me. I tried to help him, but I couldn't.'

He paused. There was a silence. Neither Mrs Kemp nor Sophie said a word. They stared into the fire. Sitting in the shadows at the foot of the staircase, I ducked my head and picked at the weals on my hands.

Pryce broke open the gun. A spent cartridge flew out; he thumbed in another. The metallic click as he snapped the chamber shut was sharp and business-like. He aimed the gun at Dr Kemp's foot.

'Martin – d-d-don't . . .'

He ignored the girl, her querulous stammering. He trained the gun up and down the headmaster's body, so that the man cringed and clenched himself involuntarily as though trying to become an invisible part of the chair.

Pryce went on, his voice even softer.

'So Jeremy won a scholarship and went to Oxford. It was a credit to him, that through all the fear and the misery of his schooldays he achieved so much. And at Oxford, for the first time in ten years, he found a place where no one knew him. No more sniggering, no more rumours, no more ugly, suggestive whispers. He thought he'd escaped all that.'

No one was looking at the fire any more, and I'd stopped studying the palms of my hands. Pryce had the full attention of the Kemps and Sophie and me. The headmaster was especially attentive: the gun was aimed straight at his head.

'But no,' Pryce said, reflectively. 'They never heal, the

scars of our childhood. Jeremy was riddled with shame. He questioned his own sexuality. The first time he met girls – and he'd never met them before in all his life – he was disturbed and agonised. It only took a glance and a smile from another man to make him snap . . .'

He lowered the gun, reached into his pocket and took out a slip of paper. He started to unfold it.

'I had a note from Jeremy last week,' he said, his voice no more than a whisper. 'His last note.' He read from the piece of paper. 'It started with Kemp. I disgust myself. I would rather be dead.'

We all gaped at him. My palms were prickling. Sophie was weeping.

'Jeremy killed himself five days ago, at the end of his first term at Oxford. Somehow – I don't know how exactly, but he must have thought it was appropriate – he contrived to strangle himself with a string he'd removed from a piano.'

Mrs Kemp put her hands to her mouth and leaned forwards. She retched, barking like a dog, then buried her face and mewed. Sophie just stared and stared at Pryce. Tears rolled down her cheeks and into the corners of her lips.

Pryce crumpled the piece of paper into a tight little ball and lobbed it into the fire. I watched the lazy, dreamlike, almost slow-motion arc of it, and then it lay and smoked for a moment before bursting into a lovely blossom of flame.

Dr Kemp watched it too. When he turned back to Pryce, he found that the barrel of the gun was an inch from his nose.

'Is the music going through your head?' Pryce whispered. 'A requiem for the souls of the dead? Is it for Jeremy Pryce? Or for yourself?' The man closed his eyes. Pryce murmured to him, '*Requiem aeternam dona eis, Domine* – Grant them O Lord eternal rest . . .'

The man started gibbering. 'I never touched him, I swear to God I never . . .'

Pryce jammed the gun into his throat. All of a sudden his voice was hard. No more whispering. There was a fleck of spittle on his mouth.

'You made him disgust himself. You were killing him right from the start. And you're doing it now, you're doing it to Alan . . .'

Without shifting his eyes from Kemp, he called across to me, 'Does he make you afraid? Alan, does he make you afraid?'

I stood up. All of my schooldays I'd been trained to stand up when a grown-up spoke to me, and now a grown-up with a gun pressed into the headmaster's throat was asking me a question. 'I – I don't know. He . . .'

'Tell me and tell him! Does he make you afraid?' Pryce started shouting at me. 'Afraid that he'll hurt you? Like he hurt you yesterday? Come here! Come here and show me, show him, show him your hands.'

Unable to protest, I crossed to the fireside. Mrs Kemp still had her head on her lap, her hair falling about her face and hiding her completely. I manoeuvred past her wheelchair, caught the hopeless, terrified look in Sophie's eyes, and then Pryce's hand lashed out and caught my wrist in a grip like steel. I felt my fingers prised open, and

Pryce shoved my palm into the headmaster's face, so close that the man could have stuck out his tongue and licked it.

'Did he hurt you? He hurt you, didn't he? Look at your hands, look at them!'

We all looked, where the blood was oozing from the scabs I'd been picking – lines of scabs, as thin as wires, more than the stripes that Kemp had given me.

'Yes, yes – he . . .'

'And you're afraid?'

Pryce was louder now, tugging me close and squeezing the bones in my wrist, jamming the gun harder and harder into the headmaster's throat.

'You're afraid he'll find out what you did to the piano? Yes, with these!'

Pryce wrenched my hand deep into the side of the armchair where Kemp was sitting, forced me to feel by the headmaster's thighs, jammed my fingers between the cushions until I found the wallet of the piano's tuning keys.

'With these!' He tugged out the wallet and held it aloft. 'I saw you hiding them, Alan, and now you're afraid he'll find out it was you and he'll hurt you again.'

'It wasn't me . . .'

'Does he make you afraid when he looks at you in the bath? Does he?'

'Sometimes – yes, sometimes . . .'

'Does he make you afraid when he sits on your bed? Does he touch you? Alan, tell me! Does he touch you?'

'Yes, he . . .'

'I never, I never!' the headmaster blurted. Pryce forced us together, me and Dr Kemp, jamming our faces together with all the force of one hand on my wrist and the thrust of the gun on the headmaster's throat.

'Last night . . .' I heard myself breaking down. 'Last night, or the other night, I don't know when – he touched me, he . . .'

'His hair was wet!' the headmaster was shouting. 'For God's sake, tell him, Scott! I touched his head because . . .'

'My hair was wet! He touched me! He frightened me!'

And we both broke down, speechless, heaving for breath.

Pryce let go of us. I fell away from the armchair and, finding that I was holding the wallet of tuning keys, dropped them onto the floor as though they were burning my fingers. I instinctively shrank towards Mrs Kemp and Sophie, who were clutching each other's hands and weeping together, threw myself down by the pile of logs I'd made and blinked into the flames. Kemp was struggling for air, a man drowning.

Pryce stood up, composed again. He sneered at Sophie and Mrs Kemp. 'Women,' he said, as though it were a dirty word he'd learned in the playground.

He sneered at me and Dr Kemp. 'Perfect pitch, look what it does for you.'

He leaned the gun against the headmaster's armchair, picked up the tuning keys and moved from the fireside. His footsteps were slow and deliberate as he crossed to the piano.

No one dared to watch him. We could hear what he was doing. It filled my stomach with a terrible sickness. With his left hand he thumped a bass chord, sonorous, menacing, out of tune. With his right hand he leaned into the body of the piano and felt with one of the keys. And then the ugliest of sounds, as he loosened and loosened one of the strings, a horrible groaning, like something wounded and dying, as he thumped with one hand and loosened with the other.

When it stopped, we all looked up. I saw him wrench a bass string out of the piano and hold it up, and it coiled and writhed in a gleam of firelight. He tugged it tight in front of his face.

He moved towards Dr Kemp. '*I disgust myself . . .*' he whispered.

I noticed what happened next, saw how Mrs Kemp and Dr Kemp exchanged a secret, furtive look of understanding distilled by twenty years of marriage. She looked from the gun – leaning against his chair – and into her husband's eyes. He looked from her eyes to the gun.

As Pryce advanced towards him, with the piano string taut in his hands, the headmaster started blustering. 'I never touched him, I never! Afraid of me? Afraid of work, more like it! I made them work, I made your brother work, without me he'd have gone nowhere, none of them would! I saw his talent and worked it! I made him what he was, I . . .'

'Shut up!' It was Mrs Kemp. She rounded on him, on her own husband, suddenly swerving her wheelchair so close that her knees were touching his. 'You're a liar and a bully! I've seen it myself for years and years! I've endured your blustering and your bullying and . . .'

He shouted back at her. His hand felt for the gun. 'I made them work! I worked them! Without me they'd be nothing!'

'Your pig-headedness, your self-importance, your self-righteousness, your . . .'

Pryce swaggered towards them. The string turned from silver to gold as he came close to the fire. He was bringing it to Kemp, delivering death.

Solemn, priestlike, he intoned, '*I disgust myself, I would rather be dead* . . .' and as I watched helplessly, I felt the involuntary movement of my hands to my own throat, as though anticipating the cutting of the wire and trying to prevent it.

The woman whirled towards Pryce. 'And you! Your excuses, your bitterness, your stories about Jeremy – I don't believe any of it! You've made it all up, you've invented it all . . .'

Pryce feinted at her with the string. It gave Kemp the chance they'd been angling for. He grabbed the gun and thrust himself out of the chair.

Too slow. Pryce saw the glimmer of gunmetal, twisted towards him and seized the barrel. There was a moment of grappling and grunting, the two men chin to chin and bellowing and the gun jerking up and down . . .

The woman lunged forwards. Her thin little hand closed on the barrel, so weak that it made only the tiniest difference to its angle. Enough difference.

There was a bang. The headmaster squealed and collapsed onto the floor, pressing both hands to his groin. Blood welled between his fingers.

Pryce hissed at the woman, 'You're fucking mad you fucking shot him!' and reloaded in an instant. Instinctively, hearing the chock of the chamber closing, Kemp lifted one of his blood-slippery hands, grabbed the barrel and yanked it hard.

There was another bang. Mrs Kemp fell back in her chair. She flopped and gurgled, utterly spastic. Pryce tore the gun free. He was yelling, 'Jesus you fucking shot her!' Blood pumped from her throat.

In the confusion, in a blur of smoke and blood and noise, I fled out of the hall.

THIRTEEN

I skidded along the corridor, navigating by radar as the
darkness closed around me. The beat of the blood in
my head, the pulse of fear in my veins, seemed to bounce
back at me from the walls and the floor and the ceiling
as I ran. I slid to a halt at the first of the lifts, where the
glow of light from inside illumined the sign on the door.
Ignoring the sign, for the first time in all my years at
Foxwood I pulled the door open and plunged inside. I
shut the door, jabbed at the button and went up.

It seemed horribly slow. The cables groaned, the cogs
and wheels clanked, the feeble light flickered. I found
myself dangling in a little cage, swaying in mid-air, and saw
the grey, cobwebby walls of the shaft go crawling by. When
it stopped at the first floor, I got out and padded along the
corridor to the landing at the top of the grand staircase.

From there, I leaned over the banister and peered down to the hall.

Pryce and Sophie were engaged in a bitter row. Face to face, lunging at each other across the wheelchair in which the headmaster's wife was slumped, they spat and cursed and shouted. Their voices blurred into one clanging duet, impossible to make out the words, but their anger and panic rose up the staircase to where I was standing. I saw Sophie bend and then kneel at the side of Mrs Kemp's wheelchair, and then Pryce, with a ghastly shove, heaved the girl away.

Hard to believe what happened next – I just goggled as Pryce took hold of one of the wheels, wrenched it upwards and dumped Mrs Kemp out of the chair and onto the floor.

The woman just lay there, as though dead. Sophie knelt beside her and turned her onto her side. Pryce had taken hold of the headmaster by the collar of his tweed jacket and was dragging him towards the wheelchair.

Too late, I recoiled from the banister. Pryce glanced up and saw me. Breathless from manoeuvring the lumpen weight of the wounded man, he crowed, 'I know you're up there, Alan – it's where I would've gone . . .'

With a sudden tug, he hoisted the headmaster up and onto the chair.

The wheels slithered and spun and he jammed them with one foot while he worked his hands under the man's armpits and adjusted him upright. All this time Kemp was grimacing horribly, his teeth clenched, pressing his hands into his groin where the blood was oozing through his trousers and between his fingers. He threw a despairing look at the body of his wife, whose place he'd taken; her face was dead white, as though already bled dry, her eyes and mouth half-open, unseeing, speechless.

'I know where you'll go next, Alan!' Pryce called up to me, without turning his head to the dark space of the stairwell behind him. 'And after that, and after that!'

He bent and addressed himself softly to the headmaster. 'I know every move he'll make, Dr Kemp. But I'm not so sure about you. Is it twenty years you've been here? You must know every crack and corner and hidey-hole – it's your place, that's what you said, and I bet you know every inch of it.'

Sophie was kneeling as low as she could, pressing her ear to Mrs Kemp's mouth. 'She's breathing, just, but n-n-not for much longer . . .' Crouching on the floor, with a smear of the woman's blood on her cheek, she snickered at Pryce like a stoat in a trap. 'She was right, Martin! You know n-n-n-nothing, you are n-n-nothing – you make up all this shit to hide behind, to disguise your nothingness . . .'

He slapped her mouth, a whipping back-hander. 'I didn't shoot her! Did I? And I didn't shoot him! Did I? They fucking shot each other!'

He regained his breath, inhaling a big lungful and pushing his hair back from his face. Sophie fingered her lips to see if she was bleeding, saw blood, thought it was hers, and felt at her mouth again.

'We'll play another game,' he said. 'We'll all play. You'd be at a disadvantage, Sophie, not knowing the place like the rest of us do, so you can be on my side, and we can even things up for Dr Kemp as well.'

He reached for the piano string, which had fallen onto the carpet and coiled itself there in the confusion of shouting and shooting. He hauled Sophie to her feet and pulled her to him. She stammered an incoherent protest, she hammered her fists on his shoulders, but she was too feeble. With a series of brutal yanks and crudely twisted knots he wound one of her ankles to one of his. In less than half a minute, they were bound together as though for a three-legged race.

They stood upright, the girl sobbing for breath, half-clinging to him for balance and half-thrusting him away from her, Pryce mugging and miming the fun of the game. Then he took hold of the handles of the wheel-chair, spun Kemp around and propelled him very fast towards the corridor. With a mighty heave, he launched the headmaster into the darkness. He and Sophie watched and listened, as the wheelchair hissed on its thin smooth tyres and disappeared into the black tunnel.

Pryce shouted after it. 'You've got a minute, Dr Kemp! Two minutes! Then we're coming for you!'

I padded back along the first-floor corridor. There were no lights in the dormitories or the bathroom, only the glow from the lift; and just as I reached the lift I'd come up in I saw it jerk into motion and start to travel down again. I stood and watched as it vanished into the shaft.

It was Dr Kemp who'd summoned it. As I leaned close to the shaft and peered down, I could just see him, moving in and out of my line of vision through the narrowest crack. Heaving for breath, utterly unaccustomed to sitting in the wheelchair and trying to handle it, he was struggling to manoeuvre it onto the ramp and brake it close to the lift. Now, having brought the lift down to him, he found it all but impossible to yank the door open while the chair tried to skid and spin this way and that, until he'd tightened the brake, opened the door, released the brake and heaved himself inside. I could see a darkening patch of sweat on the collar of his jacket, could see it spreading through the back of his thick, tweedy jacket; his hair flopped infuriatingly over his eyes. He was hot, steaming and bleeding, and he clutched at the glistening mess in his belly as though it would suddenly burst open.

He held his breath and listened, to try and hear if Pryce had started to follow him. He pulled the door shut, thumbed the button and the lift started upwards.

It loomed towards me. I heard it grinding and clanking, and I hurried back, as quickly and as quietly as I could, to my vantage point on the staircase.

In the hall, Pryce reloaded the gun. He rattled the box of ammunition and dropped it into his trouser pocket. Sophie writhed against him, enraged to have found that it was less uncomfortable to hold onto him with her arm around his waist than to thrust him away. He stroked his little finger into the blood on her cheek and dabbed it onto the tip of her nose. 'Cute,' he whispered. 'Shall we go?'

He lugged her out of the hall and into the gloom of the corridor.

I stayed where I was and peered down to where Mrs Kemp lay beside the hearth. In the moments after the shooting, I'd seen her eyes flickering, as if she were slipping in and out of consciousness: winded by the impact as she'd hit the floor, in shock from the bullet wound to her throat, bewildered by all the yelling around her. Now, sensing from the growing silence that she was alone, she opened her eyes. She took tiny sips of breath and turned her face to the warmth of the fire. She was alive, although the life in her body was trickling away and there was nothing she, or I, could do to stop it.

The waste . . . From where I was hiding, I could just see the photograph of herself and Dapple, and I thought of the little time she'd had with her husband before the accident had ruined her. It made me so sad and angry, to see how she sipped the air to keep herself alive, to know that she would die if she didn't keep on sipping, she would surely die before she would see her husband again. I watched her: every droplet of life was sweet and precious, every sip of air was a taste of her life. And I felt, in my understanding of the deadly game that had just begun, that simply by lying at the fireside, quite motionless, and by being alive, she was an essential player.

I moved back to the lift as it came up towards me, meaning to help Dr Kemp. But then, from downstairs I heard the opening of the other lift door and knew that Pryce and Sophie must be getting inside it. Both the lifts were rising towards me.

Stifling a bubble of panic that rose inside me, I instinctively ran back to the staircase and flew down it.

Before I reached the bottom, I sensed another presence in the hall. I could feel it, in a breath of cold air which seemed to fog around me.

The boy was kneeling beside Mrs Kemp.

A boy like me, dressed exactly like me, in a grey pullover and grey shorts.

I froze, paused with my hand on the banister. I saw an image of myself bent over the stricken woman. But when the image turned and looked, it wasn't me. It was the boy I'd seen in my dreams.

His face was flushed, his black hair shining in the firelight. He was holding Mrs Kemp's hands very softly in his. And she, looking up through half-open eyes as if through the haze of her own lashes, was smiling faintly, in recognition of his face and the comfort he was giving her.

The boy let go of the woman's hands. He stood up, and with a curious beckoning motion of his head he crossed the hall and disappeared into the dark downstairs corridor. I followed him.

And from then on, together, silent and unseen in the lightless corners of a building we both knew so well, the boy and I shadowed the movements of Kemp and Pryce and Sophie. I had the faintest inkling – something in the way he'd beckoned me – that he'd come back, enabled to return to Foxwood by the odd off-chance that I was still there, to play his part in the game.

A dream-boy, a ghost-boy, a flutter of cold air through my dormitory window – whoever or whatever he was, and whatever fell purpose he had for me, I sensed that he needed me, he was powerless without me.

I lost him in the darkness, although I knew he was close. I felt him nearby, in the prickle of the wire in my hands and the sting of the wire in my throat.

Kemp, arriving at the first floor, had heard the other lift coming up too. He'd gone straight back down again. Desperate to get back to his wife, knowing that Pryce had left her immobilised in the hall as a bait to lure him back there, he negotiated his way gingerly closer and closer.

I watched him, I was with him all the time, unknown to him, unseen by him. And I sensed horribly that Pryce was right behind us and would spring out at any moment.

Heaving for breath, Kemp ducked into the library and hid, futilely, between the tall bookcases. I hid with him. There was a curious shuffling footfall in the corridor overhead. For some reason, Pryce and the hapless girl were lurching in and out of the darkened dormitories. We heard a lift come down. When the headmaster snagged the wheelchair on a protruding shelf, I watched him stop and hold his breath as Pryce's crowing voice sounded just inches from where we were hiding – *Are you there, Dr Kemp, are you there?* – and a sinister cooing seemed to echo and hum through the house, up and down the lift shafts, along the corridors, everywhere – *Alan, where are you? Upstairs, downstairs, where are you, Alan . . .?*

The house was full of Martin Pryce.

My head pounded with the dread of turning a corner and confronting him, Pryce with the gun, Pryce with the piano string. And the house, which had become so familiar for all the years I'd been there, was suddenly a baffling and infuriating maze. I was filled with an insane anger at the house itself, as I moved in the wake of the terrified headmaster and saw it thwarting him with its maddening jumble, its angles and corners which caught him and jabbed him as he tried to steer past: the ramps which sapped his failing strength as he struggled up them and careered down; the lifts, one at each end of the building, with their clanking gates, their cables and cogs and wheels, going up and down from the bottom to the top of the house as Pryce toyed with them to confuse and exhaust his victims – so that the whole thing was a nonsensical game of snakes and ladders.

Foxwood Manor was a maze: a dark, cold, unfriendly maze of shabby rooms and dusty corridors. It flooded me with hatred and bitterness. And, worse somehow, an overwhelming boredom for all the time I'd been a prisoner there.

Dr Kemp leaned with all his strength on the wheels of the chair. His hands and the wheels gleamed with blood. He propelled himself closer to the hall. And as he came closer to his wife and sped towards the light at the end of the corridor, I felt my bitterness fall away – as I realised it was the chair I hated, not the house, and my heart ached with pity for Mrs Kemp, for all the years she'd endured it.

The headmaster reached the hall, peered in and saw his wife lying beside the fire.

Pryce and Sophie were at the top of the great staircase. They started to stumble down. Pryce was saying, 'Come on Sophie, this'll make it a bit more fun . . .' With a curse, as Pryce half-dragged and half-carried the girl down the last few steps, Dr Kemp could do nothing except spin the chair and accelerate as hard as he could, back into the corridor.

I hid and watched as Pryce lugged Sophie across the hall.

She was tight-lipped, her face white with anger and fear. She'd given up struggling against him, and just hobbled wherever he took her. Now he dragged her past the table and its wreckage of a Christmas feast, stepped over the body of the headmaster's wife as though she were no more than a heap of rubbish, and lifted the lid of the record player.

'This'll do it,' he said.

He took off the long-playing record that was on the turntable – Fauré's Requiem – and dropped it onto the nearest armchair, and I saw him tug out the little black disc of a 45 from under his shirt. He dropped it onto the turntable, changed the speed, stood back. And even from where I was watching, in the dusty black mouth of the corridor, I could hear the needle settle onto the vinyl, nestle into the groove. Pryce adjusted the volume to maximum, so that the crackle and hiss were loud in the expectant room.

'Oh yeah, this should do the trick,' he murmured.

Kemp had raced back to the lift and wheeled himself inside. I heard the lift go up and up, past the first floor corridor, past the second. Towards the attic.

I ran. We ran. For the ghost-boy, the dream-boy was still with me, in a waft of cold air which made my scalp tingle and my palms itch. With my eyes closed, I flew up the stairs to the first floor, knowing every step, every creak in the floorboards, every chip in the paint, feeling with my fingers up and up and onwards to the second floor, in a house so dark and blank and yet so much a part of me that when I swerved to a halt on the corridor near my own dormitory I knew there'd be a little forbidden door in front of me, with a little forbidden handle on it, and a sign that said: FORBIDDEN TO BOYS . . .

The attic. I'd never been up there.

I opened the door and flung myself inside, pulling the door shut behind me and scrambling blindly up and up a narrow staircase until my head banged onto a trapdoor. I flopped down, panting, heaving, lost in a pitchy darkness.

Through the noise of my own breathing, I heard the hiss of the wheels of the wheelchair over my head.

Kemp had taken the lift to the attic. He must have yanked open the door and thrust himself out, just as the music blared.

Music? The jagged chords of 'You really got me . . .' were so loud in the great hall that they tore into the lift shafts and corridors and filled every space in the old house. And I could hear Pryce yelling at the top of his voice – *Can you hear this, Dr Kemp? Music is the life of the school! It runs through the building!*

As the record turned, the noise built in and built a stealthy momentum, growing in volume and intensity. I could hear Kemp shouting too, as though he were grinding his teeth and shouting for the only means of help he could think of. '*Scott!* Where the devil are you? Are you there, for God's sake?'

Huddled in my safe, secret place, in the staircase only a few feet away from the headmaster, I was as astounded as Kemp to hear this music pounding through the building; astonished to hear something so appallingly, so marvellously raucous stirring the dust and cobwebs of Foxwood Manor.

Pryce's shrilly manic voice came to me from some-where far below. Kemp was calling me from up in the attic. I pushed with all my strength on the trapdoor above my head and felt the weight of something on top of it, until it opened just a little. I peered inside.

It looked as though the headmaster had given up shouting for me. Galvanised into action by the savagery of the noise that was blasting through the building, he heaved himself out of the wheelchair. He'd seen from the movement of its cables that the other lift was coming up. I saw him stumbling along the attic, treading onto piled-up junk, ducking through a line of old clothes; I heard him gritting his teeth and growling to himself, '*Where is it? Where is the wretched thing?*' – and then he was fumbling into the highest, darkest corner, reaching up to a fuse box and struggling to pull it open.

The lift was clanking up and up. He knew that Pryce was in it.

Pryce and Sophie were coming up to the attic. I could picture Pryce, with the gun in one hand, his other arm around Sophie's waist, as he yelled the lines of the song – *you really got me now, you got me so I don't know what I'm doing, oh yeah you really got me now, you got me so I can't sleep at night . . .*

The lift was almost at the second floor when the lights went out. It jerked to a halt. The music slurred horribly and stopped.

The entire house was in darkness. And silence. Only an eerie creaking as the lift dangled and swayed in the shaft. Then I heard Pryce say, 'What the fuck?'

Kemp had thrown the mains switch, turning off all the power in the house.

Now he felt his way back through the shadows of the attic, and he collapsed heavily into the wheelchair. Only the cloudiest of moonbeams fell through a snow-covered skylight in the roof, enough for me to see a gleam of tears in his eyes, tears of relief that the noise had stopped and even a twist of a smile on his lips, a moment of triumph, as he heard Pryce calling from inside the stranded lift, 'Hey, Kemp, what are you playing at? Are you up there, Kemp?'

There was a tiny tremor of panic in the young man's voice. Kemp buried his face in his hands, careless that they were sticky with blood and cobwebs, and squeezed his eyes shut.

I forced the trapdoor open further, shoving aside whatever had been weighing it down, and popped my head out of the staircase, like a marmot emerging from its burrow.

I'd never seen the attic before. Watching the head-master earlier had given me no sense of its size: a great tunnel of roof space almost as long as the house, cluttered with papers and books and crates and trunks, the jumble that a country prep-school might accumulate and then discard over three or four decades. A long rack of clothes on hangers swayed in the darkness like a queue of faceless people.

I blinked into the gloom, turning towards the head-master hunched in the wheelchair. I was puzzled, then alarmed, to see that the chair was rolling towards me.

'Dr Kemp? Sir?'

The wheelchair gathered speed. The headmaster, rub-bing at the tension in his forehead, hadn't felt the wheels turn beneath his weight as he'd flopped back into it. The chair swivelled, silent and smooth on the warp of the ancient floorboards. It moved faster towards the hole in the attic floor: the hole from which I'd just emerged.

I cried out again, 'Sir! Dr Kemp!' and he opened his eyes and turned, too late, to see where he was heading.

Above him, the snow-encrusted skylight whirled like a giddy moth. Disoriented, weak from loss of blood, he wrenched at the wheels but could do nothing to control himself. And I couldn't possibly have stopped it, couldn't have countered the force of a thirteen-stone man swoop-ing towards me. I ducked away and threw myself back down the stairs, as far as I could go.

Just in time. The man and the chair crashed into the stairwell, overturned, banged down and down and down with a series of sickening jolts and suddenly jammed.

Kemp was stuck there, somehow wedged into the narrow space. He groaned, badly hurt by the fall, 'My God my God oh God help me ...' The chair had capsized. He was hanging half out of it, upside down, both his arms somehow pinioned at his sides, his head and shoulders dangling into the stairwell.

I cowered at the bottom of the stairs. Looking up, all I could see was blackness and the bulk of the man and the chair hopelessly plugged into the hole.

'Scott, are you there? Help me, for God's sake, help me get out of here.'

'I'm here, sir, I'm down here.' I felt my way up the steps until I was just below the wreckage. 'I can't ...'

'You'll have to get through, somehow! You'll have to get past me and pull me out!'

For a split second, it was almost funny. There was a glimmer of farce. But then something happened, so awful that the whole house felt the horror of it.

As the man hung upside down above my head, dangling with all his weight, we both heard the softest, gentlest whisper of a sound – like the tearing of silk. He said, 'Oh God,' because he must have felt it as well as hearing it. The weight of his body was opening the wound. He couldn't staunch it with his hands, because his arms were trapped – and suddenly, unstoppably, the blood welled into his trousers until it spattered and dripped onto the stairs and into my face.

He started to cry. He said, 'Oh God,' again, his face wrinkling and he started blubbing *oh god oh god oh god* in a little girl's voice, and his mouth and nose were full of uncontrollable tears.

The blood from his trousers came faster and hotter. No longer a spatter but a steady trickle. He began to squeal.

I gaped up at him, my headmaster, my Dr Kemp. A pig, hanging in an abattoir. Squealing. Bleeding. A piglet on a hook, ready for slaughter.

I heard myself saying *please Dr Kemp please sir don't sir* ... but the noise of it cut through my words and all the surrounding silence. It was a sick, shameful noise, and it grew louder and more dinning, quite unearthly, the cries of a dying animal from the mouth of a middle-aged man in a tweed jacket and a shirt and tie.

Tie. I lunged up towards him, grabbed his tie and started to force it between his teeth.

Unable to free his arms, he snarled and snapped at me, trying to fend me off. *Please sir please stop sir please stop stop stop* I was shouting into the horrid twisted piggy-face, and I stuffed in the tie, timing it as he snatched a breath to carry on squealing. He gargled and gagged and blubbered and I forced more and more of the tie into his mouth and silenced him.

Until he just hung there, whimpering. He stopped wriggling, his breath calmed as he inhaled through his nose, and the trickle of blood from his groin slowed and stopped.

A silence. I lay on the stairs and listened to it.

FOURTEEN

Ten o'clock on Christmas Eve. The whole place, and everybody and everything in it, had stopped dead, as though it were gripped and seized by the deadening cold.

Foxwood Manor, cut off from the world by miles of woodland and deep snow; no telephone, no electricity.

Pryce and Sophie, uninvited, unwanted guests, prisoners in a cage in a cobwebby shaft.

Dr Kemp, hanging in a narrow staircase, half-in and half-out of a wheelchair, with his own tie stuffed into his mouth. Me, a blood-spattered twelve-year-old boy, huddling beneath him.

Mrs Kemp, dying in front of the fire in the great hall.

In one of the stables, a crash-landed, convalescent crow; in another, a splendid, useless car.

Outside, an eighteen-year-old labrador, frazzled to death and already buried under the cold cold lawn.

No one was going anywhere.

'Kemp? Alan? What the fuck's happening up there? What are you doing?' Pryce shouted suddenly.

His voice sounded very loud and close in the deadened building, although he and the girl were still encaged in the lift. It stirred me and the headmaster alive again. I clambered up to him and pushed with all my strength to force myself past the wreckage. I snaked one of my arms through and wriggled past the man's body, feeling the frame of the chair chafing the skin on my belly as my shirt rode up. At the same time, Kemp found one of his hands was free and, retching hoarsely, pulled the tie out of his mouth.

The voice came again. 'Alan, are you with me and Sophie? You aren't afraid of Kemp any more, you can get us out of here!'

Then Sophie, chiming clearly. 'Alan, you've got to help Mrs Kemp!'

There was a gasp, as though Pryce had wrenched her into silence. He shouted, 'Your wife's dying, Kemp! You shot her, remember? Turn the power on and you can go down in the lift! It's the only way! Don't you want to see her again? Don't you want to say goodbye before she dies?'

Kemp had managed to find some leverage and pushed at me with all his might. His bloody, sticky hand slid on my thigh, then found a place on my belly to shove and shove. I heard myself cry out, the chair cutting into me, but still I writhed upwards, inch by inch. Kemp was grunting, 'You can do it, Alan, you're there, you're there

. . .' and he found a breath to shout, 'The boy's with me, Pryce! He'll get me out, you murderer!'

Pryce yelled back. 'I didn't shoot her! You did!'

The defiance in his voice faltered slightly. There was a tiny wobble of petulance. It was unmistakable, the sound of it, and the sense that his arrogant power was slipping. When he shouted again, there was a shriller note of desperation like the squalling of a spoilt child. 'Alan, leave the old man and do what I tell you to do! Didn't you hear what happened to my darling brother? Is that you, now? Are you Kemp's little darling? Has he got his dirty hands on you, like he did with Jeremy?'

Kemp was still pushing me. I'd reached through and grabbed a banister, something to pull on, to squeeze myself through, and the man's fingers were rough on my bare skin. At last I wriggled past and up, through the trapdoor and into the attic.

Pryce was ranting. 'Is he touching you now? Are you his little Dolly Boy? You're a tease, aren't you Alan, letting him touch you, making him do it – his darling Dolly Boy . . .'

I crossed the attic to the lift shaft and peered down. There was a dim yellow glow, some kind of emergency light that had come on when the mains power had been switched off. And I could see obliquely into the lift itself, which had jammed to a halt just a few feet below me.

Pryce was staring up the shaft. He was pasty-faced, his long hair damp with sweat. And he saw me. Before I could step back from the shaft, he caught the movement of my body and his eyes met mine.

'*Dolly Boy!*' he hissed.

All of his bitterness towards Kemp, the jealousy of his brother, all of the bile inside him he spat towards me. His voice was poisonous, and at the same time I could just see Sophie's hand, her arm around his waist, stealing closer to the trigger of the gun.

'*A good name for Jeremy and a good name for you – and it was my idea, for Kemp's fucking angel with perfect fucking pitch – and I made sure it stuck. It was me. I hated him and I hate you Alan you fucking Dolly Boy you . . .*'

The gun went off.

The report was sharp and very loud, amplified in the lift shaft. As the echo faded, Pryce said very softly, 'What've you done, Sophie?' He dropped the gun and the box of cartridges, and he slid to the floor.

He clutched his left foot. There was a blackened, smouldering bullet hole in his boot and blood was welling out. He whispered, 'Why is everyone fucking shooting each other?'

Sophie kicked the gun to the opposite corner of the lift. While he was stunned by the impact, still in shock, she knelt beside him and deftly unwound the piano string from their ankles. I heard her heaving as hard as she could on the lift door, until she wrenched it open. The lift had stopped just above the second floor: there was a nine-inch gap. Ignoring Pryce, who was wheedling at her, 'Help me, Sophie, hey help me!' she skidded the gun across the floor and through the gap and it fell with a clatter to the corridor below.

And then she was out of my field of vision, out of the crack of light I could see down the shaft and into the lift. But the wires trembled, the cage swaying with the force of her little body as she struggled to push herself through the gap and out. I saw Pryce roll after her, the slick of blood he left behind, and he was begging, 'Hey Sophie Sophie . . .' as he tried to prevent her escape. But his hands were hot and slippery from the wound in his foot. The lift shuddered – and there was a thud as the girl, wriggling like a fish away from his grasp, squeezed out and landed with a thud on the second-floor corridor.

Pryce was mad. I could just make out the writhing of his body and see him forcing his head into the gap she'd slipped through. It was too small, but he forced his head into it. And he roared, like a medieval madman with his head in the stocks, *'You'll never get out Sophie you'll never get out Jesus I'm fucking stuck help me Sophie help me you're no fucking angel Sophie for fuck's sake help me . . .'*

He couldn't move, either back into the lift or through the gap.

I hurried back to the trapdoor and looked down into the hole. Sophie had moved swiftly along the corridor, seen the little staircase, heard the gasping breath from inside it and immediately climbed in to investigate. I could see her in the darkness, peering up at the bizarre tangle of headmaster and wheelchair.

'Dr Kemp? Alan?'

The man hissed back at her, 'Oh God, is he there? Pryce?'

'He's stuck – he can't g-g . . .'

'And I'm stuck! Push me, for heaven's sake! And Scott, are you up there? Help me, help me . . .'

With a new, concerted effort, Sophie shoving with her shoulders from below and me reaching down from the top to pull at the chair with all my strength, we shifted the wounded man out of the wreckage and up towards the attic. He moaned, he stifled a yelp of pain; sometimes he pressed his fists into his groin where the wound had torn wider open. I leaned in and caught at his wrists, I heaved and heaved while the girl pushed from underneath. Until at last the headmaster crawled out and flopped on the floorboards, his whole body heaving, the breath rattling in his throat.

Sophie wriggled past the wheelchair, which was easier to shift without the man jammed in it. As she got by, she kicked and kicked at it until at last it was freed, and it went bouncing down the staircase and landed with a crash in the corridor below.

She scrambled up into the attic and knelt by the headmaster. He blinked at her, struggled to raise himself on one elbow and stared with horror at the black hole in the floor, the staircase from which he'd just emerged. 'Is he down there? Pryce? Is he coming up?' he gasped.

'I told you! He's stuck! Halfway out of the lift! He'll g-g-g-get out unless . . .' She stood up and peered into the strange shadows of the attic. 'Did you t-t-turn off the power? Where is it? Where's the . . .?'

There was a sudden rattle and roar from the lift shaft. No words, but the bellow of someone trapped, someone fighting with every nerve and sinew to force a way through the tiniest of spaces.

'He's getting out!' the girl hissed. 'Where's the p-p-power? Show me!'

She pushed through the boxes and books and clothes. As she passed under the skylight, for a second she glanced up at the pane of glass, and the moonlight fell on her face. Then she saw the fuse cupboard, open, and lunged towards it.

'Halfway out?' Kemp was jolted into action. Somehow he lurched to his feet and stumbled after her. 'You'll kill him! For God's sake, don't . . .!'

He fell headlong over the jumble of junk and crashed to the floor. Just as Sophie threw the switch.

With a slurring groan, the music started – *you really got me you got me so I can't sleep at night* – louder and more raggedly menacing than it had seemed before, and the lights flickered on. The lift shuddered, the wheels groaned, the cables squealed, and the cage moved up and up the shaft.

The three of us stared at the door of the lift. The music rose to a deafening climax – *you really got me you really got me you really got me* – and its four madding final chords, as the cage reached the attic.

There was silence. The door didn't open. Kemp whispered, 'You've killed him.'

Sophie moved forwards and pulled the door open. The lift was empty. Only a boot, and a scatter of cartridges.

She stepped in, bent to the floor and picked up the boot. It was wet with blood. 'He's alive,' she said. 'He must've forced himself through.' She dropped the boot with a thud. In a moment, as Kemp just gaped at her, she was back in the attic and reaching for the fuse box. She turned off the power again.

Darkness. Only the delicate moonlight and the yellowy glow of the emergency bulb inside the lift.

Silence. Only the hoarse breathing of the stricken headmaster and a lovely lull of noiselessness.

'He's alive,' Sophie said. 'And he's down there, waiting for us.'

I hadn't spoken since Pryce's ranting tirade, the horror of the gunshot, the struggle to get out of the staircase. My mind had gone blank, paralysed by the awfulness of the headmaster's screaming and by Pryce's toxic words. I wanted nothing more than to hide in a dark corner of the attic, or crawl into an old trunk and pull down the lid until I thought it might be safe to come out again – but, as I glanced once more into the open stairwell, I saw the glimmer of a movement in the corridor below.

Not Pryce. It was the boy.

For a second, I saw his upturned face, pale, anxious. His eyes met mine, long enough for me to see the beckoning in them. And then he was gone.

I heard my own voice say calmly and clearly, 'Stay here, Dr Kemp. I can get help. I think I know how.'

I started down the stairs.

FIFTEEN

At the very bottom, I peered out, froze and held my breath.

Pryce trod slowly along the corridor. He was a bent, lurching figure, oddly half-lit by the little bulbs in the ceiling.

He stopped and leaned against the wall. He was so close I could smell the sweat in his hair. He seemed light-headed, confused. With a groan of pain, he peeled the sock from his left foot and dropped it onto the floor. He listened to the silence, cocked his head this way and that like a sparrow, and then he continued towards me. Every other footstep left a perfect bloody print on the lino.

He came to the wheelchair, which lay on its side in front of him and blocked his way. For a long time he stared at it and frowned, as if it were the first time he'd seen it and he didn't understand what it was: a chair with wheels, capsized, one of the wheels askew, the spokes distorted, and the other turning and turning very slowly. He stood and stared until the wheel stopped, then he moved forwards and set it upright. Using the handles to support himself, he pushed it ahead of him. And it squeaked – a rhythmic, plaintive *squeak squeak squeak* – as he limped away, along the corridor.

At last I took a breath. Kemp and Sophie had heard him too, had strained to catch the uneven footsteps and known that Pryce was at the bottom of the staircase. Now, as he took the chair away, the squeaks receded into the distance – tinier, fainter, like a mouse skittering through the wainscot. And then gone.

'What's he doing?' Dr Kemp, slumped on the attic floor, was hissing down the stairwell to me. 'I have to come down, I can't leave my wife . . .'

'No,' I hissed back at him. 'Stay up there. He . . .'

'My wife! How can I just sit and do nothing?'

'We need help,' I said firmly. 'We can't beat him on our own. Stay there.'

Sophie was coming down. I saw her body against the attic skylight, as she manoeuvred into the hole. Just as she negotiated the first few steps, backwards into the darkness, the headmaster leaned to her and caught her wrist. For a split second, she stared up at him, horrified, because it was the same grip with which Pryce had manhandled and bullied her. I heard him say, 'Please, Sophie, just tell me, please tell me –' and she gasped as he squeezed her wrist tighter '– the note, the note he said that Jeremy had written . . . Is it true? Do you know?'

'You're hurting me,' she said. He let go. She seemed to have difficulty composing her reply. There was a pause, long enough for me to see in my mind's eye, as though against the perfect blackness of the hole in which I was huddling, the slow arcing flight of a ball of paper and its sudden eruption into golden flame. I watched the flame blossom and die. When at last she spoke, her voice was flat and strong, without a trace of a stammer. 'It isn't true. There was no note. Jeremy didn't kill himself.'

She ducked away from him, and as she felt her way down and down towards me, I heard the headmaster gasp to himself, 'Thank God, thank God.' Then he called after her, as loudly as he dared, 'I never touched him, I promise, I never . . .'

Sophie and I trod softly away from the attic staircase and into the corridor. She felt for my hand, gripped it warmly and whispered, 'Where are we going? What are we doing?'

I knew that Pryce was nearby, indeed I thought I could hear the squeak of the wheelchair somewhere ahead of me. And so I said to her, 'Where's he going? What's he doing?' She squeezed my hand even harder, and I could sense in the fierce desperation of her touch that she knew, that she was too afraid or appalled to tell me.

Pryce was there, only yards away, and yet, as we stole behind him, he seemed quite oblivious of the real world around him. We shadowed him, hiding and watching as he stopped the chair and peered about him. He was lost. In a building where he'd spent five of his childhood years, a house whose every room and cupboard and corridor he knew as intimately as I did, he'd lost himself. The wine, the pain in his foot, the darkness – for whatever reason, the reality of Foxwood Manor had slipped away and left him bewildered and frightened in a long black tunnel. He squinted ahead of him, where it narrowed and closed into nothing but blankness. He turned and looked behind him: the same. Overhead, high in a cave of shadows, a dim yellow light illumined a skein of cobwebs and not much else.

Lost, fumbling through the dim, cobwebby tunnel of a half-remembered, half-forgotten childhood.

There was a door open beside him, so he left the wheelchair and limped inside. I tugged Sophie closer, and we peered into a room whose coldness and emptiness seemed to yawn in front of us. We watched him shuffle forwards, heard him bang into something hard, and in the ghost-light from the dormitory window we made out a long row of beds – the skeletons of beds, stripped to nothing but their bare black frames.

He moved slowly past them, one after the other, trailing his hand on the cold iron as he limped by. As I leaned in, the room swam around me. For me too, the reality of it was fading, replaced by a fractured dream vision of what it might have been. And as he bent to one of the beds and stared at the place where the pillow should have been, I heard him whisper, 'Jeremy? Jeremy, are you there?'

There was no answer. There was nobody. But when he lifted his hands to his face and smelled the blood on them, I saw the boy appear beside him.

Pryce knelt at the side of the bed, as he'd done every single night for all the years he'd been at Foxwood. And the little brother he was searching for stood dimly over him, as he mumbled the words which were ingrained in his head forever.

'*Lighten our darkness, we beseech Thee, O Lord, and by Thy great mercy . . .*'

It didn't sound like a prayer. He only sought comfort in the hiss of the words in the silent room, their familiar shape in his mouth. He struggled to his feet, whispering, repeating the phrases like a spell as he moved back towards the door, and I felt my own lips moving to the rhythm of the phrases I knew so well. The boy had disappeared, and this, together with the shuffling approach of Pryce, brought me once more to my senses. Just in time, I pulled Sophie away, and we withdrew into a pool of shadow.

Pryce stepped into the corridor, blundering straight into the wheelchair. He clenched his teeth and hissed, and I saw how he shuddered with the pain in his wounded foot, how it flickered through his body and into the very dome of his skull. The present moment and a realisation of his surroundings came back to him with a jolt. He stared around, wild-eyed, then shoved the chair ahead of him and into the adjacent bathroom.

He knew this place. It must have had many memories for him, from a distant long-ago boyhood to the vividness of the previous night. He stumbled past the baths, which looked like empty alabaster tombs in the darkness, and felt for one of the sinks. He turned on a tap and doused his face with water. Over and over, he plunged his head into the basin and splashed his face and his neck and hair. When at last he emerged, spluttering, gasping at the icy cold, he stared into the mirror: the eyes of a dead man, a dripping, bloodless face.

As though he were afraid of himself, he smeared at the glass with the heel of his hand and left a smudge of watery blood. He stared again, disbelieving. 'Jeremy?' he whispered. 'Is it you?'

He moved faster now, pushing the chair ahead of him along the corridor. When he reached the landing at the top of the staircase, he leaned over the banister and saw, far below, how a flutter of firelight played on the shabby rugs of the great hall. That was the only light, for there were no more emergency bulbs. He wheeled the chair to the brink of the staircase, held tightly to the handles and started to bump it down.

Softly, softly, *bump bump bump*, he lowered the chair down the stairs. Sophie's hand was hot against mine as we both peered after him, saw how he paused for a breath at the first-floor landing and appraised the figure of Mrs Kemp lying by the hearth. She was not moving, she had not moved. *Bump bump bump*, he continued down.

He wheeled the chair across the hall, past the Christmas table, to the fireside. He knelt and studied the motionless woman, who was sprawled exactly as she'd landed when he'd dumped her onto the floor. Even from our vantage point, high above the scene, her hair was very beautiful, for it had fallen away from her face in a spray of silken gold. Her skin was white, without a trace of colour in it; all the flush had faded, all the blood had drained. Indeed, from the wound in her throat a good deal of blood had run into her clothes and onto the carpet. It gleamed in the movement of light from the flames.

He bent very close, so close that her hair stirred a little as he breathed. Not a sign of life. He said into her ear, 'It's me, Mrs Kemp, it's me,' and touched her cheek with his lips.

Her eyes flicked open. She looked at him with such suddenness and clarity that he flinched from her. And then she closed her eyes again, as though he weren't worth the effort.

'Good,' he said. 'You're still part of the game.' He stood up, wincing at the pain in his foot, and leaned on the wheelchair. He pushed it away from the fire and out of the hall, and it went *squeak squeak squeak* on the linoleum floor as he disappeared into the bottom corridor.

I mouthed at the girl. 'Where's he going? What's he doing?' And when she bit her lip and shook her head dumbly, I mouthed again, 'You know! Tell me!'

Quickly then, I led the girl by the hand, down the staircase to the hall. She veered towards the woman, but I pulled her with me, determined that we should try to keep Pryce in sight, that we should not lose him, that we should at least have some idea of where he was and his intentions. What I dreaded most was the nightmare of not knowing, just the sick feeling that he was somewhere in the building, somewhere close, a kind of murderous ogre who could strike from any shadow. We followed him into the corridor, ducking into the library as he stopped and turned. If I'd thought his purpose with the chair was to move Mrs Kemp, to relocate her elsewhere in the building as part of the gruesome game of hide and seek, I'd been wrong: because the chair was empty as he squeaked it rhythmically, steadily, along the bottom corridor and further away from the hall.

Together we cringed in the darkness, sheltering between shelves of ill-assorted books: dusty tomes, never opened, never touched, blocks of musty paper stacked like bricks; a jumbled collection of comics and annuals, dog-eared and thumbed by generations of small boys who'd sought a haven there on rainy afternoons and long wintry evenings. For a moment I thought of Martin Pryce, a lost and lonely boy huddling in this very corner; and I thought of his brother Jeremy, who'd also hidden there, seeking a little respite from the torment of bullying and abuse.

I held the breath, thick with dust, in my nostrils. Every mote was the misery of a boarding-school Sunday, the stink of homesickness, the hours and days I'd moped in the library: the longing for home that only a boarding-school boy can truly know.

I felt for Sophie's hand. It was warm and soft, like my mother's. When her fingers entwined into mine and squeezed, I felt a rush of love for her. It flooded my body with warmth, like a transfusion of blood. It gave me strength as well, a sudden steely determination to survive. So that, when she whispered to me, 'The woman, we have to help the woman . . .' I was amazed how calmly I replied, 'No, she's dead.'

I tugged her by the wrist, past slabby walls of encyclopaedias and atlases, to the further end of the room.

We moved out of the library and into the adjoining classroom. I knew that wherever Pryce was heading, Sophie and I would be faster than him, nimbler through the obstacle course of the pitch-dark school. We were the only two, of the five players in this Christmas game, as yet unscathed by gunshot, unhampered by loss of blood. We slipped swiftly and silently from room to room. I knew every desk in every class, every floorboard that might creak underfoot and give away our whereabouts, and so I led the girl through deep shadow, over splashes of snowlight and moonlight from high windows, further and further away from the great hall.

'Where are we going?' she murmured.

We were in the changing-room, so dark that even the ghostly figure of my coat on its peg was just a piece of the enveloping gloom. Her palm pressed against mine, and I guided her forwards.

'What was that?' I stopped dead. She said again, 'What was that? Did you hear it?'

We'd both heard it: a heavy thud from somewhere high in the house. It checked us for a moment, as we wondered what it could be, then I urged her on again. I unbolted the door at the back of the changing-room and together we burst into the stable-yard.

I knew what had happened. As Sophie and I stepped from the stillness of the building into a blinding blizzard, it came to me with utter certainty that Dr Kemp had come down the attic staircase.

He'd sat in the attic for as long as he could, ordered by a small boy to stay where he was. How long could he stay there? How long could he obey the instructions of a twelve-year-old? Not long, or not at all.

Grinding his teeth at the pain in his groin, he must have thought of his wife, shot in the throat, tipped from her wheelchair, her life-blood pooling at the fireside. And I knew he could smell her, he could touch her: because, as he'd slumped and groaned among the jumbled boxes, as he'd stared at the skylight blotted with snow, he could have reached to the clothes which were hanging there and pulled them down to him – her riding outfits. I'd seen them and I knew what they were, and I knew he must have hung them there himself, with care and tenderness, soon after her accident, when she'd known she would never ride or walk again.

I imagined him, a frightened, stubborn, middle-aged man, lying in a dusty moonbeam. He'd stretched up and tugged down a jacket and a pair of jodhpurs and pressed them to his face. The scent of her, the warmth of her, the lingering energy of the horses she'd ridden, the sense of the shortness of the time they'd had together before she . . . I thought of him inhaling deeply, intoxicated by the love of his wife and the need to hold her again, and then crawling to the top of the stairs and starting to bump himself down, feet first.

Agony in his belly. The grease of sweat and blood on his hands. A swirl of giddiness in his head.

When I heard that thud, I knew in my heart – because I knew Dr Kemp – that he'd pitched into the hole, banging and crashing head over heels, and landed at the bottom of the stairs.

Sophie and I seemed to swim through the snowstorm. The pale moonlight through the blur of the blizzard made our shadows flicker like old newsreel. I pulled her across the yard, where the snow was deep on the cobbles, and in seconds I was struggling with the latch of the far stable. Ignoring her questions, the sound of her voice somehow muffled and woody in the snowfall, I pushed the door open and we fell into the darkness.

She leaned on me, hopelessly lost and confused by what I was doing. The stillness in the stable was a comfort, however. It simply felt better and safer to be out of the school building, blanketed by the snow outside and the silence inside. The girl didn't know where she was; she had no choice but to trust me as I lugged her unceremoniously through strange and secret places to a temporary refuge. She listened, holding her breath, as I scratched and scratched a match, saw it flare and smoke, and she watched as I held it close to the wick of the lantern. The flame licked and fluttered, steadying into a warm golden light.

She stared around the dusty interior of the stable. It felt warm, although there were no animals, and the floor was bare, uneven cobbles. No straw, no feed, nothing alive to breathe and steam and stamp and keep the air from freezing – until she caught a tiny tinkling, fidgeting movement in the far corner and saw the bird staring at her.

'Take this.' I handed her the lantern. No time to explain. She followed me on tiptoe, and when we were close to the bird I bent to the floor and picked up a feather. I whispered over my shoulder, 'Just hold up the light, that's all you have to do, as still as you can.'

Fascinated, she did what I said. As though hypnotised by the flame and the gleam of the jackdaw's eyes, she obeyed me without questioning the connection between the horror of the game and this calm, oddly irrelevant business with a bird in a stable. If there was a connection, for the moment she gave up trying to understand it and just stood with the lantern.

I stroked the jackdaw's belly. With the tip of the feather I caressed its throat. I whispered, 'Are you ready for this, my little imp?' and with my other hand I untied the leather thong that attached its leg to the perch. With a tinkle of bells, the bird sprang to my wrist.

'My imp, my imp . . .'

And then the sweet, blissful moment was over. There was a crash outside, the sound of the changing-room door being banged open, and the slam of it falling shut. We heard the crunch of footsteps in the stable-yard.

'The lantern! Blow it out! Quick!'

Sophie blew and blew. The flame died, then fluttered alive again, obstinately tall and strong. She blew harder and it went out in a plume of smoke.

The three of us, boy and girl and bird, peered through a crack in the stable door. Pryce was shoving the chair through the snow. It slewed and stopped, the buckled wheel stubborn and hard to control.

Cursing, he bent all his strength against the handles, too much, so that the chair slid sideways and fell over. He cried out, in anger and frustration, and kicked at it with his right foot, so that the good wheel spun fast and threw a spray of snow across the yard. His left foot, still bare, was a mess of blood and blackened skin. He righted the chair and forced it on and on, until it was close to the opposite stable door.

He unlatched the door and pulled on it with all his weight. It refused to move: the snow had drifted deep against it. Oblivious of the cold, his wound numbed by it, he scuffed and scuffed at the snow with his bare foot then pulled on the door again. This time he dragged it wide open. He manoeuvred the chair close to the boot of the red Jaguar.

Sophie said, 'Oh Jesus,' and clapped her hands to her mouth as though she were going to vomit.

And the jackdaw, reacting to the terror in her voice, erupted from my wrist. It beat and beat in the air, it screeched, and then, as I tried to control it by drawing in the jesses, it dangled upside down and thrashed its wings in a blind, hysterical panic. The bells were loud in the still air of the stable.

Pryce heard them. He turned from the car and stared through the falling snow towards the door from which the sounds were coming. He limped across the yard.

The bird gripped my wrist so hard that its claws drove into my flesh. Stifling a yelp of pain, I folded its wings under my arm, grabbed its leg, silenced the bells. I grabbed Sophie in turn, and we scrambled as far as we could go into the furthest corner of the stable and ducked behind the empty stall. We could do nothing more but crouch there, stare at the door and wait for it to open.

The footsteps came closer. The door opened. Pryce was a looming silhouette.

'Who's there?' he said. He took a step inside, caught his wounded foot on the cobbles and hissed like a cat. He stared into the darkness. He sniffed the air, as though to distil and distinguish the whiff of the lantern from the other unfamiliar smells in the stable. He heard a rustling, fidgety movement.

'Who's that? Alan, is it you?' He came on. Step by step he moved deeper into the shadows. When he reached the stall, he bent around it and felt the air with his fingers, so close to my face that I could smell the blood on them.

I let go of the bird. It seemed to explode, a nightmarish screaming creature, a raggedy black piece of the night with wings and a tearing beak and raking claws. As Pryce staggered away, it scrabbled and clung at his face so that he covered his head with his arms and fell back to the door. At last it whirled past him and out of the stable, trailing the jesses and the bells attached to its foot.

With a yell, Pryce disappeared into the snow. I tugged Sophie to the door, and we saw him stumbling across the yard. He was a hunched, wretched figure, shaking his head to flick the blood from the fresh wound on his face, still leaving a bloodied print from the wound in his foot. The blizzard whirled around his shoulders.

'We've done it,' I mouthed at Sophie. She blinked at me, uncomprehending. While Pryce huddled in the shelter of the other stable and wondered what it was that had cut him, I took the girl firmly by the hand and we padded across the yard to the door of the changing-room.

We slipped inside. Sophie groped in the darkness and threw the bolt, and then she bent and dry-retched into a corner. Anxious to see what Pryce was doing, I peered out of a window.

He was leaning wearily on the bonnet of the car. Then, with his back to the stable wall, he put his right foot onto the long red snout and pushed. The flat tyre squelched, the rear wheels crunching into the snow, and then he bent and shoved with both hands under the front bumper. The car slid out of the stable and stopped in the yard.

The snow was still falling steadily, although the whirl of the blizzard had slowed. He limped outside and moved the wheelchair close to the back of the car. In just a few moments, his hair was whitened with big soft flakes.

He took a deep breath, opened the boot, peered into it and then stretched in with both his arms. There was something heavy and awkward inside and he struggled to lift it out.

Sophie pulled me away from the window.

SIXTEEN

S till intact, we moved silently through the house.
I remember a strange feeling, the tiniest inkling of
triumph, at the thought that for a short while we'd
regained the territory. I knew that Pryce would come
back, the bolt on the door would not stop him; but just
then, as we padded through the changing-room and past
the chapel, into the main building and along the bottom
corridor with staffroom, library, music practice rooms
and classrooms, Pryce was out and we were in. And I was
determined to maintain the initiative, earned by my local
knowledge and the way I'd led the mission to release the
jackdaw from the stable, so I immediately made for the
boys' staircase and started up it. Sophie followed me. She
only muttered, 'What about the woman?' as we saw the
glow of firelight from the great hall, far ahead along the

corridor, and then demurred when I said firmly, 'No, let's find Dr Kemp.' She was right behind me as I climbed the stairs, unerring even in the deepest darkness, up and up, past the first floor and onto the second, to the little door at the foot of the narrow staircase to the attic.

I expected to find Kemp lying unconscious, or dying, or even dead. He wasn't there.

We paused together and listened to the silence in the house. We could see, in the feeble glow of the overhead bulb, that the lino was smudged with footprints and tyre-prints, all smeared in a mess of blood: a lot of blood, from Pryce's foot when he'd dropped out of the lift and pulled off his sock; and then a long, wide swirl of it, as if something had been dragged along the floor. The sock was there, black and sodden.

I put my head into the staircase. 'Dr Kemp, are you there?' I called, hoping I'd been wrong and he was still sitting meekly in the attic. No answer. I clambered up and looked. Nobody.

I came down. The steps were sticky with blood. From where Sophie was waiting for me, from where she stood in the swash of blood and urged me to follow her, the trail of it glistened into the darkness – a gruesome brush stroke painted onto the lino by the slither of the headmaster's stomach as he'd dragged himself along the corridor.

We reached the landing and craned over it, in time to see him bump and bump on his backside down the last few steps into the great hall. From the top to the bottom of the staircase, he'd left the round, fat print of his blood-soaked trousers.

'Dr Kemp!' I hissed down to him. 'Sir!'

I didn't know why I called out to him, or what I would have said next if he'd looked up and seen me: it was an instinct, to make contact with him, either to reassure him that we were there or to lessen my own fear. In any case, he didn't hear, he didn't look up. Having reached the hall, he sat in the mess of his own blood and slowly rolled onto his back, groaning as though the effort of every movement were killing him. He dug his fists into his wound; he coughed and coughed and spat a gobbet of blood onto the carpet. From the way he clutched at his chest, I thought he'd bruised or broken his ribs, and I imagined again how he'd cartwheeled down the stairs from the attic and thudded into the corridor.

'Where is she?' Sophie hissed into my ear. 'Where's the woman?' From the top landing we could see the flicker of a dying fire, but no sign of Mrs Kemp.

I gazed down, and my head swam. I squinted at a dark pool by the hearth – it could have been shadow or blood – the place where she'd been lying. She wasn't there.

I trod down to the first-floor landing. Saw what Kemp had already seen.

His wife was sitting in an armchair beside the fire. Her head was propped against a cushion and her eyes were closed. She might have been sleeping. Indeed, if the old dog had been snoring at her feet, it mightn't have looked so different from any other wintry night in the great hall at Foxwood Manor: Mrs Kemp relaxing before bedtime, the glow of the embers on her face and in her hair.

But there was no dog. There was a Christmas tree draped with shattered bulbs; a lot of broken glass from the photographs and trophy cabinets; an abandoned dining-table; plates and bowls of congealing fat and greasy gravy; spattered pools of candle wax. There was a slick of blood on the rug.

'Sarah,' the headmaster called softly. He heaved himself to his feet and groped his way across the hall.

'No, sir! Please sir!' Those were the words I wanted to call out, as he blundered forwards and I knew he was enmeshed at last in the trap that Pryce had laid for him. But no words came. Pryce must be there – only *he* could have moved the woman into the chair – and now he was waiting, watching and waiting. My lips moved, but I just gaped and stared, dumbstruck with fear, and I felt for the warmth and strength of Sophie's hand.

I felt into empty air. She'd gone.

The headmaster knelt at his wife's feet. 'Sarah, Sarah!' he whispered, and he took them in his hands – her icy feet, his hands like fire – willing all the life and heat of his body into hers.

And suddenly the lights flickered on. The music started.

There was a deafening blast from the record player. It was inches from the headmaster's ear. The sound had been rude and ugly enough when he'd heard it from high in the attic; now it was a physical assault. Jagged chords, a primitive beat, an uncouth, snidely insinuating voice – *you really got me you got me so I can't sleep at night . . .* Thrown off balance, Kemp let go of his wife's feet, fell away and rolled backwards onto the blood-soaked rug.

Sophie must have thrown the switch. In the time it had taken me to realise she wasn't there beside me, in the short, holy moment which Kemp had been allowed with his wife, she'd flown up to the attic, reached for the fuse box and turned on the power.

Kemp had forced himself upright. In the gloom of the Christmas tree at the further end of the hall, he saw a figure sitting at the piano – motionless, so bizarrely hunched in the wheelchair that its forehead was resting on the keyboard, the face hidden by a fall of dark hair.

The woman's eyes flickered open. Kemp reached for her hands, and, despite the hellish cacophony, for a second they gripped each other's fingers – her lips moved, she tried to smile at her husband, but only a trickle of blood oozed from the corner of her mouth. He lifted her hands to his face and kissed them.

The last glimmer of life faded in her eyes. Then it was gone.

He had no more time with her. There was a rush of movement from the piano, and when he turned to see what it was, the dark figure in the wheelchair was careering straight at him.

Kemp couldn't move out of the way. The chair rammed into him, two bony knees catching him full in the chest and smashing him back into the record player. The speed jolted down to 33 rpm. But still the record turned, ear-splittingly loud but horridly slow, the words just a ghoulish groaning.

Kemp lunged at the wheelchair. All of his anger and hatred erupted inside him. The pain, that had been salved in the few moments he'd had with his wife, now flared through him, dazzling hot. It was the pain he needed to mobilise every last ounce of his strength.

'Damn you! Damn you!' His hands grabbed at the flopping hair, twisted and yanked, clawed at the face and throat. He shoved and bellowed so that the chair spun away from him. 'Damn you, Pryce!'

The music stopped.

I'd seen it happen, unable to believe what I was seeing. Martin Pryce, appearing from behind the piano, stepping forwards, lifting the needle from the disc.

He loomed over Kemp, who'd collapsed onto the floor, heaving with rage and exhaustion. Kemp stared up at him. Then he looked at the figure in the wheelchair. He did a double-take, from the one to the other and back again.

Martin Pryce leaned over, put his hand under the chin of the body in the wheelchair and tried to lift it. But it was too stiff to move. He pulled the curtain of hair to one side.

A swollen, purpling face. Bruised lips. Eyes staring, glazed. Blackened skin. A dead face. The gleam of a piano string, embedded in the flesh of the throat.

'Don't you recognise him?' Pryce said.

With a terrible wrench of one hand, he grabbed Kemp by the hair. With the other hand, as if by magic, he dangled a piano string. He looped it around the headmaster's throat.

'It's Jeremy, your little Dolly Boy – I've brought him back for you.'

He tightened the string. Kemp squirmed and flopped, like an animal caught in a trap. He clawed with both hands to try and stop the wire from cutting. But it cut deep. And it was easy for Pryce, who was tall and strong and on his feet, while the headmaster crumpled to the floor, gurgling, gagging, tongue out, eyes popping – so easy for Pryce that he could reach with a free hand, drop the needle randomly onto the record and restart the slowly grinding blast of sound.

He dropped the headmaster onto the floor, jamming him against the wheelchair. Kneeling suddenly, he tore off his dead brother's left shoe and sock. A second later, he'd melted back into the shadows behind the piano.

I'd seen it all. Sophie hadn't. She'd left me and gone upstairs to turn on the power – and for something else, a thing forgotten and lost while the house had been in darkness. When I blinked over my shoulder and up to the top landing, she was standing there with the gun.

She came down the stairs and flew right past me. I was on my feet, grabbing at her arm and trying to stop her, but she was too strong, too quick.

She reached the bottom of the stairs before me. She saw Mrs Kemp slumped in an armchair. She saw the figure hunched in the wheelchair, its left foot bare and swollen-black – hunched over the body of Dr Kemp, who was gurgling, twitching, flapping pathetically at a piano string tight around his throat.

She strode forwards. At close range, she raised the gun and fired just over the headmaster's head. The bullet slammed into its target.

'Help me! Alan, help me!' she yelled. 'Quickly!' She threw down the gun. As I hurried forwards, as I tried to drag my horrified eyes from the figure in the wheelchair, she knelt to the headmaster and struggled with the piano string.

Too late, too late. She couldn't do it. The string was too tight and deep in his flesh. As she fought with the wire, Kemp rolled his bloodshot, bulging eyes at the ceiling. His blood-filled mouth opened and closed, and his final breath was a long bubbling cry. At the end of it, his head rolled slowly forwards onto his chest.

The music stopped. Silence, at last.

We knelt for a long, lovely minute. The sense of peace was almost overwhelming. I knew that Martin Pryce was looming nearby, I knew Sophie would soon realise that her bullet had found the wrong target. But I didn't care. A great weariness settled on me. The whole building breathed an exhausted sigh at the passing of Dr and Mrs Kemp, its guardians for the past twenty years. The only sounds were the flutter of the fire and the click-click-click of the disc turning on the record player.

I looked long and hard at the dead headmaster's face. The features, which had seized so grotesquely as he'd struggled to breathe, had now softened. His eyes were closed, and there was a dribble of blood from his lips. In repose, he was just a shabby, middle-aged man, bundled awkwardly in his shirt and tie and tweed jacket, grey flannels and suede shoes. His hair needed cutting: it was greasy, and where it fell over his collar there were flecks of dandruff. There were tufts of bristle in his ears and nostrils, his nose was red, his cheeks were marbled with veins, and a fine white stubble covered his chin. In the left eyebrow, there was a scar almost an inch long, perhaps from a childhood accident or sporting injury, which I'd never noticed before.

Staring at him, I realised I'd never looked so closely, through all the years I'd been a boy at Foxwood.

I picked up his right hand; inexplicably, I wanted to touch him, to be touched by him. This was the hand that had held a little cane and swished it sharply onto my backside. It had wielded a wooden clothes-brush and smacked it on my buttocks. With these fingers, now tacky with blood, he'd rapped my knuckles with the ivory baton, as I'd tried my best to sing in tune or to master my scales on the piano. I picked up his left hand, where two of the fingers were curled hard into the palm, an injury which all the boys had noticed and never dared mention, a secret he'd only divulged to his most precious pupils – to *me*, who'd been precious to him. Somehow amazed, oddly moved, I examined the hands of this man I'd often feared, sometimes hated, but whom I'd never really seen before: Dr Kemp, headmaster of Foxwood Manor School, deceased.

As the body sagged, as the last of the life drained from it, we knelt in the silence and knew that he was dead.

Sophie appraised the figure in the wheelchair. She ran her eyes from the long dark hair which hid the face, over the lean body which was so twisted and still; the long legs, bent on either side of the dead headmaster; the bare left foot, mottled purple.

She bent closer and touched the foot. Ice cold. No wound. The stink of death.

She recoiled sharply. We both turned and stared across to the piano, as Martin Pryce stepped from behind it.

'You as well, Sophie? Can't you tell us apart?'

She turned back to the man she'd shot, whose hands were so black, whose face beneath the flopping hair was swollen and black. She saw the glint of the wire in his throat. She recoiled in horror and disgust. She looked from the dead, cold Jeremy to the living, bloodied Martin Pryce.

'You wanted to kill me,' he whispered. 'Hard to believe.' With a couple of lurching hops, he covered the distance between himself and the girl. Before she could get to her feet, he grabbed her arm and yanked her to him. 'We're in this together, Sophie, we always have been . . .'

She writhed away from him, but he was too strong. He lugged her to his chest and squeezed her to him, so hard that she could barely breathe. 'I love you, Sophie, and you love me, remember? That's what got us into all this . . .'

She squirmed in his arms, flailing at his face with bloody fingers. 'No, I never loved you! Maybe I could've loved Jeremy! And so you killed him! I hate . . .'

There was a horrible groan. The dead headmaster, who'd been propped against the legs of the dead Jeremy, now slid to the floor. The air in his lungs was forced out in a gurgling sigh, and, as he flopped onto his side and his head bumped hard on the floor, a bubble of bloody mucus the size of a golf-ball formed at his lips and then popped.

We all stared. And Sophie stamped as hard as she could onto Pryce's left foot.

She broke away from him. He raged at the pain and clutched the blackened wound. He yelled after us, me and Sophie, as we fled across the hall, 'You can't get away! There's nowhere to go!' But we slipped into the shadows of the corridor.

Sophie disappeared ahead of me. I could hear her in the distance, as far away as she could get from the horrors in the great hall. An awful sound – not weeping, not retching, but the whimpering of a wretchedly wounded animal. The misery of someone destroyed by the mess of her life.

Pryce hobbled to the dining-table. I watched, as I'd done before, indeed as I'd been watching him since he and Sophie had arrived at Foxwood Manor. He tried to muster a few drops of wine from the bottle and glasses. He licked out the dregs.

He bent to Kemp and sat him upright, leaning him against the armchair on which Mrs Kemp was sitting. He took her left hand and the headmaster's right, and twined their fingers together. In this way, husband and wife were joined.

The fire had almost gone out. He built a scaffold of holly twigs on the embers. They caught immediately, so dry from waiting their turn at the side of the hearth. Onto the new blaze he leaned some bigger pieces of wood and watched as yellow and blue flames licked around them.

Click-click-click – the record was still spinning on the turntable, the needle riding an endless groove.

He moved to it and picked up the needle. He was about to drop it again when he paused, with an expression of the greatest disgust on his face, snatched up the 45 and tossed it onto the fire. Immediately it folded into the flames.

He picked up the long-playing record which had slipped off an armchair and onto the floor, blew off the dog hairs and placed it on the turntable. The needle hissed and crackled, and then the music started.

Lovely beyond words, the first haunting melody of Fauré's Requiem filled the hall. Pryce fell to his knees on the hearth rug, and his face was twisted, tormented, as he looked at the crumpled figure of his dead brother, at the dead headmaster and his dead wife sitting hand in hand and strangely serene. The music swelled around him, so strong and sure, so human, so alive.

He stared into the flames, where the molten black plastic fizzled and flared, and he wept. Hot, uncontrollable tears ran down his cheeks and into the corners of his mouth.

SEVENTEEN

I searched the house for Sophie and found her at last. Like a dying animal, fatally poisoned and wracked with pain, she'd crawled into a dark corner and huddled there.

She was in my bed, in the furthest corner of the highest dormitory. When I tiptoed into the room and whispered for her, I made out the mound of her body under my blankets, with her face to the wall. I heard her laboured breathing and came closer, and she shuddered at my touch on her shoulder, thinking that at last Pryce had come for her. But when she knew it was me, her body eased. She didn't move, she didn't turn towards me, she just exhaled long and slowly and whispered something into the pillow. I bent to catch what she was saying. She was almost too exhausted to speak, enmeshed in the fear and horror of what had happened, of what might yet happen, but she whispered again, 'Hold onto me, please, just hold on . . .'

I kicked off my shoes and slipped under the blankets. When I wrapped my arms around her, her body seemed to melt. She wept like a child.

Slowly her sobbing subsided. She fell into a stupefied sleep, the only hiding place she could find.

The music continued. As Pryce had said, it crept up the stairs from the great hall, crawled along the corridor and slithered under the door of the dormitory. I thought I could feel it coiling itself under my bed. And yet it was so familiar, so much the sound of an ordinary bedtime at Foxwood Manor, that somehow it smudged and blurred the reality of the nightmare that Pryce had brought with him. Or maybe it was the comfort of lying so close to the warm body of the girl. I felt myself drifting asleep . . .

And the boy came to me.

He stood in the doorway of the dormitory, dressed like me in grey pullover and grey corduroy shorts. And yet, framed in the darkness of the corridor, he had a kind of gleam on him. His face was pale, the glow of a mushroom pushing its head from the soil of a forest, and his black hair was shining. Spectral, he beckoned to me. I slipped out of bed, careful not to disturb the girl, and followed him.

Along the corridor, down the stairs and into the hall. Without a glance to left or right, he crossed to the front door and paused for me to join him there. His hand was cool and dry in mine as he took me through the door and outside.

The snow had stopped. The woodland lay still and hushed, a pristine world. The trees swayed and groaned, and as they moved they shifted the weight of the snow and showered it onto the ground below. As the blizzard had died, the clouds had frayed and torn until the last tatters had blown away, and now the sky was perfectly clear. A gibbous moon had dipped to the horizon, leaving a swirl of stars.

There was a movement in the pool of shadow beneath the copper beech, and Wagner padded across the lawn towards us. He was wagging his whole barrel-shaped body, so pleased to see us, and when he lifted his face to my hands and then to the boy's his teeth chattered with joy.

I followed the boy and the dog into the woods. He meant me to see everything. So far I'd missed nothing: with my own eyes I'd witnessed every turn of the action, peeping and peering, pursuing, shadowing, recording every move of everybody on the screen of my mind. And now the boy had come for me, in my sleep – not to wake me, but to show me in a dream – so that I would see for myself the unfolding of the story.

A mile from the school, a man was sleeping. He lay inside an old caravan, beneath the bare boughs of an oak tree. The caravan was covered with a deep layer of snow; all the angles and corners had been softly rounded so that it looked like a huge boulder, or a barrow that men had made hundreds of years ago, an ancient piece of the forest. There was a little window, minutely ajar, but no light from inside it.

The boy gestured me to the window. I smudged at the frost on it and looked in.

Roly stirred under a mound of blankets. He was completely covered, even his head buried. It looked, in the shadows of the jumbled little space, more like the den of a bear than the habitation of a human being, and through a crack in the window I caught the smell of stale bedding, unwashed clothes and an unwashed body.

I willed him to wake up.

Roly pushed his head up, twitching his nose like a ferret. He blinked, scratched his tousled grey hair and he listened.

He knew the sounds of the forest. He'd lived in the woods for years, given the use of the caravan and a monthly pittance by a feckless landowner. Now, he could tell that the blizzard had stopped by the unearthly silence that surrounded him, an absence of sound made more profound by the secret whispering of the trees as they shivered the snow from their branches. And something else.

He lay there and listened until, despite the effort it took to push the warm blankets aside and get out of bed, he stood up and pulled on his trousers. His breath was white in the freezing air. He put on his shirt and a thick pullover, stomped his feet into his boots, took his old waterproof coat from the peg on the back of the door and was ready to step outside.

And something else, he needed something else. Again I pressed my will on him, so that, as he picked up a torch and shone it around him, the beam fell on the shotgun which leaned at the side of his bed. He picked up the gun and loaded two cartridges.

Roly trudged through the forest. He inhaled the cold, clean air, to clear his head from the fug he'd been breathing under his bedding. And we followed him, two boys and a dog, silent and unseen, for we were not a real part of his waking world. Our feet made no sound, no imprint on the snow. The sound he'd heard was a tinkling, like the splintering of ice except for its odd insistence, again and again with a shake and rattle. He waded knee-deep where the snow had banked against fallen timber, he pushed through nettle beds and bracken, and he flashed the torch into the enveloping darkness. The light gleamed back at him from the silvery columns of birch and the blackened pillars of beech and ash.

The sound grew louder. He was getting closer.

I willed him on, I willed him to look upwards. And when the little bells rang over his head, and he saw in his torchlight a fluttering like a piece of rag caught high in the branches of a venerable holly, he leaned the gun against the tree, switched off the torch and slipped it into his coat pocket, blew on his fingers and started to climb.

The bark of the tree was slippery, but the branches were gnarled and knobby and easy to grip. Roly moved steadily upwards. As he climbed higher, it was harder to find places to lodge his boots, and the clustered leaves prickled at his face. Near the top, he jammed himself against the trunk and felt for the torch in his pocket. He shone it through the highest branches, an icy, brittle place, and fixed the beam on the struggling jackdaw.

The crippled crow I'd rescued from a tangle of thorns. An imp, delivered into my care by some mischievous spirit of the forest.

The bird had tangled its jesses, and now it was dangling hopelessly upside down. Too weak to scream, it hung there, panting, hissing, wasting its strength in futile spasms of anger as it thrashed its wings against the sharp leaves. The bells tinkled through the snow-muffled forest.

Roly reached up to the bird. Wrapping an arm around the trunk of the tree, he pointed the torch with one hand, stretched with the other and fumbled for the jesses. But they were snagged, entangled by the jackdaw's frantic movements, and as he tried to undo them it stabbed at his hand with its beak. He leaned out as far as he dared and tried to seize the stump of its missing leg. For a moment the bird was free from the tree and righted itself, and it gripped his forefinger with the last of its strength. He swore, dropped the torch, let go of the trunk and lunged for the bird with both hands. By chance, in the darkness and cold and the flailing of wings, he found its legs with one of his hands, pulled it towards him and folded its body against his.

I was shouting, Wagner was barking, the boy was shouting too – we could see the breath in front of our faces. But Roly couldn't hear us. None of us could warn him or do anything to help him, as his foot slipped from its precarious perch. Just as he managed to bundle the bird inside his coat and hug it close, the branch on which he'd rested his weight snapped and gave way.

He fell sideways, away from the trunk. With a breathtaking impact, his ribs struck a bigger branch, which arrested his fall and gave him a second to grab for a handhold. The branch cracked beneath him – and from there on, he banged and crashed and slithered down and down, through the limbs of the tree, his body and his boots smashing a way from the top to the bottom.

He landed flat on his back in a deep drift of snow.

He lay still, and I knelt over him, searching his eyes for a flicker of movement. He groaned and stared right past me, blinking at the stars through the splintered branches. Winded, he stayed where he was and tried to regain his breath. When he felt a sudden writhing inside his coat, he sat up, shook the snow out of his hair and struggled to his feet.

The torch was still shining where it had fallen. He picked it up, turned it off and put it in his pocket. He didn't need it. The starlight and the gleam of the snow were enough for him, and he knew every inch of the woodland. Within the warm and pungent darkness of his jacket, the bird stopped squirming – my imp, released into the woods to summon the only help there was.

Roly took his shotgun and started the long, slow walk towards the school.

And in my dream, I was there before him.

Wagner had gone. On the lawn in front of the house he'd licked my hands and the boy's hands and limped into the shadows of the copper beech. He disappeared, a big black dog absorbed into a deeper blackness. Returned to the reality of death.

I was inside the house again. Pryce had left the great hall and gone to the chapel. The music followed him – and I was with him too, a kind of dream-shadow. He'd turned up the volume as high as it would go, so that every part of the building was filled with the swelling sound, and he knew it was clear and loud in the dormitories because he'd heard it a hundred or five hundred times, and he knew that it thrummed in the lift shafts and up to the big hollow space of the attic in the very roof of the house. The music moved with Martin Pryce, comforting and warm like a cloak around his shoulders, as he limped down the corridors and past the classrooms and library and staffroom, when he started in fear at the sight of a single coat looming like the figure of a man in the shadows of the changing-room.

He reached the chapel. The dust and cobwebs stirred as he crossed to the vestry.

Starlight pierced the stained-glass windows. The bell rope dangled in front of him, and for a moment he felt the smoothness of it, the grip and the sweat of all the palms of all the boys who'd tugged it. But he didn't ring the bell – although he'd done so many times in those long-ago years – because the music was so full inside him: it was all the sound he needed, all the sound he would ever need. I watched the tears run down Pryce's face, as he reached for a surplice and cassock from the pegs in the vestry.

He tried them all and they were all too small. His frustration grew as he took one after the other and pulled it over his head, tried to force it over his shoulders and chest. Too small. Time and again, he tore off a red surplice and threw it into the corner of the room, ripped off a white cassock and tossed it aside, until, in anger and bitterness, he forced his arms through and his head and wriggled his body until he stood there, mouthing to the music through the sobs that rose into his throat – an overgrown choirboy, weeping, stuffed into a surplice and cassock he'd grown out of eight years before, illumined in a beam of starlight.

He limped up the aisle, between the rows of pews where generations of boys and teachers and parents had sat, and he left his sticky footprints on the cold floor. He found his place in the choir-stall: not the coveted place of the head chorister, where I had sat, where Jeremy had sat, because he'd never won such distinction. He sat in the darkness of his little corner, from where he used to sit and watch his exalted brother.

And then the music drew him back to the great hall.

It was a tumult, full blast, so loud that it was the only sound in my dream. Even for Pryce the sounds of the real world were blanked out. Indeed, when he stepped on some broken glass with his bare foot, when he cried out and leaned so clumsily on the dining-table that a wine bottle toppled over, it was all in a kind of silence. Grimacing at the newer, even fiercer pain, he hobbled to the fireside, where he lifted Mrs Kemp from her armchair and into the wheelchair.

An oblong of golden light fell from the front of the house and far across the lawn as Pryce pulled open the front door. He let the weight of the woman in the chair tug him down the ramp and then he leaned and crunched the wheels through the snow. It was deep, unmarked by the print of any bird or beast. He manoeuvred the chair to the mound which was the only sign of Wagner's grave, and he lifted the woman out and laid her there. She sank comfortably into the snow, as though she were asleep on a feather bed.

He went back for Kemp. It was a struggle to lug him into the wheelchair, because the man was sitting on the floor and much heavier than his wife. Then he rolled him out of the door, so fast down the ramp that he fought to control the chair in case it might tip over, and he heaved with all his strength to push it across the lawn to the copper beech. He stood beneath the branches, leaning on the handles of the chair, gagging for breath, until he was ready to pull the man out and plump him down beside his wife.

I watched him: a gangly choirboy trussed in a red surplice and white cassock shoving a wheelchair once and then a second time across the lawn, leaving a dead woman and a dead man in the snow. I heard the lovely music, and I saw, in the light which fell from the front door of the school, the glistening of tears on the choirboy's face.

With the utmost tenderness, Pryce lifted the body of his brother onto the chair. The body was curled like a foetus, from being brutally buckled and bent into the boot of the car – only just possible when the spare wheel had been taken out and left behind. Completely stiff, it hunched in the chair, its head almost touching its knees. Pryce wheeled swiftly to the door and down the ramp, and this time, the third time, it was easy to follow the existing tracks and roll smoothly to the graveside.

Jeremy's body was light. He levered it out of the chair and onto the snow, beside the bodies of Dr and Mrs Kemp. And then he knelt and kissed the purpled face, the blackened fingers.

As he did so, I felt the cold, dry fingers of the boy squeezing mine. I turned, and I saw in his eyes that there was yet one thing I must do for him, that he couldn't do for himself. It was why he'd come back.

The music built to a marvellous climax as Pryce wielded the spade, as he drove the blade at the ground. He swung it from over his shoulder, beating and beating with an increasingly desperate and futile rhythm. It was useless. The earth was frozen. The iron of the spade hit the iron of the ground with a terrible, jarring force, and made no impression at all.

At last the music faded. The spade clanged a few more times, until the overgrown choirboy was exhausted. Sobbing, he flung the spade down and fell to his knees.

EIGHTEEN

C hristmas morning. It was very dark in the great hall
of Foxwood Manor. The fire had gone out. Bitter
cold. The door was wide open to the wintry dawn.

Still wearing the surplice and cassock, Martin Pryce
was asleep in an armchair. He looked wretched, with his
head thrown back and his mouth agape. There was a welt
on his cheek where the bird had torn him, and his skin
was deadly pale. His hands dangled and his fingers
twitched, and they were mottled white, blenched by the
snow. His bare foot was scoured: all the blood was gone
from it, and the gunshot wound was raw meat.

As Roly came closer to the school he could see the tall
chimneys of the house through the woodland. He trudged
through the snow, which had been treacherously deep on
the uneven ground of the forest, and at last, as he

approached the building from the back and crossed the playing fields, he found good footing.

He paused there, and he surveyed the tops of the beech trees beside the school. Something was different, something was missing, and for a few moments he couldn't decide what it was. And then he had it. He was often up and moving through the woods at dawn, and in the darkest days of winter he would catch the crows still roosting in the high branches: this morning there were none.

He came behind the school. He didn't want to meet anyone, to disturb anyone, and, in any case, his business was only in the stable-yard. The jackdaw stirred inside his coat as he turned the corner and felt the cobbles under his boots, and there he stopped dead at the extraordinary sight in front of him.

A car full of snow. Long and low and smoothly rounded, it seemed to be abandoned there; having no roof, the inside was filled with snow. The boot, wide open, was also full of snow.

Roly squinted at the car. Where a slab of snow had slipped from its flanks, he could see that it was red, and the wheels had silvery spokes and silvery hubs. He touched the rim of the steering wheel, then recoiled and swivelled around in case anyone had seen him do so. One of the stables was open, and he could see from the tracks that the car had been pushed out of it. The snow all around was a scribble and scrawl which made no sense at all; narrow tyre marks too, and a smudge where something had been dropped and dragged, even some bare footprints tinged the softest pink.

Roly frowned, pushed back his cap and scratched his hair. He crossed to the corner stable, pushed the door open and went in.

The jackdaw bated as he took it out of his coat, such a whirl of screaming and thrashing that all the dust in the stable clouded around him. Quite calm, he just held its jesses and held it at arm's length, his head turned away, as though it were a firework he'd lit in his hand, showering sparks all over him. 'Be good, be good,' he whispered, and he moved across to the perch and swung the bird gently in the right direction. With the momentum of one of the swings, the jackdaw beat itself upright in mid-air and clawed at the perch, scrabbled with its claws and gripped.

At last it stood there, chest heaving, tattered and ruffled and very angry, glaring at Roly with mad black eyes.

He tied the jesses to the perch and stepped away. There was a wry, weasly smile on his face. 'Don't look at me like that, all huffy,' he said softly. 'I didn't do it for you, I did it for the boy, all right?'

He picked up the shotgun and came out into the yard. As he turned the corner of the house, a great cloud of crows rose from the lawn.

There was an enormous commotion. The birds whirled into the air in such chaos that some of them snagged in the branches of the copper beech. And then, startled that the man with the gun had suddenly appeared, they went clacking and cawing into the tops of the woodland trees, where they clamoured and slowly settled. Roly stood there and watched them, puzzled to see so many and so early, when they might have been roosting still.

He crunched through the snow to see what they'd been doing.

He saw the overturned wheelchair, a spade, and the marks that a spade had made on the hard ground. Mrs Kemp was lying on her back. Her hair was lovely, but she had no eyes or nose or lips: only holes in her face, where her eyes and nose had been. Her teeth were long and yellow, like a horse's, and there was a gaping wound in her throat, which surely the crows had not made. Dr Kemp lay beside her. The birds had had his eyes as well, although they'd left his nose and attacked his cheeks instead. Their beaks had gone into the flesh, broken it open and worked into the gums, pulled his tongue out sideways, through the cheek, because his teeth were so tightly clenched: yellow teeth, exposed to the roots. It looked as though, curiously, the crows had ripped his trousers and pecked into his belly: a mess of blood. And there was a third person, curled oddly into a ball and lying on his side: a stranger, a young man with long dark hair. The birds had picked off his ear, and the flesh around it was black.

Roly stared at the three dead bodies, so grotesquely disfigured. He glanced up at the birds in the high trees, and his first reaction, in shock and disgust, was to raise his gun and . . .

He heard a noise from the house. He lowered the barrels of the gun and turned round slowly.

*　*　*

I woke from a strange dream.

The commotion of the crows had woken me, and I found myself lying in my bed with all my clothes on, with my arms enfolded around a sleeping girl. I rolled out of bed and pressed my face to the window. Roly was on the lawn, pointing his gun up into the trees. I rapped on the glass, and he lowered the barrels of the gun and turned round slowly.

When I beckoned to him, he lifted his hand in a kind of wave and trod across the lawn. He could see from there that the front door of the house was wide open.

'Sophie, Sophie!' I shook the girl awake. Her befuddled face turned towards me. Her cheek was striped from the pillow, her eyes wild and frightened; I could smell her mouth. 'Roly's here!' I hissed at her. 'He's come to help us!'

She had no idea what I was saying. She didn't know who Roly was. But when she stared at me, reached out and touched my neck, there was a tiny jewel of blood on her fingertip. 'Who? What?' she said. 'What is it?'

I spun away from her. There was no time. But as I hurtled across the dorm and out of the door, I could feel the welt around my throat and the blood welling from it, the prickling of the stripes on my palms – the stigmata of my dreams.

I skidded to a halt on the top landing. Far below me, the hall was very dark. I tasted the air rising from it, dank and stale like the air from a cellar.

Swallowing hard, almost gagging, I moved down to the next landing. Roly came through the front door, stepped inside and stopped. He sniffed and shuddered and exhaled: the building was deathly cold, somehow colder than the world outside. He peered into the gloom, making out the empty chairs, the gape of the hearth, a dinner table with glasses and plates and an overturned bottle. Beyond that, it was as black as a cave.

He said softly, 'Scott, are you there?' and took another few steps. I tried to answer, couldn't. His boots crunched on broken glass. With a quiver of fear in his voice, he called towards the staircase, which curved up and up to where I was standing, 'Scott, where are you?' He started to climb.

Silent night. Holy night. A few muffled notes from the piano. No more than a whisper in the great hall, but a whisper that made Roly stop on the stairs and turn back.

Silent night . . . holy night . . . The first two lines, only the melody, played on muted bass keys. And then silence.

Roly stared back into the hall. He stepped from the staircase, towards the dimly echoing darkness from which the sounds had come. 'Is that you, Scott?' he said.

It started again, the plangent melody of the carol. A bit louder, as though the fingers on the keyboard were drawing Roly closer and closer towards the piano. 'What's happening?' he said. Glass crackled under his feet. One of his boots caught a tin cup that was lying on the floor and it clanged against the hearth. 'Scott, are you all right? I saw them outside . . .'

I trod down to the foot of the stairs. I couldn't speak. The playing got louder. Not so lovely, the melody skewed, distorted, an ugly sound – *all is calm, all is bright* – played on one finger, wrongly, and then stopping.

'Stop it,' Roly said. 'Stop it, boy, and answer me.'

I tried to call out, to warn him, but it felt as though the wire were tightening in my throat. I could hardly breathe, my hands were fighting it and the wire was cutting my palms. Roly banged into the corner of the piano, hardly seeing its angular bulk in the shadows. He fumbled around its edges, reaching to where he thought I must be. Nothing but empty, cold air. There was no one.

His fingers blundered onto the keyboard, startling him so much that he jumped away as though the piano had bitten him. He whirled around, sensing someone very close.

And then he heard footsteps. He turned and saw a dim figure coming down the stairs.

'Who's that?' he said. 'Who are you?'

Sophie moved past me. She said in a high, clear voice, 'Thank God you're here. Please help us.'

'Help you? I don't know . . .'

Roly's breath was cut off. A black shape rose behind him, sudden and misshapen like some ghastly spectre conjured from inside the piano itself. It whirled a gleaming wire around his throat and pulled it tight with a terrible strength.

Sophie cried out – *No Martin no!* – and flew across the hall.

Roly grappled with the wire, one of his hands scrabbling hopelessly as it cut and cut into his flesh. In his other hand, the gun came up.

There was a crashing detonation.

The blast lifted the girl from her feet and flung her

backwards. She landed with a sickening thud in the fireplace.

The explosion rocked the whole house. Outside too, the crows erupted from the treetops in a panic of raggedy wings and hoarse voices. And then there was a long beat, as the report echoed and faded and a kind of silence resumed.

Roly was gurgling, spastic, flapping his arms and legs like a puppet. Pryce dropped him onto the floor.

'Sophie – oh Jesus, Sophie . . .'

He lurched to the hearth, a hunchbacked creature in the half-light, still bundled in the bloodstained surplice and cassock and dragging a swollen, purpling foot. He leaned into the fireplace and embraced her.

'Sophie, I didn't mean – I didn't want to . . . Oh Jesus, Sophie, I love you I love you please . . .'

He held her tightly, although she was utterly limp in his arms, and buried his face in her chest. The side of her head was a welter of blood, the ear and hair scorched off. For a full minute he shuddered and sobbed with the horror of it, and the words spilled out of him, as though he himself had been burst open and everything inside was broken. '*Lighten our darkness, we beseech Thee, O Lord, and . . .*'

A shaft of light fell across him. He turned his face into it and blinked, quite dazzled.

He saw a boy silhouetted against the window. A gleaming boy with a halo of dust.

'Jeremy? Is it you? Are you here?'

I opened the shutters wider. I'd come into the hall in the aftershock of the blast. With a glance around the room I saw Roly lying beneath the piano, where he'd crawled in the final throes of his struggle with the wire. I saw Sophie, crumpled and bloody in the fireplace. Pryce, the choirboy, huddled against her, squinting into a gleam of snow.

'Jeremy?' he said. 'Alan? Alan, it's Sophie – it's Sophie, look!'

I bent to the floor and straightened up with the shotgun.

'Help me, Alan, help me! She's . . .'

I hefted the gun in my hands. The weight and the warmth and the smell of it were oddly satisfying. It eased my breathing, it soothed my hands. And I could feel the boy with me, in me, guiding me, using me.

'Alan, I didn't mean this, you know I didn't – look, Alan, I . . .' Pryce moved from the fireplace, on his knees, dragging himself towards me. He wheedled, 'I never wanted this, I didn't come here for this – I never meant those things I said . . .'

I stood perfectly still in the cold sunlight. Craven, toady, Pryce slithered closer. 'I'm on your side, Alan, I know what it's like to be here, in this place, with these people! I've been you, and you'll grow to be like me, to *be* me! Alan, you *are* me!'

'No.' I levelled the gun, sighted, held my breath – as my father had taught me to do, as the boy wanted me to do.

The voice changed. It was a sneer, full of loathing. 'No, you aren't me. You're Jeremy, you're Kemp – you're Kemp and Jeremy with your perfect fucking pitch. Do you know how *im*perfect you've made me feel?'

He lunged forwards. I squeezed the trigger.

At close range, the blast hit him full in the mouth. He spun away and crashed back into the fireplace. He lay there, obliterated, his arms and legs flung out, flopped against the girl; side by side, they looked like a couple of rag dolls that had been dropped down the chimney. For a few moments his fingers opened and closed, and then stopped.

It was done.

A silence grew. Slowly, all the dust in the air settled, and so did the ash that had been blown out of the hearth. The smoke from the barrels of the gun was a dim blue haze in the light that fell between the shutters of the tall window.

I glanced to the open front door, thinking I'd seen a movement there. There was a flutter of cold air, as though someone or something had passed through the door and gone outside. And then a silence in the house that had not been heard since the game began.

It was all over.

I stood for a minute, for two or three minutes. It made no difference: the passing of time could make no difference to what had happened. Once the din of the explosion had faded and even the ringing in my ears had gone, I just stared in front of me and my mind was blank.

My breathing was easy. When I felt at my neck, there was no blood, no wound. The prickling on my hands was just an itch.

I dropped the gun onto the floor. I heard the faint sound of a regular, rhythmic clicking, trod to the record player, picked up the needle from the spinning disc and put it gently on its cradle. I switched off the turntable and watched it slow down and stop. Then I closed the lid of the walnut cabinet.

The world was a still, utterly silent place.

NINETEEN

The telephone rang.

It was so loud, so unexpected, that I just blinked and stared. It was the sound of faraway, of somewhere beyond the miles and miles of snow-covered forest. I let it ring for a long time, before I picked up the receiver and lifted it to my ear.

A woman's voice, bright and blithe. 'Hello, Foxwood Manor?' A pause, then, 'Dr Kemp? This is Jennifer Scott, Alan's mother . . .'

I held the receiver away from my ear and examined it in my hand, as though it were a piece of technology I'd never dreamed of. The little voice tinkled into thin air. I said into the mouthpiece, 'Mummy?'

'Oh Alan, you're there! I'm so sorry, darling, I haven't been able to make it, I'm still in Austria . . .'

Somehow the stream of words was too quick for me. It was a language which had no meaning for me at that time, in that place. A warm trickle ran through my hair, down my forehead and into my eyebrow, from where it dripped onto the strange black object I was holding. I stared at the blood, and I studied the odd, crumpled dolls in the fireplace: the girl-doll was still quite pretty, but the choirboy-doll had no face at all. Under the piano, a figure in an old waterproof jacket and boots lay very still.

There was broken glass everywhere. Bullet holes in the walls and the ceiling.

And blood. It dripped from the mantelpiece, from the edges of the hearth, from the furniture, and it pooled on the threadbare carpet. It dripped from my eyebrow onto the mouthpiece of the telephone.

The voice was quite foreign to me, a breathless prattle: '– ringing to wish you a Happy Christmas, and of course your birthday! A teenager, thirteen today, a big man! Congratulations, my darling!' And then singing, as soft and sweet as the voice of an angel. '*Happy Birthday to you, Happy Birthday to you . . .*'

I put the receiver onto the lid of the record player. There was a gasp from the fireplace, and I saw Sophie's eyes flick open. I knelt quickly to her, and with the ball of my thumb I wiped the clotting of ash and blood from her lips. She coughed, inhaled very deeply, and stared at me, reaching up to touch my cheek.

'It's all right, Sophie,' I said, 'you'll be all right,' and very gently I prised her out of the hearth. She stumbled to her feet, wobbling like a newborn foal. As I helped her across the hall to the front door, my mother's singing continued and followed me. I could still hear it very faintly as we stepped outside, into the gleam of sunlight and snow – 'are you there, my darling Alan?' – a voice from hundreds of miles away, oblivious, as though from another planet.

A beautiful, beautiful morning.

The sky had cleared from grey through silver to an exquisitely pale blue. And the snow was lovely on the lawn and in the woodland. The crows had come down again, a squabble of wings and claws and sharp black beaks beneath the boughs of the copper beech. Although they'd risen in panic when the man with the gun had appeared, they hardly flinched from me and the girl. They only fidgeted and flapped when we emerged from the door, before settling again to their Christmas dinner.

I sat Sophie on the front steps of the school. She leaned back and turned her face to the full light of the sun. I said, 'You're safe now,' but she couldn't hear me. I could see from her eyes that she understood.

I skirted the lawn, turned away from the front of the house and went round to the stable-yard. One more thing to do.

The car was there, mounded and filled with snow. It looked as lithe and perfect as new; all of its scars and wounds had been healed over. I pushed open the door of the stable, and a stripe of sunlight fell through it and onto the bird. It was perfect too, from the tips of its blue-black claws, the shimmer of its plumage, to the blink of its beady eyes and the gleam of its beak. I whispered as I crossed the stable, and it shivered with the anticipation of my touch. 'My little imp – this time it's real.'

The jackdaw consented to having my fingers on its leg. Indeed, it closed its eyes in a kind of swoon as I untied the jesses from the perch and the bells tinkled for the last time. I held the jesses with one hand, and the bird sprang onto my wrist.

Together we stood in the stable-yard. We smelled the air, so cold and clean that it burned in our nostrils, and we narrowed our eyes at the bright sky. I undid the jesses from the bird's leg and dropped them onto the snow.

The bird gripped my arm, untethered now. It ducked and shuffled, making a curious mewing sound, cocked an eye at me and then at the treetops beyond. I said very softly, 'Go on, go on, you're free . . .' and it beat its wings so hard that the sunlight dazzled and glittered around my head.

The jackdaw leaped from my arm, up and up, onto the stable roof. It scrabbled and hopped and slithered, fell off – and as I hurried forwards to catch it, it swerved away from my hands. It climbed into the air. Gaining height, it flicked from one end of the yard to the other, skimming the roofs of the stables. Then it banked sharply, up and away, and was gone.

I waited, in case the bird turned and I'd see it again for one more second. It did not. I was alone. I breathed deeply, easily, and the sun felt good as I lifted my face to the sky.